DEAD AIR

THE DAY THE MUSIC DIED

Kelly Orchard

Dedication

To Ken Orchard, my Dad—With whom I worked for over 40 years. His knowledge, guidance, and love for radio shaped my view and inspired this story.

"Isn't this clever?"

Acknowledgments

This novel is the culmination of countless influences, guidance, and encouragement from a community of remarkable individuals, and I'm deeply grateful to each one of you.

To all the radio broadcast engineers I've met over the past 25 years, particularly those in Los Angeles who inspired the origin of this story:

- **Mike Callahan** of KIIS FM
- **John Paoli** of KFI
- **John Russel** of KTLA TV

Though no longer with us, their legacy lives on in the details and spirit of this book.

Special thanks to **Paul Sakrison**, veteran Los Angeles engineer, now retired, for sharing your expertise on personal drones and their use by hobbyists.

To **Howard Fine**, for your invaluable knowledge of towers and signal strength.

To **David Oxenford**, Federal Communications Commission attorney and partner at Wilkinson Barker Knauer LLP, for answering my questions about the Emergency Alert System and legal matters surrounding emergency broadcast law.

I owe immense gratitude to **Libby Gill**, author and leadership speaker, for encouraging me to write this story and for guiding me toward educational programs that helped me bring it to life.

To **Kris Paulsen**, author, accountability partner, and dear friend—thank you for your wisdom in self-publishing, editing services, and unwavering friendship.

To my oldest and dearest friend, **Lanae Alderete Richter**—thank you for your never-ending support and for giving me a safe place to land while finishing the draft.

Thank you to **Doc Searls**, photographer, for allowing me to use one of your stunning photos for the cover of this novel.

A heartfelt thanks to the subcontractors through Reedsy and Fiverr who provided editing and design services to bring *Dead Air* to its polished form.

To **Mike McVay** of McVay Media Consulting—thank you for enthusiastically championing *Dead Air*, diving in with both feet to help spread the word, and promoting it throughout the radio industry. It would not have been as fun or effective without you.

Finally, to the radio insiders who joined the launch team early, ARC readers, and social media supporters—your encouragement and participation have made you feel like family.

Thank you all for making this journey possible.

Table of Contents

Prologue

Juan Garcia was enjoying listening to the morning show on the FM classic rock station of his radio group when the audio abruptly went dead in the middle of a song.

He shook his head, walking out of his office and into the studio to see what the problem was, but the morning-show team just stared at him as if they expected him to fix it. He did a quick inspection of the broadcast equipment and toggled a few buttons and switches but accomplished nothing.

He wasn't happy. He'd have to cross town to get to the Empire State Building, where the station's transmitter was located. In New York City, that meant it would take at least thirty minutes to get there from the main studio location, not to mention having to endure going through security.

The thirty-minute drive down seven blocks was excruciating for Juan as he continued to hear nothing but a dead signal on the radio. Flipping through the frequencies, he discovered that nearly all the FM stations in New York were off the air, too.

Confused and concerned, as he made his way through the lobby of the Empire State Building to the security office, he showed the familiar security officer his credentials and informed him that this was an emergency and that he needed to rush up to the transmitters.

"Oh, are you here for the other guys?" the security officer asked.

"What?" Juan asked.

"Yeah, one of your engineers was here not too long ago with some other men. They said you sent them to do some sort of inspection. Is everything alright?"

Juan didn't even answer the security officer as he dashed to the elevator that would take him to the very top floor where the transmitters were housed. He pushed the button to call the elevator to the bottom floor. Suddenly, there was an unusual, distant clanking noise from above, as if something heavy had shifted unexpectedly. The sound echoed down the empty elevator shaft, and he looked up in confusion.

As the elevator descended, the noise grew louder and more alarming, the initial clanking turning into a series of loud metallic crashes. The shaft seemed to amplify the sounds, making them resonate with an almost physical intensity. Even the floor was vibrating.

He stood in shock as he heard the elevator crash into the floor on the other side of the door. Somebody had cut the cable.

"What the hell is going on?!" he said, running back to the security desk. "The elevator just came crashing down!"

Chapter One

We've Been Hijacked!

The Beatles song that Mike Harris set as the alarm to notify him that one of his radio stations was off the air startled him awake. "Help!" blared from his smartphone at his bedside. After a long night at the transmitter, he was tempted to hit the off button to get a few more minutes of shut-eye. But he was too awake now to ignore that there was a problem with one of his stations.

He turned on his clock radio, which was already tuned to KLCL FM, one of the eight radio stations for High Point Media that he handled. The station played the popular music of today, but this morning, there was absolutely no audio. That he awoke to silence surprised and concerned him. Dead air was an utter sin in radio.

"Who isn't paying attention?" he wondered before he sat up, rubbed his eyes, and shook the grogginess out of his un-caffeinated head.

His phone ringing was something he expected. A few years ago, the radio industry changed, stations merging as big broadcasting corporations formed in order to develop a new competitive edge. In what felt like a blink, he'd gone from engineering two radio stations to overseeing the technical operations of eight radio stations, along with directing five engineers and an apprentice. His phone was pressed to his ear most of the day.

"I think we've been hijacked, Mike!" the morning-show board operator yelled.

"What do you mean, we've been hijacked?" Mike said, annoyed. "You've got dead air, that's all." It was Monday morning, and it had been a long weekend working at the radio stations' transmitter sites, troubleshooting a glitch in the new installation of the latest technology in broadcasting.

"No, that's not it. Something's wrong. I think we've been taken over or something."

"We're a friggin' radio station, for Christ's sake! Nobody hijacks a radio station." Mike threw off his covers and swung his feet to the floor, sitting on the edge of his bed and searching for his glasses. Looking at the clock, he saw it was

6:13 AM.

What day was it?

Monday.

What was the date?

April 1st.

Oh, what? Was this an on-air prank?

Mike had thought the days of jocks playing April Fools' pranks on their listeners were over. He hadn't even had his morning jolt of caffeine from his ritual Big Gulp of Coke from 7-Eleven.

The "children" were always panicking about something. In his thirty years as an engineer for radio stations in Los Angeles, he'd spent so much time and effort training one intern or board operator after another, hundreds of them, that he'd learned it was more effective to speak to them as if they were in kindergarten.

"No, really, Mike, I'm not kidding!" the board operator said. He was a kid, intimidated by Mike's experience and authority at the stations. The board operators secretly called Mike the Professor.

"Tell me what's going on," Mike said. He needed to calm this kid down so he could get a straight answer.

"Well, we were just getting ready to play back the traffic report just after 6:00 when, all of a sudden, the audio went dead, and I can't figure out why."

"What do you mean it just went dead?" Mike looked toward the clock radio on his nightstand and turned and looked over at his wife, Shelly, who was also awake now. She reached over to rub his lower back.

"Are you positive you haven't flipped the wrong switch somewhere?" Mike asked.

"I'm certain of it," the board operator said. "I've been working here long enough to know now what to push and what not to push. I don't know how to get us back on the air."

"What do you hear in the studio?"

"Everything on the computer screen looks normal, as if we're just playing what's programmed. I can even hear it through the studio speakers.

"Alright."

"But it's not on the air. There's just a low hum."

"Okay, let's assess this again."

Mike had learned over the years to instruct the board operators just enough to empower them to do their job but not enough to inadvertently sabotage a broadcast. Patience was not his strongest attribute, and sometimes, in his effort to be patient, he could become very condescending. Troubleshooting with these kids was the worst!

"Tell me what you see on the computer screen," Mike said.

"It—it shows the commercials that are supposed to be running, and when I switch the audio to what's playing in the studio, I can hear what should be on the air. But when I switch back to what's on the air, it's just dead air."

"Where's Stevie?" Mike asked. Stevie Gold was the morning-show personality and tended to be very high-strung. He was overpaid with an ego to match, but Mike had to admit he got the job done. KLCL FM had the highest ratings in Los Angeles, and the audience and sponsors loved him.

"Oh, he's right here, and he's freaking out! That's why I'm calling you," the board operator said. "He's yelling at me as if this is my fault. I need help!"

Mike could hear Stevie stomping and pacing in the background while he likely waved his arms like a petulant child. "What do I have to do around here to get my goddamn show to run right? Who's the knucklehead in charge?"

Stevie let out some profanities, and Mike felt sorry for the kid. Talent could be like that, especially in a major market like Los Angeles.

"Okay, I'm going to check the transmitter and try to find out what's going on. You call Gunner in programming and let him know I'm on top of this apparent malfunction and that I'll be there as soon as I can."

Mike already knew this wasn't a transmitter issue. Just as he was starting to open the app on his phone that enabled him to control the transmitter remotely, his phone rang for the second time.

His engineering buddy Tom, from another radio group across town, appeared on the caller ID. He ignored the call as he tried to connect to the transmitter remotely.

Mike loved this remote technology and especially appreciated it when it was too early in the morning to even be awake. The industry introduced remote-control transmitter tech many years ago, enabling radio and television stations to control and monitor the transmitter without ever needing to get out of bed. It also allowed the station to save money on staff because, as part of the federal government's rules, they used to have a live person at the transmitter in case there was ever an emergency.

Mike's eyebrows curled as he waited in bed for the app to connect, the crease in his forehead tightening. He couldn't access his remote dashboard. It was as if he'd been blocked out or it had been disabled. *What's going on? Another malfunction up there on the mountain?*

He and his apprentice Albert had just spent the weekend on Mount Wilson at the transmitter troubleshooting some problems with their recent installation, but they hadn't touched the remote-control unit, so their trip didn't explain his remote dashboard being disabled.

His phone rang again. "Yeah," he said, growing more and more concerned. He didn't like these kinds of pranks, or whatever this was.

"Mike, this is Paul. We have a big problem." Paul was one of Mike's engineers who worked on one of their eight stations. "KSSP is off the air. I just got a call from the morning board op complaining of dead air."

Mike sighed. He didn't want to make that trek up to the transmitter again today. If this was an April Fools' prank, it was a terrible one, and whoever was pulling it off was pissing off a lot of people.

He stood and turned to Shelly, who looked just as concerned as he did. She never liked the crazy hours he worked to keep these radio stations on the air.

"What's going on now, Mike?" she asked, sitting up.

"I gotta go."

"But you worked all weekend! Don't you remember what the doctor said about your heart? Too much work is why you had that heart attack in the first place!" She sounded angry, but Mike knew it was only panic. She worried about him, and rightly so.

"I know, I know…" He'd heard it a thousand times in the last three years.

"I know you love your work, Mike, but you're not taking care of yourself. That company works you too hard."

"I'm in crisis mode right now. I gotta go." He looked around for the pile of clothes he'd discarded the night before.

"Okay," she said, "but I'm going to start pulling out those brochures on condos in Hawaii again." The idea of retiring in Hawaii was a dream they concocted together right after Mike's heart attack a few years ago. Shelly had recently retired from her teaching job and was eager for Mike to hang up his job, too. He just wasn't ready to stop any more than he was ready to eat healthy, exercise, and stop drinking soda.

Mike dressed in his standard blue jeans, T-shirt, and ragged tennis shoes, grabbed his phone, clipped it to his belt loop, and didn't bother combing his scraggily thinning hair.

Confident that he'd get this prankster under control soon, Mike almost grinned at the thought of how the jocks and programmers were responding to this. He pictured them pacing, fuming, stewing. Their show had been disrupted, and they now had no purpose. It bordered on comical.

Mike walked out to the garage and over to his workshop. The counter and floor were a disorganized clutter of components, tools, and equipment that he liked to fix and refurbish. Not only was he a radio engineer by day, but he also liked to tinker with equipment in his downtime. He felt it especially rewarding to find an old piece of equipment and make it work again. He picked up a couple of pieces of testing equipment and opened the garage door, climbing into his messy Ford Explorer, which was cluttered with equipment, wires, cables, miscellaneous components, and discarded Big Gulp cups. He turned on the radio and scanned the FM dial to listen to other stations as he drove to the corner 7-Eleven store for his morning ritual of a Coke to start the day.

But his calmness quickly morphed into distress as he listened, the situation becoming more and more alarming as he found dead air after dead air on numerous FM stations around Los Angeles.

He looked at the frequencies of the stations that were off the air. He'd been an engineer in Los Angeles long enough to know one simple fact: all the affected FM radio stations were broadcasting from one major antenna site.

Mount Wilson was the primary broadcast transmission antenna array in Southern California. About thirty FM radio stations and every television station in the Greater Los Angeles area had their transmitters and broadcast sites up there. Almost half of the broadcast transmissions in the market came from the top of Mount Wilson in the Angeles National Forest.

What the hell was going on?

Mike was boiling with anger. Who would wreck Los Angeles radio like this? Was it a prank, or was it some sort of an outage on the mountain? But they had triple backups in case of power outages, so an outage didn't make any sense.

Abandoning the stop for his Big Gulp, Mike pulled his phone off his belt loop, held the wheel with one hand, and called his counterpart, Tom, at one of the other stations that was off the air.

"This is Tom," came the voice on the other end of the line. Tom and Mike had known each other for years. Tom worked for another large broadcast company that had as many stations in LA as High Point Media. All of their FM had dead air as well.

"Hey, man. Sounds like you have the same problem as I do. We should head up the mountain and see what's up," Mike said, having determined that making a stop at the station first would be a waste of time.

"Yeah, I've been trying to figure this thing out," Tom said. "This just doesn't make any sense. I was on my way to the station when our morning news guy called me, and I'll admit, I'm perplexed."

"I'm assuming it's some April Fools' prank. Well, I'm not amused, and someone's ass is canned."

"I'm on my way to Mount Wilson. How about we meet at the ranger station and ride up in one vehicle?"

"Fine by me."

Mike loved that broadcast engineers helped each other out. It often seemed like the only area of the broadcast industry where competition didn't truly exist. Well, except that all technical people liked to brag about the latest toy they were installing. They all loved to compete in the area of sound quality and signal strength. It was a game of "my signal is bigger than yours." But when it came right down to it, broadcast engineers had the same goal in mind: do whatever it took to keep these stations on the air and put out the cleanest signal possible.

He tuned his car radio to High Point Media's AM flagship station, AM 790 KLAR. As one of the largest radio companies in the United States with stations in all the major markets and ancillary markets across the country, High Point Media has dominated the vast majority of broadcasting since radio consolidated back in the 1990s. Their Los Angeles stations alone brought in nearly a billion dollars in revenue the year before. AM 790 KLAR was California's emergency broadcast station. But right now, even KLAR wasn't reporting on the other broadcast disruptions of the other stations.

Good, let's not give those clowns the satisfaction of making news. He knew it wouldn't take too much time to figure out what they'd done and fix it.

His phone vibrated on his hip again. It was Roy Longly, the market manager for the eight radio stations. He was in charge of everything and only concerned about revenue and profits, a corporate suit that Mike merely tolerated and was grateful not to cross paths with all that much. He unclipped his phone and answered the call.

"What's going on, Mike?" Roy asked.

"I don't know yet."

"What do you mean you don't know yet? Don't you have all those fancy gadgets and backup systems so things like this don't happen?"

Even Mike knew that this amount of lost airtime meant lost revenue. And this wasn't just one station; it was four. They'd be losing hundreds of thousands of dollars an hour, and who knew how long it'd take to get them back on the air? He was glad he wasn't the one who had to answer to the advertisers and clients this morning.

"Well, obviously, something has happened since our audio has been cut."

"Well, how long until you can get these stations back on the air? We're losing money and pissing people off!"

"It's not that simple. We aren't actually off the air. The transmitters are on."

"What's the fucking difference?"

"I've tried to access the Burk remote-control unit up at the transmitter for KLCL. Nothing. I called the landline, but it appears to be disconnected. I'm on my way up there."

"So, how long do you think it'll be until you get us back on the air?" Roy asked, clearly under pressure to get answers and handle this situation. "We've been off the air for forty-five minutes now, and we've got listeners calling and texting, asking about why they can hear the stations on the web but not on their radios."

Mike looked at his watch. It was 6:45 AM, and his other line was ringing. It was the studio. He ended the call with Roy and answered the board operator who'd called him earlier.

"What's happening?" he asked. By now, the board operator was frantic. Stevie had left the studio in a huff and told him he'd be back when they were back on. Not wanting to abandon his post, the board operator remained alone in the studio, waiting for help.

"Just like I thought," Mike said. "The remote-control units are malfunctioning or something, and the transfer of control is at the transmitter."

"What do you mean 'control is at the transmitter'?" the board op asked.

Mike wanted him to understand, always the professor. "Well it's like this: just like when you watch TV at home, you have a remote control that allows you to change the channel and control the volume and to turn the TV off and on. If the remote control is broken or the batteries die, then you have to get up off the couch and turn on the TV or change channels."

"So, what does that have to do with why our stations are off the air?"

"They aren't actually off the air. The transmitters are on but the audio has been cut directly up there. Control of our transmitters is now at Mount Wilson. Either someone is playing a prank up there, or something has gone terribly wrong. Someone has disconnected my ability to control the transmitter remotely and has taken over all programming from the transmitters."

"Then you can take care of this problem in a short amount of time, and we'll be back on? Can I tell Stevie that?"

"I think you'd best tell Stevie not to hold his breath. I have no idea what I'll find when I get up there."

"Wish me luck." Stevie was hotheaded, and the board op clearly didn't want to get the brunt of his rant when he heard this news.

As Mike drove through town to the freeway, he'd already tuned in to several stations, all of which had dead air. He was tired of the silence. In his world, silence equals failure.

Thankfully, he got a gorgeous mountain drive to Red Box ranger station at the base of Mount Wilson. Early spring in the Angeles National Forrest was beautiful, and he considered it one of the perks of making trips to the transmitter.

He arrived at the ranger station only moments before Tom, who parked his truck, grabbed his gear from the back seat and climbed into Mike's Explorer.

"Everyone at my station is panicking," Tom said.

"I'm sure we'll be seeing the engineers from all the other stations up here soon, too," Mike said.

He maneuvered the vehicle around sharp turns and avoided the jagged rocks on the passenger side of the very narrow pathway leading up to Audio Road, where the dense array of radio towers and transmitters were. He'd been up and down this mountain thousands of times over the past thirty years and could almost drive it with his eyes closed. Almost. Danger lurked around every narrow curve. He'd seen rockslides where he had to get out of his vehicle and move big rocks off the path, and he'd encountered deer in the road and snow that led him to put chains on his tires.

He went slowly around a switchback and slammed his foot on the brakes when he saw the obstacle just ahead.

"What's that? Mike glanced at Tom, who looked just as confused as he did. He put the Explorer in park and stared out the windshield, awestruck.

An abandoned box truck was blocking the entire road. It appeared to have slammed up against the rocky hillside and been crushed by fallen boulders, which littered the area around the truck's front end, along with scraps of vehicular debris. The wheels had been removed, too. Mike and Tom got out of the car, utterly perplexed.

Neither one said a word as they looked at the mountainous barricade in the road. Now, it looked like someone had deliberately parked the truck diagonally and removed the tires, which had been slashed and strewn on the other side of the truck. There was an odor permeating the spring air, an odor Mike had never experienced up here in the forest. It smelled like sulfur.

He walked closer to investigate. He'd seen rockslides up here before, but these were bigger boulders that had tumbled down from the mountainside as if there had been a blast.

He looked up at the side of the mountain and saw where the explosives had been planted just twenty or thirty feet above. He was dumbfounded. There was no way they were getting up to the transmitters.

"What's on the other side of this?" Tom wondered, and Mike did, too.

Tom tried to make his way around the back end of the truck, which was facing the forest and not pinned up against the side of the mountain. Before he could make it around the truck, they heard gunshots coming from above in rapid succession.

Mike hit the ground just as a bullet zoomed above his head. He lay still, frozen in fear. There was no time to think at all. He didn't know how long he froze in shock, but it felt like forever.

"What the hell?!" he shouted as he shot a glance over at Tom and saw the same fear in his eyes that he felt himself. They were stunned and confused as a spatter of bullets hit the ground and rocks ricocheted chaotically.

Tom was on the ground near the disabled truck's back bumper. He wasn't moving. Mike sprang into action and ran around the Explorer to take cover behind the driver's door. He looked over at Tom again and saw that he was bleeding all over his T-shirt. His breathing was rapid and labored.

"Hey! You've been shot!" Mike hollered. Now, he was in a panic. He'd never seen somebody get shot before, but he knew a bullet had hit Tom. There was no doubt.

Another rapid burst of gunfire sounded off, and Mike knew they had to get out of there. Tom screamed out in agony and was losing a lot of blood, beginning to turn white.

The mountain was covered in rock, and two steel vehicles were on the road.

He knew one thing for certain: these bullets only needed to hit something to ricochet and get him, too.

When the gunfire stopped, he figured it was his opportunity to make a getaway. He had no time to be a hero. He ran around to the other side of the Explorer, opened the back passenger door, and threw all his cables, equipment, and clutter into the back. Then he ran over to where Tom lay on the ground.

"We gotta get you into the car!" Mike yelled. "Are you able to get up?"

Tom managed a breathless "yes" and let Mike put his arm over his shoulder. He got him up and hoisted Tom onto the back seat, hoping he'd be able to get him out of there fast and in an ambulance before he died.

Chapter Two

It's Out of Our Control!

There was no time to waste. Mike had experienced nothing like this except for what he'd seen in movies or on TV shows. The sound of clattering automatic weapons and zipping bullets flying from above felt like they'd been ripped from a war zone or a drive-by shooting.

All he felt as he ran back around the Explorer was fear that the rain of bullets would start again. He knew he needed to get out of here now! There was nothing but rock and metal in this tight corner, and the road back was narrow and winding. They were more than twenty miles from help and on a mountain highway with no cell signal until they got back down to the main highway.

Losing blood had already weakened Tom. Mike imagined he would go into shock and was suffering a lot of pain.

He got behind the steering wheel and looked back at Tom, who was struggling to breathe. Blood was oozing from his belly, and his T-shirt was soaked in blood. Mike reached behind him and grabbed a rag he had kept behind the passenger seat, along with some of his cleaning supplies for the transmitters.

"Here, take this and keep pressure on the wound to help stop the bleeding."

Tom didn't answer, but he looked at Mike and held on to the rag as if his life depended on it.

"I have no idea what I'm doing, Tom, but in every TV show I've seen where there's a gunshot wound, they tell them to keep pressure on it."

Getting the Explorer turned around on the narrow road was going to be incredibly stressful, but so far, there hadn't been any more bullets. It took a lot of maneuvering and seemed as though it was taking a long time. Relieved, Mike drove as quickly as he could back down to the ranger station, which was unoccupied at 7:45 in the morning. He made a mental note that Tom's truck was still parked there as he continued driving to the bottom of the mountain.

Once he regained cell signal, he dialed 911 and requested police assistance and an ambulance. With one hand on the wheel and the other holding his phone, he told the emergency operator that there had been a shooting at Mount Wilson. He provided the location of where he was going to meet them. Help was on its way.

Then he dialed Roy Longly.

"Someone... someone shot at us!" Mike said, breathless. "We didn't get two miles up the mountain when... when we came upon a destroyed moving truck blocking access the rest of the way!" He looked back at Tom, who looked pale and weak and was losing a lot of blood.

"Are you guys okay?" Roy asked. He wasn't sure what Mike had said; he just knew he sounded frantic.

"No! Tom was shot in the gut. I called for the police and an ambulance as soon as I could get down from the mountain and got cell service again. But I don't know, he doesn't look so good."

"What? What do you mean you were shot at?" Roy was confused. How had dead air escalated to a shooting? "We need to not only notify the police, but higher authorities." This had just become a bigger deal than Roy had realized earlier. "I wanted to believe it was a prank, that it'd be resolved as soon as you got up there."

"This is a big deal," Mike said. He knew this would be a federal issue now, as they didn't own the property. Not only did they not have control of their stations, they didn't control the property either, so it was out of their hands.

"I'm on my way to the station. I'll start making phone calls. You get back here as soon as you're able," Roy said. And as an afterthought, he added, "I hope Tom is going to be alright."

As Mike reached the bottom of the hill and drove closer toward civilization, he could hear the siren of the ambulance. He pulled into the parking lot of the cafe where he'd told the paramedics he would meet them.

Mike looked at the sign as he drove up. *Hill Street Café*. It had been a meeting place for engineers for years. They'd often gather here for a meal before going up Mount Wilson to work. Now, rather than meeting fellow engineers, he was here to meet the police and an ambulance for his friend and colleague.

Mike parked and leapt out of the Explorer, waving the medics over and opening the back door so they could get to Tom.

"What happened?" a medic asked as he approached Mike with a gurney and a bag of medical supplies.

Mike gave his account as he watched one of them examine Tom's injury.

"Are you injured too?" The medic nodded to Mike's blood-soaked T-shirt.

Mike paused for the first time since seeing the moving truck on the road, and the shooting began. Was he injured? He looked down at his shirt and felt all around his body. He hadn't even realized that he had Tom's blood on his shirt. But other than that, he hadn't been hit.

"I don't appear to be." He was relieved to determine that he was not injured and grateful he wasn't going to take an ambulance ride today.

The medics wasted no time getting Tom onto the gurney and into the ambulance. Mike shuddered as he watched them wheel him away. A flash of memory crossed his mind, back when he'd suffered his heart attack and was taken away in an ambulance. He was concerned for his friend, then felt a pang of guilt, and he was glad it wasn't him in the ambulance right now. It drove away before Mike even had a chance to check on Tom one last time. He didn't even know what hospital they'd take him to.

The ambulance left, and the police remained, waiting for his statement. Mike told the officers his account of the events for the past two hours and made sure they knew Tom's vehicle was still at the ranger station.

In a state of shock, Mike could feel the adrenaline coursing through his body. Out of the corner of his eye, he saw people milling around. Some had their phones out, while others even had mics and headsets. These were independent news reporters who must have police scanners.

For the first time, it consciously dawned on him that this was going to be a major news story.

He quickly provided his statement, emphasizing the importance of returning to the radio station. There was an even bigger emergency waiting for him. He still had a job to do, and there were a lot of people who had questions. He had a lot of his own questions, and he wouldn't get answers to them standing here talking to the police.

Scared and shaken, Mike drove back to the station in silence. It was the first time in thirty years as a broadcast engineer that he didn't listen to the radio or scan the dial. His thoughts were too loud for him to hear anything anyway.

Who took over Mount Wilson and why?

Why just take off programming? What did that prove?

Had anyone else even noticed all these FM radio stations were off the air?

Why had they shot at Tom and him?

How could he get up to Mount Wilson now?

If it wasn't a prank, what was it?

He arrived back at the office building at 8:25 and parked his vehicle in the parking structure. By now the parking spaces had just about filled up. He felt sick to his stomach as he parked the Explorer in his assigned space. He took a moment to sit in the silence, needing to catch his breath. He stared through the windshield and shook his head, just now noticing the crack and a bullet hole in the top right corner of the windshield.

He honestly felt guilty that he hadn't been shot, too.

Still feeling nauseous as he got out of the Explorer, he walked toward the elevator that would transport him up to the station. Unable to keep the bile from coming up, he turned to a nearby trash can to vomit, then collected himself and rode the elevator up to the main floor of the station. He walked down the hall from the main lobby off the elevators and made his way to the main conference room, where the station staff was now converging. The day had only begun for some, but it already felt like an eternity since his wake-up call just a couple of hours ago.

He stood in the doorway and looked at his engineering team. They were all seated at the enormous conference table, looking back at him, ashen-faced and in shock. They'd begun arriving after he'd already left for Mount Wilson. Any of them could have taken that ride up the mountain with him. It could have just as easily been one of them that had been shot and left with their life hanging in the balance.

But where was Albert? Mike's right-hand guy, his apprentice, was not here. The only one on his team unaccounted for. Mike was just with him at the transmitter last night. Then he remembered Albert had been complaining to Mike about how late they were working because he was going on vacation before dawn.

"Come on in, Mike," Roy Longly said. "We have a bigger problem."

Chapter Three

We Are Not Alone!

8:30 AM

Mike forced himself to take a seat alongside the others at the oversized conference table. As he sat down, his body made it feel like he'd already been dealing with this crisis forever. He was still stunned and in shock and appeared to the others confused, even dazed. He looked disheveled. His shirt was stained with Tom's blood, and he didn't even notice or care.

This was an unimaginable development. He knew he couldn't get up to the transmitter site to fix the problem, which made him feel even more helpless than he had when he and Tom were getting shot at just ninety minutes ago.

The conference room wasn't a place that Mike frequented at the radio station. Too formal for his taste. It was an enormous room with glass walls and doors on each side, a space affectionately called the "war room" because that was where sales and programming held most of their strategic meetings. The openness allowed passersby to see who was in a meeting, which was designed to be intimidating. Mike thought it was too much like a fishbowl.

Twenty high-back leather chairs surrounded the large modern conference table. At the far end of the room there was a video screen and whiteboards for training, wired for multimedia presentations for clients and recording artists and their labels. At the back end of the room, there was a counter with cabinets for storage. The staff would put out refreshments on the counter for daily briefings.

Roy stood at the helm, ready to lead his staff in the most important meeting of his career. A conference call with headquarters was just starting, and a seat had been reserved for Mike.

The engineers, program directors, and other department heads filled the chairs around the conference table. It was standing-room-only as any staff who had straggled in had taken chairs around the perimeter of the room or been forced to stand in the corners.

They'd sure gotten here early. Mike glanced at his watch. It was 8:35. His stations hadn't been broadcasting for two and a half hours.

He struggled to quiet his confusion so that he could focus on what was actually happening at that moment. But he was still distracted by the flashes of visions. The drive up the mountain road. The discovery of the mysterious truck and the boulders blocking the path. The smell of explosives was present as they got out to investigate.

The sound of gunfire, as if it were still happening, and then an image of Tom bleeding.

The call with corporate had started as the teams from the other markets in the country were all joining the call. In any other circumstance, Roy Longly would be in his element, but his demeanor was different today.

Mike and Roy had worked together in radio for a long time now, but in quite different departments, so they'd little interaction with each other. Roy was undeniably a corporate man, a long way from where he'd started in the sales department. Dressed in an expensive suit and polished shoes, his hair was slicked and combed back. He looked like a movie star, and in a way, he was. He was one of the rare individuals that thrived in sales and building relationships, working his way through management in the Sacramento radio market until he'd been named market manager for the cluster of radio stations owned by High Point Media in Los Angeles. He played the game well with his arrogance and ego, but Mike could see that he was under a lot of pressure all the time and was glad he didn't have that job.

Mike tried to snap out of his shock, eager to learn the details of the events of that morning and regain control of his radio stations. He hated feeling powerless.

"So far, we have reports of five large cities that have experienced a disruption to their broadcast transmission facilities," a voice came from the speaker in the middle of the enormous table. "Los Angeles, San Francisco, New York, Chicago, and Dallas. It all started simultaneously, and engineers at about a hundred radio stations have experienced similar situations. Each site has been barricaded, and no two sites are identical. The FBI has been called, and they're on their way to investigate."

"Wait! How many stations also can't get access to their transmitter sites?" Mike asked, cocking his head toward the speaker, the lines on his forehead furrowed. He knew some of these installations because he'd either visited them or worked with their engineers at one time or another. In San Francisco, Mount Sutro was similar to Mount Wilson, with many broadcast sites. It was an amazing installation, the best in the country. The building to house the transmitters was as secure as a fortress.

"What sites have been taken over?" He was on a roll. The million questions that had run through his mind on the drive over now spilled out of him like an unstoppable faucet. "How is the FBI going to help us get control back?"

"We're just gathering data right now," came a different voice from the speaker. It was the director of engineering and operations who was on the landline from corporate headquarters in Dallas. They'd been hijacked too, right at their own building. He announced that the FBI had been called in as this was a federal concern. The properties weren't owned by High Point Media and the licenses belonged to the FCC. The situation was out of their control.

What they knew right now was that Mount Sutro in San Francisco, two high-rises in Chicago—the Sears Tower and the Hancock building—where stations had their transmitters, the Empire State Building in New York City, and the top of the High Point Media Center in Dallas had all been taken over and every FM radio station broadcast at those locations was dead.

"This is just unbelievable! How can this be happening?" Roy shook his head. "Los Angeles, San Francisco, New York, Chicago, Dallas, all top markets in the country. It can't be a coincidence that we're talking about an enormous population of listeners!"

"Of course, it's not a coincidence." The voice through the speaker was angry. "If and when these hijackers make their demands, this could affect as many as fifty million people, and we're desperately working on getting to the bottom of it."

Mike wasn't sure if Roy and corporate were actually concerned about the dead air and the takeover of the transmissions or about the revenue that these stations would lose because they couldn't air any commercials.

"Well, at least half *our* stations are on the air," Mike said. "How have they secured the high-rise buildings and taken over those transmissions?"

"It's pretty much the same scenario in Chicago as it is in New York," a voice said through the phone.

Mike was losing track of who was speaking, his mind racing. This coordinated effort took planning, precision, and communication. Who? How? Why? How did they get guns past security in those buildings?

Everyone in the room had been told that the broadcast transmitters located at the top of the Sears Tower, and the Hancock building in Chicago and the Empire State Building in New York City had all ceased their programs at the same time as Los Angeles, San Francisco, and Dallas.

Roy looked over at Mike. Was the trauma written all over his face? Mike wasn't sure. He was trying to hold it together so he could get some answers. The conference room went silent as they listened to the accounts from the other stations across the country.

Security in these critical buildings had been beefed up since the attack on the World Trade Center in 2001. Each high-rise building that accommodated radio and television broadcast transmitter equipment had a strict security policy in place.

Taking the elevator to the roof where the transmitters were located required approval, and only the security office had the key card to access the elevator. Every engineer was required to check-in. Once they were up on the top floor to the roof, the perpetrators had broken the hoist rope on the elevator so that when the elevator was called down again, it crashed. No more access to the roof unless the engineers climbed the stairs, and those had been barricaded, too.

Everyone on the call remembered the situation in New York when the World Trade Center went down. Nine radio and television stations whose transmitters were located on the rooftops had lost their transmitter sites and gone off the air.

"It's three hours later back here." The CEO was now addressing the group. "So, when the engineer showed up with the 'supposed' inspectors at close to 8 AM, security didn't question their visit. These guys simply informed security that they were there to conduct an inspection. Security issued the pass to get to the top floor. An hour later, all audio ceased. When the chief engineer arrived and tried to access the floor, the elevator just came crashing down."

"Well, this is definitely a coordinated plan." It was a voice from the standing-room-only gallery.

Mike closed his eyes as he shook his head. "Ya think?"

"Yes, it was very coordinated, and we have multiple layers of concern," the CEO said. "We've just begun to get all the information together and interview the personnel of these stations. It's obvious there's a connection, and we'll work closely with the FBI and the major groups in each of these markets to find out just what that is. Agents are being sent to each of our markets, so you can expect them to show up soon. We're hoping and anticipating no other cities will experience this problem because we've had no other reports, but there are no guarantees."

Surprised it hadn't already been brought up, Roy asked, "Has anybody else been shot at like Tom and Mike?"

"Yes," the CEO said. "Unfortunately, a couple of engineers in San Francisco went up to Mount Sutro and found a blockade right at the base of the entrance. They caught rapid gunfire from an automatic military-grade weapon. No one was injured, though. They appear to have been warning shots only."

"My god!" Mike said, reminded once again that he could have easily died just a short time ago, but his life had miraculously been spared. It made him feel even sicker. "We're broadcast engineers, techno-geeks, not soldiers in a war zone."

"What about our building in Dallas?" Roy asked.

"That one's different because High Point Media actually controls the roof of that building," said the CEO. "So, whoever did this in Dallas had total access to it without having to go through security. We're considering this an inside job."

"Okay, I have a lot more questions," Mike said. "Who then is responsible for this? What do they want? Why hijack our airwaves? And why just dead air? What's the point? And what's our emergency plan for something like this?"

"We're only in the beginning stage of info gathering until they come forward with demands, but maybe we can help resolve the problem before it escalates." Said the CEO.

The call had to end when the CEO and VP of operations from the Dallas office had to leave as FBI agents had shown up at their building. They informed the other markets to be expecting the FBI there soon too. Roy was eager to get on a private call with his boss to learn what they wouldn't say to the entire crew.

The call concluded with a final statement from the CEO. "Listen, I know you feel helpless and under immense pressure to get your stations back on the air, but the more we know, the better equipped we'll be to solve this. Just keep your eyes and ears open and cooperate with the authorities when they arrive."

Chapter Four

Preparing for a Hurricane

8:45 AM

The war room was quiet now, and Roy looked around at his staff. This was his domain. If this was an inside job, as alluded to by corporate, who on his staff was part of it? He had his core team, but often, the sales department, promotions and marketing department, board operators, and apprentices were a revolving door. As he looked out among them, he realized he didn't know the names of two-thirds of them.

Mike was doing the same thing, scanning the room. Who? He wasn't surprised that Albert Braun wasn't here. He'd been with him last night at the transmitter and had left for vacation first thing this morning. He was probably on an airplane right now, headed back East to see his family.

Gunner Jeffries, the director of radio programming, broke the silence. "There are a lot of listeners wondering what the heck is going on. This is going to affect a lot of people here in LA."

"No kidding," Roy said. "We're talking about millions of radio listeners. Are you even aware of how much money we're losing with every minute of dead air?" He'd been assessing how many commercial units had been lost since the four stations ceased their programming more than three hours ago. All stations combined added up to a loss of nearly half a million dollars. Add those numbers together in all five major markets and these radio stations were losing millions of dollars an hour.

"Our four AM stations are operating fine, still on the air, and playing their regular programming," Gunner said.

"It's just the stations whose transmitters are located up on Mount Wilson that can't control what's on the air," Mike said. "I think we should secure the AM transmitter sites, don't you?"

"Brilliant idea," Roy said. "But shouldn't they have already been secure? Isn't it the law?"

Mike didn't appreciate Roy's sarcasm. He'd been battling with him over the lack of a budget for better security at the transmitters for years, and it always fell on deaf ears.

"We should ask the cops to send a police car to each of the sites to make sure they're secure," Mike said. "The AM sites are spread out all over the southland, so it would take all day for us to go check on them."

A rookie salesperson standing against the wall raised her hand. "Can I ask a question?"

"Of course, you can," Roy said. He didn't know who she was, but if she was in this room, that meant she was part of his staff.

"Why can't you just get back on the air from here?"

This was such an elementary question for Mike. All he wanted to do was get back on the air. Didn't she realize that?

He got up from his seat and walked over to the whiteboard at the front of the conference room while Roy handed him a dry-erase marker and took Mike's seat.

Mike drew a basic diagram of the transmitter site. It was like giving a broadcasting lesson to his kindergarten kids again. Although he knew he needed to be cooperative, all he really wanted to do was go to his workshop, find a clean shirt and a Coke, and be alone with his thoughts while he figured out how this could've happened.

He spoke slowly while he drew a box underneath the mountain and in the box wrote, *radio station*.

"The transmitter is set to a specific frequency and sends the broadcast into the airwaves where receivers receive it, which is what you hear on your radio. The radio station"—he pointed to the box marked *radio station* on his diagram—"sends the program up to the transmitter." Then he pointed to the towers he'd drawn on the mountain. "The transmitter is what sends out the actual broadcast."

"Then whoever pulled this off would need to know a lot about broadcast engineering," Roy said. "Who do you know that might be capable of this?"

A discomforting hush filled the room as all eyes looked upon the group of engineers, who remained silent and slow to respond as they considered the question.

"Any broadcast engineer would know how to disable the remote-control access and begin broadcasting from the transmitter," Mike said. "We work with that kind of equipment every day. It's their job to install it, repair it, and ensure its function. Hundreds of engineers could pull this off."

"Broadcast engineers who work up at Mount Wilson have complained that the site has been vulnerable for years," one of the other engineers chimed in, "with construction projects going regularly. A lot of unfamiliar construction workers coming and going."

"Although there are padlocked gates to secure the area, it's been an ongoing concern that no one seems to be alarmed by the lack of security up there." Mike had been complaining about it for years. "But who would do such a thing, and why?"

"Maybe it's a disgruntled engineer who lost his job," Roy said.

"But resort to violence? Come on!" Mike was confounded. No, this was not as simple as a disgruntled employee. It couldn't be. Disgruntled employees sued for more money, but they didn't hijack transmitter farms and cease programming. "This is not just one lone engineer. This is a team of highly trained engineers in different cities and numerous locations. That's the only way this could be pulled off."

"I can't even imagine anyone that I know of who would do something like this," said an engineer from one of the AM stations. "It just doesn't make any sense."

Mike looked around the table at his coworkers. "There has to be another answer! Why kill the programming?"

"What about Albert?" Paul asked. "Albert isn't here! Do you think he has something to do with this?"

"There's no way he would have any part of this," Mike said, knowing Albert would be sitting right here at this conference table if he knew this was going on. "He's on an airplane right now, not on top of Mount Wilson."

"Well, we're not going to just sit on our asses and pretend nothing is happening," Roy said, looking at Mike. "You better get this figured out and get control of our broadcast. This is going to be a financial bloodbath. We need to fix it now!"

"Don't you get it?" Mike snapped back, pointing at his fellow engineers. "I got shot at trying to get up the mountain. We can't do anything without the police now."

Roy fumed. "Our FMs may be gone for now, but we still have a job to do with our AM stations. We have to prepare as if a hurricane is coming. So, what are we going to do next?"

Roy had always been in the sales division of the radio stations he worked for over the years, primarily in the Los Angeles area. He'd never been on the news or programming side of radio, but he'd been in the business long enough to know how stations prepared to report on big news stories. This wasn't a natural disaster like an earthquake, where reporting would come after the event.

"This'll be a news story in a quick minute if it isn't already," Gunner said. "Anyone think to check yet?"

Phones came out of pockets around the room as the group checked news sources and social media. There was news about the "outage", as the media was calling it, but national headlines and concerns weren't being brought up yet. Some were still reporting that it seemed like an April Fools' prank to gain attention for the radio industry.

Roy and his team knew differently. "Let's set up a broadcast command center right here in the conference room," Roy said. "I want enough receivers here to monitor as many radio stations as we can at once. I want to know what everyone in town is doing."

The engineering crew moved out of the conference room to bring the equipment and components from various rooms and studios to the conference room. There was always spare or discarded equipment stored in empty offices, the workshop, and additional equipment rooms.

"Next, let's get some breaking news reports on our AM stations that explain why so many stations in Los Angeles are off the air," Roy said, then looked at the program directors, who were all sitting together at the table. "I'm counting on you guys to get us through this."

"I've already got a plan going in my head," Gunner said. "People will tune in to AM for news. However, we have to be careful how we present it so as to not disrupt or impede the investigation. The stations are also the victims here."

"Bullshit!" Roy said. "Let's try to keep it status quo as best we can. No sense in removing programs that generate money if it's not necessary. We're going to have angry advertisers and clients soon. I'd like to minimize the damage as much as possible."

"We don't want to frighten or alarm our listeners," Gunner said. "Yeah, we have a duty to inform them, but also to protect them. We may have lost our FM stations for now, but we can do battle with our AMs."

"Well, what do you think is going to happen?" Roy was incredulous, seeing his year-end holiday bonus flying out the window with every minute of dead air.

"Something bad," Mike said as he came back into the conference room carrying two radio receivers and a bunch of wrapped cables in his arms. "We were shot at; let's not forget that."

Gunner had some ideas about how to manage the on-air programs but knew that Roy wouldn't like them at all, toeing the company line in order to mitigate any more financial losses. But they all knew what they had to do: report the news while avoiding mass hysteria.

"And until we report it, we're the only ones who know," Roy said.

As far as they were concerned, no one — not listeners or advertisers — knew these stations had been hijacked. The public only knew that they weren't airing any programming.

And with that, Roy left the conference room and hurried to his office on the fourth floor, eager to speak to his boss in private. He knew there was more going on than what had been said on the conference call. There always was.

Bracing for Impact

9:15 AM

The cables and power cords strewn all over the floor of the conference room snaked their way to an array of radio receivers and small speaker on the cabinet, turning the conference room into Roy's temporary war room where the "enemy" was being monitored.

Mike constructed towers of receivers, stacking them five or six at a time next to each other, arranging them from largest on the bottom to smallest on top. In total there were five towers of thirty-five receivers. It still wasn't enough to monitor every single station within the area, but that didn't matter. They could at least monitor enough to know what was happening.

Mike tuned four receivers to just the FMs owned by High Point Media and heard the low hum on all of them, indicating that the transmitters were still on. Then, he switched the dials of a stack of receivers to the AM band and tuned the frequencies to their AM stations. Thankfully, the news of the hijacking hadn't been on the air yet. The morning talk shows, news shows, and sports shows were nationally syndicated, with local news segments at the top of the hour, but they hadn't started reporting on their own hijacking yet. He still had several station frequencies to tune to and stopped the dial on a handful of stations across the LA area of influence, the ones they competed with most for listeners.

He tuned to the FM jazz station. The smooth piano, cymbals, and sax tempted him to turn up the volume to counter the clutter in his head. He moved on to the next receiver and tuned it to another FM with an "oldies" format similar to one of their top FM stations. A low-level competitor, but competition just the same. They were playing an Elton John song.

Up to that point, no station had reported on the situation with the broadcast media in Los Angeles, which struck Mike as peculiar given the presence of apparent independent journalists hanging around after he'd descended from the mountain to rendezvous with the police and ambulance for Tom. What had happened to those people, and why hadn't the news leaked out yet?

It was only 9:15 AM, and regardless of what happened now, Mike felt like this was only the beginning of a very long crisis. He'd already been shaken up at dawn and shot out of a cannon into hell. He could barely manage his anxiety as he tried to dismiss the cyclonic thoughts of the truck blocking the roadway, Tom hitting the ground, all the gushing blood, losing control of the station, panic rising from his gut...

He'd already experienced enough trauma before knowing that other markets had also been taken over. The internal rubber band that twisted around and around in his chest was on the verge of snapping. This situation was only going to get bigger and worse. He didn't know what, but something was brewing. He took a slow, deep breath and let it out even slower.

"This is surreal, isn't it?" Mike said but didn't take his eyes off the array of receivers. "I can't just stand around waiting for orders when there's nothing here for me to do."

"Well, what do we do now?" asked Paul, the KSSP engineer.

Mike took his attention off the radios and looked around the room. This wasn't the typical Monday sales-and-strategy meeting that was usually the first order of business for the week. The sales management team and staff would occupy the conference table and celebrate wins and commiserate over losses. He never attended those meetings, though. He usually didn't have any business in this part of the building.

"That's my question, too." Mike pursed his lips and blew out a puff of air. He rubbed his chin while considering their lack of options. Nothing like this had ever occurred. He had no one to call upon about their next step. He looked down at his bloodstained T-shirt and wondered about Tom.

The room began clearing out except for the engineers installing the command center and the programming department collaborating around the conference table. The staff who had shown up at the station for their normal workday had discovered the stations were in crisis and realized that no work would be done today. Some of them took the opportunity for a day off while others lingered in the halls to discuss what was going on and spread rumors about what could be happening.

"I don't want to wait for a report from the police about our AM transmitter sites," Mike said. "How about you guys take a couple of vehicles and go check them out."

"Don't you want to come too?" Paul asked.

"Yeah, I want to go, but I also want to be here when the FBI shows up," Mike said. But what he really wanted was to hunt down a clean shirt and wash off Tom's blood. "Do you have a gun?" There was a touch of sarcasm in his words but also a hint of sincerity.

******

"Here's what we know so far," Gunner Jeffries said after gathering his team at the other end of the conference table, away from Mike and the engineering chaos. "The majority of the FM stations in LA aren't broadcasting. For now, the news hasn't broken about the shooting at Mount Wilson, but we're going to fix that as soon as we can get straight on how we're going to manage this."

Gunner was the head of all programming for the eight-station cluster, leading a team of four to manage them all. Years ago, when large radio companies began merging to gain a competitive edge, the elimination of staff was used as a cost-cutting measure. Now, rather than one individual being responsible for a radio station's programs, that same individual might be responsible for what goes on the air for two or more. Gunner alone directed all the content for three of the stations, while the other program directors oversaw the remaining ones.

"What do we have?" asked the program director of the Spanish language station.

"We have two of the most top-rated news stations in Los Angeles; that's what we have," Gunner said.

"Yeah, but no actual news staff," complained the program director for one of the FMs, not broadcasting.

"I don't think we have many options right now," said the program director for the AM sports talk station.

"Roy is going to flip out, but I don't see a smarter alternative," Gunner said. "We don't know what's going to happen or how we're going to regain control of our signals again. We don't get to run that show; the authorities do. I think we'd be smart to combine what's going on the air and simulcast all four of our AM stations." Gunner's first instinct for managing the over-the-air content was to shrink the chances of broadcasting varied reports and opinions. He wanted

38

complete control of what they put out over the air until this catastrophic hijacking was resolved.

"Why would we do that?" one Program Director asked.

"Because the media usually covers and reports the news of a crisis, but today, we're the news, and with an audience this size, we've got to keep it under control."

"What are you afraid of?"

"Yeah, for all we know, they're gonna come back on the air playing polka music."

A couple of them chuckled until Mike interrupted them. "Hey! A friend and I got shot a couple of hours ago. Tom is in the hospital. He could die. This is no laughing matter."

"We don't have any idea what they might do," Gunner said, trying to admonish his team for the joke and in doing so, apologize to Mike. "I do *not* want our stations to be responsible for some sort of rhetoric that develops into rumors and innuendo. We need to make sure we keep our reporting and information factual. We not only have a responsibility to report what's going on, we have a duty to protect our listeners as well."

"Roy clearly said he wants the status quo on the AMs so that the company loses no more money," the programmer from the sports station said. "How am I going to just ignore this massive news story with sports programming?"

"We need to pull our resources, and all be working for a common cause," Gunner said, ignoring the comment about Roy's instructions. "It's just more efficient to simulcast. Fewer moving parts, and easier to manage one on-air personality and run prepackaged calls and comments. We've got to handle this delicately, so we don't cause a crisis ourselves."

"You mean like a commentator spouting off their opinions about a corrupt government conspiracy or something?" said the program director for the news station. Laughter went around the table again.

"Exactly. We're not going to create or promote propaganda. Remember the 'War of the Worlds' radio program in the '30s? We don't want a repeat of that kind of chaos with false programming."

Despite the crisis, they still had a job to do. But Gunner just knew. Something bigger was coming. These pirates who'd taken over the broadcast of five major markets hadn't just killed the programming—and shot at people too—just to let it sit there like this. The FBI wouldn't be coming here if this was going to be over soon and all would be back to its regular broadcast as usual.

"We have no FM programming, that's clear. And I think that if we simulcast the four AM stations so that we're broadcasting the same content to all our listeners, we can be consistent with the message. You guys gotta believe that this is going to get bigger, right? It's not just about dead air. More's coming, and we need to be prepared."

"You think Roy will go for that? All that loss of revenue on top of this?" asked the Program Director from the sports station.

"This could run away from us at the speed of light if we don't manage the content on air," Gunner said, adamant. "I'm not at all worried about how Roy is going to feel about it. If we lose advertisers or listeners because of a crisis programming decision, then I'll lose my job. I really don't care."

Regardless of the crisis, radio stations still had to operate under federal law. No matter how frightening the circumstance, like first responders, they had a duty to perform. He also couldn't put anyone on the air with a report until they had a plan, a narrative, and an anchor for the broadcast.

"We cannot simply rely on callers. We need a 'man on the street' approach too, someone who'll be an objective reporter. That way, we can control some of the content. We can use our AI program to give us more studio voices."

"I think we need to have one voice on the air here as an anchor," said the programmer for one of the AM news stations. "I could send out some of our people with remote equipment to talk to those out on the street and report back what they see or hear."

Gunner waved and got Mike's attention from across the conference room, but the guy appeared to still be in shock as he stood there talking to the engineers and staring at the equipment set up on the counter. "Hey, I need you guys to set us up to simulcast," Gunner told Mike.

A momentary pause. Mike's train of thought was broken. "What time do you want the simulcast to begin?" he asked.

"10:00. All stations point to AM 790."

Mike left the conference room, followed by his four engineers. Flipping a few switches in Master Control was all it would really take. The stations were already set up for it as KLAR AM 790 was California's emergency alert station, responsible for being on the air to inform the public of all emergency information and in case the president of the United States needed to address the nation.

"We also need to manage social media and control what's happening on our internet radio stream," Gunner told his team. "In order to dispel confusion, I think it's best to cut off the regular programming so that it's not airing over the internet. It's already beginning to gain some traction. We're already getting calls from listeners questioning why so many stations are off the air, and somebody's going to report on it very soon."

It just made sense to Gunner to limit their exposure and the risk that someone would say or do the wrong thing on the air and set off some sort of chain reaction. Nobody had a clue what that might be, but most had been in the radio news business long enough to know how unpredictable situations could be, and this situation, in particular, was unprecedented. They truly had nothing to prepare for.

The group discussed the potential dangers of reporting too much information to the public. After all, the hijacking of their transmitters was an ongoing investigation. Because they were technically victims, they weren't permitted to share details from law enforcement, which conflicted with their responsibility to inform the public for safety reasons.

"We'll write some scripts and talking points in order to control the messaging," Gunner said. "We don't know moment by moment what will develop, so we have to control what we can. One broadcast message on all four frequencies is manageable."

He looked at his watch. 9:30. If he wanted to get a handle on this by 10:00, they had to get moving; end of discussion. Against the wishes of his team, he'd made the decision. The biggest programming decision of his career.

And he feared that it just might end it.

"So far, the public is not yet aware of what has happened. They don't know that we have no control over our transmitters. It's only dead air."

They finally agreed that the content they put on the air would guide their communities through this. The messaging had to be consistent, congruent, and easy to digest. They'd be reaching out to a wider audience now, which meant they needed a unified message that appealed to everyone.

"Who should we call on to be that one voice?" asked the programmer from the sports station. "Certainly not a commentator, but I bet we could find an athlete. People listen to them."

"How about Stevie Gold?" suggested the one in charge of KLCL. "He's already here and has been in the jock lounge all morning. He's pumped up and ready to get back on the air."

Gunner knew he'd have to make a final decision. It was the job of his team to know their on-air personalities and their audience intimately. And although he trusted their input and suggestions, ultimately it was going to be his decision on how to present their message to their combined listeners.

"Stevie is all wrong for this," Gunner said, taking a swig from his water and coughing a little as it went down. He wanted to be fully transparent with his team and knew that Stevie just didn't have the maturity to be an anchor. "You know, he's just a morning-show personality playing pranks and hosting fun. He'd be too unpredictable and wouldn't have the trust of our older audience. This is just too serious of a matter."

Cutbacks through consolidation had gutted their live news department years ago. Although there were anchors and political pundits who were on the airwaves through syndication from a studio on the East Coast, they would not be focused specifically on the LA market. Gunner believed news anchors and political pundits would only stoke the fire of controversy, and the music personalities might make light of the situation or use dialogue that would need to be censored. And, while all their talk-show hosts were smart and informed, some of them followed conspiracy theorists, and Gunner couldn't take the chance that they'd start frightening listeners. No, it had to be someone who would be a calm and authoritative voice over the air.

They discussed the virtues of each announcer on their staff of eight stations: a couple of news reporters, talk-show hosts, and radio personalities. They reviewed their characteristics, how they handled pressure, and even their political ideologies and personal hang-ups. The thing Gunner and his team could agree on most was that they had a very diverse cast of characters at their disposal and wanted to make sure they chose the right voice to represent their message.

"We can send our reporters out of the station if and when we end up needing to. But we need someone live and local, someone who knows and loves LA and its people, and our listeners."

"How about Edward Dunagan?" the program director for AM News talk 1290 said. Dunagan had experience and integrity in LA, hosting a mid-morning legal analysis program called "He's Done It Again with Edward Dunagan."

"He's a lawyer," Gunner said, shaking his head. "That's as bad as a political pundit. We don't need that right now."

"Without a full-blown news department, we don't have an experienced anchor to put behind the mic." Said Gunner

The mention of another afternoon reporter's name was brought up, but Gunner wasn't happy with any of their options. He had a vision in mind.

And suddenly, he knew what he wanted to do.

He wanted to bring in Jackie Shure, his midday personality, on the urban music station. He'd been working with her on developing a podcast as a side project. She didn't want to be pigeonholed, and he'd promised her he'd help her become a talk-show host.

"I think we should go with Jackie Shure," Gunner said.

"She's not an anchor, she's a hip-hop jock!" the news programmer complained.

"Exactly!" Gunner slapped his hand on the table. "Experience brings arrogance and cynicism. Jackie is neither of those. She'll listen and be objective. She has an impressive range of appeal."

He felt the midday personality on KSSP just might be the best choice. The younger generation was more likely to act out in panic. They'd also be more likely to respond to a voice like Jackie than that of a legal analyst. But, of course, he knew he was biased. Three years ago, he hired her after a stint in Las Vegas at an urban station. He'd discovered her while listening to a local station when he was up there to attend a broadcast conference and liked her persona on the air. She was smart as a whip and had the professional demeanor and soothing voice like the "mama" that they needed right now. Gunner reminded the group that her audience was loyal and large, and whenever she was out in public, people flocked to her, and she responded in kind. He was confident she was the right choice.

"I don't know if it's such a good idea to bring her in as the voice of our station. She doesn't have the same integrity that Dunagan has." Said the program director for the news station.

"Dunagan knows the law. That's it," Gunner said. "Jackie knows people, and she's great on the mic and connects with her audience. Plus, she has a degree in psychology and wants to be a talk-show host. Dunagan's ego alone will get out of control. I can manage Jackie."

Gunner wouldn't budge. He wanted the other programmers' agreement but was willing to go against their consideration if he had to. He knew he could guide her and that she'd be able to deliver.

Finally, the other programmers conceded, knowing full well that Gunner had the final say and there was no convincing him to go with someone else. They weren't certain that Jackie was the right choice, but a decision needed to be made. The clock was ticking.

Chapter Six

Jackie's Moment

9:15 AM

Jackie looked at her reflection in the mirror. She just got a text from the boss that she needed to get to the station as quickly as possible because of an emergency. He needed her to be there before ten o'clock. She'd already been getting ready to go in, even though she knew they weren't on the air. She'd been texting with her producer pals from the station and knew they weren't broadcasting—but that didn't stop her from going in to see what's up.

Rumors were already starting, but Jackie paid no mind to rumors. She would get to the truth, and for that, she needed to be close to the action. With no time to spare, she chose not to bother with her usual style of makeup today, opting for the bare essentials on her face and realizing she preferred it that way.

Dressed in comfy brown office slacks and a cream-colored tunic, she slipped into her gold sandals and matched the ensemble with gold earrings and a bracelet. She may only be on the radio, but she always liked to dress as though she was going to make a public appearance. Her radio persona was as authentic as she was. She may not be a famous radio personality hosting her own talk show—yet—but that didn't mean she couldn't dress the part.

Anxious to get to the station now that Gunner had summoned her, she gathered her bag, phone, keys, and notepad and looked herself over once more in the full-length mirror before hurrying out the door. As she made her way downstairs from her apartment, she was glad she'd found this place in North Hollywood three years ago when she moved back to LA from Las Vegas. It was just a short commute, only a fifteen-minute drive up Victory Boulevard to the High Point office in Burbank.

She flipped through the frequencies on the radio in her silver late-model Lexus sedan and turned onto Victory Boulevard. The sun was shining, and it looked like a typical spring morning in the Southland. Jackie tuned to her own station, where she would normally listen to the "Bad Boy Hip-Hop Show" to get her day going and mentally and creatively prepare for her shift behind the microphone that started at ten o'clock. But instead of the crazy morning show, it was nothing but dead air, and it had been this way for nearly four hours.

She asked Gunner what they were doing about the dead air, and he only texted back with a short answer: *We're working on it.*

Jackie arrived at the parking structure and maneuvered her way through the garage to her assigned space right next to the entrance to the elevators that led to the lobby of the multi-story, multi-company office building in Burbank where the eight radio stations owned by High Point Media were located. The parking situation in Los Angeles presented many issues, and Jackie was always immeasurably grateful that her assigned parking spot for work was right next to the elevator. *Perks of being an LA DJ*, she noted as she danced her way to the elevator. *You get to park near the front door.* A great parking space in LA was a treasure to be celebrated.

The elevator brought her up to the lobby, and she made her way to the bank of elevators that went to the third floor, where the station's studios and offices were located. Once the elevator doors opened, Jackie hurriedly walked down the corridor to the conference room, where she saw the group of program directors sitting around the table while the station's engineering employees milled around by the back corner. The hallway was bustling with activity as other staff mingled while drinking their morning coffee.

As she scanned the room, she saw the wall of receivers stacked on top of each other. It was an impressive display. Nobody looked up when she walked in and nearly tripped on the cables lying on the floor. Her heart started to race, and for the first time, as her eyes opened wider, she was filled with panic, "Oh my god..." she whispered. "This isn't a prank; it's for real! What the heck is going on?" she asked her boss, eyes darting around the landscape of the room to take it all in and keep Gunner's face in sight. A shudder rolled through her shoulders as she attempted to mentally process everything she was seeing.

Gunner got up from where he sat at the conference table and led Jackie to his office on the other end of the third floor.

Jackie Shure had been the midday air personality on the urban station for High Point Media in Los Angeles for three years now. Her warm and confident rapport with her audience had made her a household name with the station's target audience. "This is Jackie Shure, sure to be with you and sure to make you groove", was her opening line each day.

"Sit down." Gunner pointed to a chair at the round table in his office, reached into his mini fridge, and pulled out two bottles of water before he joined Jackie at the table, who was looking confused and stunned. She pulled out a chair and sat down, but only on the edge, and with perfectly straight posture. There was nothing here to feel relaxed about.

Gunner's small office was neat and tidy, and there was only room for his desk and the table with two chairs. Photos and posters of music stars and concerts that the stations promoted adorned Gunner's walls. His desk was small, not like the monstrously enormous desk she'd seen in Roy Longly's office. In fact, by comparison, Gunner's desk was miniature. The bookshelves against the wall behind him displayed a few books on programming and audience statistics, but the focal point was the award he received when he was nominated for Program Director of the Year by his peers a few years ago.

She'd sat at this table a hundred times with Gunner, going over her show and discussing ideas, music, and promotions the station was involved with. This wasn't their typical show prep meeting.

"What is all of this?" Jackie asked. "I just thought there was some joke being played on the radio stations in town. You know, April Fools' and all."

"No. Stations in five major markets have been hijacked by some terrorists or something like that," Gunner said. "We have no control over our FM transmitters located up on Mount Wilson, including KSSP."

He spent a few minutes explaining the chain of events and what they knew right now, driving home the gravity of the situation. Jackie's posture never changed, remaining upright and stiff as she listened. She shook her head in disbelief, even though she knew what he was telling her was indeed happening.

"So, what can I do?" she asked. Eager to be put to work in any capacity, Jackie Shure was always ready to jump in and help wherever she was needed. Feeling motivated to persistently prove herself, she felt great personal satisfaction when she was appreciated, even for the smallest of things. She prided herself on being a people pleaser, and it showed in her work ethic.

"Right now, we're anticipating some fallout with radio listeners, and most likely advertisers too. We don't know how this is going to develop or when we're going to regain control of the transmitters and resume normal programming. It's not as if the public is unaware that these stations aren't broadcasting anything, but we're helpless to get access to Mount Wilson, and while the FBI and our engineers are trying to figure it out, we need to implement our emergency plan."

"What's the plan for an emergency like this?" she asked. She knew there were policies and procedures that radio stations needed to follow because of the FCC but was unfamiliar with the specifics.

"Well, the emergency plan has essentially been thrown out the window. There never was a plan drafted for what to do in case your airwaves are hijacked, only for natural disasters, so we're operating on instinct now," Gunner said.

Jackie nodded.

"The programming plan for now is to give as much information as possible without alarming the audience with unnecessary facts or half-truths. And we've all agreed that to manage that, we're going to combine all our stations into one broadcast using one anchored voice. And we unanimously agreed that it would be you." He leaned over the table and touched her hand. He needed her to be ready and confident and to know that he had her back.

"I want you to go on the air and be yourself," he said. "You already know how to present the information. You'll explain what's happening and give out any emergency information as it comes in. You'll be the voice representing our stations."

Gunner knew what this meant for Jackie. It was a rare opportunity to step into the spotlight. She'd been an excellent team player, and he'd enjoyed working with her as she developed. He didn't know how long this broadcast would last, but he knew she was up for the job.

"But I thought you said we have no control over KSSP?" Jackie's mouth suddenly felt dry, and she took a sip of her water, hiding her fear that she wasn't as ready as she thought for this responsibility.

"Right, we don't. You're going to be on all four of our AM stations. We'll start simulcasting all four signals coming up here at ten o'clock. I've got some scripts and talking points for you, and I need you to prepare yourself by getting up to speed on the events of the last few hours."

"I don't feel so good," she said. Her stomach was flip-flopping every second. "I'm not an anchor, I'm a hip-hop jock. A personality."

Fear ripped through her. This was what she'd always wanted, so why was she afraid of it?

A small voice in Jackie's mind reminded her of her mother mocking her when she was a young girl. She flashed back to a memory of her sitting on the floor in front of the TV while she watched her favorite inspirational talk-show host when she'd turned around and looked at her mom sitting in the recliner behind her.

"I'm going to be just like her one day!" Jackie said.

Her mom just laughed and said, "Who do you think you are? You'll never be like her, and you'll never be that famous!"

Here, Gunner was handing Jackie a big break on a silver platter, but it was coming at a time of crisis, with a responsibility far larger than any she'd ever dreamed of. And she didn't even have the luxury of celebrating her unexpected promotion because of just how seriously she had to take this event.

"You're going to be great, Jackie!" Gunner said. "This is who you are!" He stood and motioned for her to follow him.

Speechless, she followed him out of his office, up the corridor, and into the main studio for AM 790 KLAR, the number one news and talk station in the Greater Los Angeles area.

Her thoughts raced as her mind processed the importance of what Gunner had just assigned her to do. The volume of potential audience numbers astounded her as she added them up in her head. Jackie Shure was about to get her big break, and she was nervous as hell. She was going to be the voice that everyone, *everyone*, was going to be listening to in LA, at least on the High Point stations.

Although the circumstances that had elevated her were frightening, she also couldn't help but feel excited because she knew what this could mean for her broadcasting career. This was her chance to change everything. Jackie had always wanted to be more than just a disc jockey playing music. She was born in Los Angeles, and when she earned her way back here three years ago, she was thrilled to make it to the big leagues. Now here she was, being asked to speak to the greater LA area about a seriously frightening situation, and it had nothing to do with music. No one knew what was happening.

She followed Gunner through the heavy soundproof door into the KLAR studio. Each studio in the station was practically identical, so Jackie knew her way around the board, but this was still unfamiliar territory, and she felt overwhelmed. It didn't have the same branding and look, and it smelled different.

The wall hangings, mic covers, and labels were stamped with *KLAR*, not *KSSP*, as she was used to seeing, but other than that, the space was designed the same them, but other than that, the space was designed the same way as the KSSP studio she was familiar with. In fact, the KSSP studio felt so much like home to her that she kept a pair of slippers stored in the cabinet for when she really wanted to "get comfortable with her audience."

The KLAR studio was large enough that one could easily walk around the humongous console in the center of the room. She walked to where the microphone, computer, and other components were situated in such a way that it resembled the cockpit of a jetliner. Thankfully the engineering department labeled every button, dial, and knob in the same fashion in each studio, which made it fairly easy to move from one studio to the next and still know where everything was.

"What's on the air right now?" Jackie asked. She put her purse on the chair behind her and reached in for her phone and notepad, then placed them on the console board in front of her. Touching the button to increase the volume in the studio, she discovered the station was airing a traffic report that led to a commercial for a local car dealership. The ten o'clock hour was only 120 seconds away.

Gunner handed her a few papers as she adjusted the microphone boom so that the mic reached her mouth at just the right position. She reached for the headphones and placed them around her neck.

"How am I to handle all this?" she asked Gunner. Her body was shaking from the adrenaline flowing through her veins. She realized that this "hijacking" could grow into a bigger crisis as she read the material that had been given to her. She read through the script, and the message became much more real as she practiced out loud the pre-written words warning listeners what was happening.

"You will not be alone. We only have one job here today, and that's to inform the public," Gunner said. "For now, you'll just read from the script and use the talking points we've provided. Until something changes, this is all we can do. There really is no 'emergency' as far as the public is concerned. We just have to broadcast this to address the undeniable fact that forty percent of radio and television stations in Los Angeles are not airing any programming."

Just then, one of the part-time board operators walked into the studio. "Help and support is here!" he said, and Jackie felt relief to see she was getting reinforcements.

"Travis is going to assist you for the time being with whatever we need," Gunner said. "We're going to set up interviews with local and national authorities." Travis settled in on the other side of the controls from Jackie and placed his headphones over his ears.

"We're pulling all our collective resources together for one broadcast, so don't worry," Gunner continued, "we have plenty of people screening and pre-recording calls. In fact, that's what we've got the other show hosts and reporters doing in the other studios."

"Wouldn't one of the actual news reporters or talk-show hosts from KLAR be better suited for this?" she asked.

Gunner placed his hands on her shoulders, looked her straight in the eye, and said, "This could potentially become dangerous. We're blindly considering all possibilities, but the fact is, people have been shot at, and more than a hundred stations are off the air. This has the attention of the FCC, FBI, and Homeland Security. It may turn into an international incident or a national security issue, at the very least. I have no time to contend with egos. We have to proceed with caution and transparency. We can't have pundits doling out their personal opinions today. We need someone who will follow directions and just be calm, not go off the rails."

Jackie knew she sounded like an insecure little girl. Most of the time, she could mask her insecurities with humor and laughter, but today, she wasn't able to hide it. Inside, she was freaking out.

"I've been in this business for a long time," he said. "The entire programming department carefully considered the options of whom to put on the air today. We can't have egos stepping all over one another, and the listeners don't need political pundits speculating about how the government failed to protect us or anything about our company being too cheap, or whatever sort of dialogue they might try to start.

"What we need is someone our listeners will trust. Someone who sounds calm and reassuring. That's you."

Gunner glanced over Jackie's shoulder at the clock and removed the hand he'd placed there to give her reassurance. It was 09:59:50. "Ten seconds to air," he said, moving away from Jackie with a smile and thumbs-up.

Jackie pulled the headphones over her ears and adjusted the microphone to her lips. As the red light flicked on, indicating they were live on the air, she felt her breath catch and her stomach twist. It lasted only a fraction of a second before she opened her mouth to speak.

Chapter Seven

Beneath Suspicion

10:00 AM

The events of the morning had left Mike's body worn out. He found himself torn between the endlessness of this day and the disbelief that it was only ten. It had been four hours since his abrupt wake-up call. He hadn't even eaten anything yet today. He needed to fix that.

The men's room on the third floor was empty, and he was thankful no one was in there when he arrived to change his shirt and get cleaned up. He locked the door. He needed some quiet right now, some time to decompress.

He hadn't heard about Tom's condition yet, nor had he had a moment to inquire about it. Mike was simultaneously concerned for his friend and relieved it wasn't him who'd been shot. The conflicting emotions were exhausting.

He carefully tugged the soiled shirt with Tom's blood over his head. The water coming out of the faucet was warm, and he wet some paper towels and washed the streaks of blood from his arms and chest. As the minutes passed, Mike's questions only grew. His anxiety peaked when his phone vibrated: a text from Roy to meet him in the conference room.

The FBI has some questions for you.

Good! I have questions for them, too. Mike splashed water on his face and ran his wet hands through his scalp to get his scraggily mess under control. He pulled some dry paper towels from the dispenser, dried off and put on the clean radio-station T-shirt he'd gotten from the promotions department. At least he'd brushed his teeth this morning and now had on a clean shirt. That was the least he could do. He looked at himself in the mirror and gave himself one last check before he left the silent solitude of the bathroom to return to the conference room to confer with the FBI.

He stopped at his office first and dropped his dirty shirt on his desk, looking longingly at the Big Gulp cup of warm flat Coke. No wonder he was so tired. Would it be possible to sneak out of here in a while and get his morning jolt?

Mike entered the nearly empty conference room where Roy and two men in suits were seated at the huge table. The audio receivers were all set up, the volume turned down to level one, and the crowd that had flooded the room earlier had left. Roy was explaining to the FBI agents how he had instructed his crew to set up the stacks of receivers so they could monitor all the radio stations, off and on the air, so if and when something changed, they would hear about it as it occurred. He was proud of how quickly and cleverly his engineering department had rounded up every piece of equipment they had at their disposal and created a functional receiving command center in record time, and wanted the authorities to know it...

Roy greeted Mike, and all three men around the table stood up as if he were somebody important. Mike wasn't typically the guy that authority figures stood up for. He was a quiet engineer that minded his own business, no more, no less, not someone who was part of important meetings like this—unless there was a technical issue, but those meetings were never held in the conference room.

But now the room no longer felt like a radio station, having taken on the appearance of a command center, with the equipment on the counter and the authorities here to investigate. Mike leaned over and grabbed a water bottle off the center of the table. Water would have to do for now.

"This is FBI Special Agent Chuck Forrester," Roy said, "and this is his partner, Special Agent Jacob Dominguez."

Mike just nodded, pulled out a chair, and joined them at the table.

"Roy has filled us in on the events of the morning, and we have some questions for you as we conduct this investigation," Agent Forrester began. He sat down across from Mike as if he were interrogating a suspect. "You were the first responder, is that correct?"

"Yes," Mike said, twisting the cap off his water bottle and taking a swig. "I got a call this morning just after 6 AM that one of our stations was off the air."

"And what did you do next?"

Mike recounted his actions during the earlier hours. It sounded like make-believe to him as the words poured out of his mouth. His radio stations had been hijacked. He'd borne witness to a shooting. Everything was out of control. He wanted to know about Tom. "Do you have any word on him?"

"Not yet," Forrester said. "Describe for me the details of the events leading up to when you arrived here at the station."

Mike told them everything he could remember, but he was still in shock. Some of the details were fuzzy.

"What do you mean the remote control to the transmitter was disabled from the mountain?" Forrester asked. "I understand this is probably an elementary question for you, so please forgive me, but can you explain to me how that works?"

Once again, Mike, the resistant professor, pushed his chair away from the table, stood, and made his way to the whiteboard. He picked up a dry-erase marker, removed the cap, and picked up where he'd left off with the drawn diagram earlier.

"Every station that transmits from Mount Wilson has had their programming disrupted." He watched their eyes glaze over like a couple of high school kids who couldn't grasp physics.

"But wait!" Forrester said as if he'd just had a brilliant idea. "Can't we just have the electric company cut the power off at Mount Wilson?"

Mike found such a naïve question amusing.

"That would be an idea, Special Agent," Mike said. "If simply cutting the power off was even an option, I would've suggested it once we lost control of the stations, but we have backup generators at our transmitters."

"Backup generators for every station?" Forrester seemed surprised.

"Yes, we all have backup generators to operate the transmitters in order to keep the stations on the air in case of an emergency or a mass power outage. Some stations have tankers underground with as many as thirty thousand gallons of diesel fuel. They could stay on the air for months."

"But there are some stations that are still on the air," Forrester said.

"Yes, our AM stations," Roy said.

"And what are those stations playing right now?"

"Just a little while ago, at ten o'clock, we veered away from our regular programming on all of them and combined the signals. We're now simulcasting one program on all four of the AMs," Roy said, still unhappy with the decision Gunner had made. Combining what was on the air for four radio stations into a single stream only made the company lose more money.

"This really is uncharted territory here. We need to consult with higher authorities," Forrester said. "But we cannot express enough how imperative it is for you to narrow your commentary to just the facts and keep that as a 'need to know' for your audience."

"Narrow our commentary?" Roy said. "That's impossible. We're a media company; we report news and information. We won't keep this under wraps. That's ludicrous!"

"Understood." Forrester held up his hands in a gesture of surrender. He then looked over at Mike, who was sitting quietly, tearing the label off his water bottle and taking it all in. *This is a nightmare.*

"Roy tells us that your apprentice"—Forrester paused to look at his notes—"Albert Braun is not accounted for. When was the last time you saw him?"

"Albert and I were just up at Mount Wilson last night," Mike said. "In fact, we'd been up and down the mountain all weekend. I didn't even get home until after midnight."

"Did Albert drive himself up there?"

"Yeah."

"Did he leave when you did?"

"Yeah, I locked up the transmitter building, we walked to our cars together, and he followed me down the mountain."

"What happened after that?"

"I got home and went to bed."

"And Albert?"

"He was actually headed to LAX. He'd been bitching at me about how long we were taking because he had to get to the airport. He's headed back East to visit his family."

"Vacation?" Forrester said. "That's convenient.

"What's that supposed to mean?" Mike was angry. "There's no way that Albert has anything to do with this!" And yet, flashes of conversation rang in Mike's ear.

Albert loved to talk about conspiracy theories and how "they" were going to take over the world.

"So, tell us more about this Albert Braun." Agent Forrester shot a glance at his partner, with a silent nod, instructing him to check the man out. Agent Dominguez nodded and picked up his phone.

Mike leaned back in his chair, covered his face with his hands, and slowly shook his head. He took a deep breath and lowered his hands, letting out a long sigh. "Albert knows the whole ball of wax about Mount Wilson. I taught him everything up there.

"We've worked together for about a year and a half now," Mike continued. "He's brilliant, and I've enjoyed working with him. Heck, he even came to our house for Thanksgiving last year when he couldn't get home for the holiday. I just cannot believe he would have anything to do with something like this."

"We'll get more background information on him now," Forrester said. Domínguez dialed a number on his phone and quietly spoke to who Mike assumed was an agent on the other end, giving them Albert's name.

Mike filled Agent Forrester in on how Albert had come to work for him a couple of years ago. High Point Media had been working on the plans to build their new facility and move all eight of their radio stations to this new location. Mike had needed an assistant for the project, so he'd hired Albert, who proved to be a critical addition to the engineering team, doing his fair share of the new transmitter installations. They'd been under enormous pressure to get modern technology installed and operational under the deadlines that corporate demanded. Albert's eagerness to go up to Mount Wilson at all hours to work in order to keep up with corporate's demands had proved to be invaluable for Mike. They'd been working at Mount Wilson for weeks installing new equipment.

"Where did you find him?" Forrester asked.

"He answered an ad," Mike said.

"Did you do a background check? I'd like to look into his personnel records. We're sending agents to his address right now to investigate."

"You're wasting your time, I'm telling you."

"Has he ever said or done anything that has made you question him? Anything suspicious at all?" Forrester asked.

Would being a conspiracy theorist count? Would that make Albert suspicious? Mike decided to keep that to himself—for now.

"There are a lot of engineers that could have done this," he said. "Why do you think it must be Albert? I know he's on an airplane right now. I just saw him last night!"

"We're exploring every lead, and since Mr. Braun is the only engineer not accounted for from your staff, we need to check on him and find out where he's at."

"Why do you suspect Albert anyway?" Roy asked. Even as he sat here with Mike and the FBI, his phone was vibrating with voicemails, texts, and emails. He didn't even need to look. He knew it would be filled with angry clients.

"What we do know so far is that your company is a common denominator," Forrester said. "High Point Media is the only group owner with stations located on all five transmitter sites in Los Angeles, San Francisco, Chicago, New York, and Dallas. If this is an inside job, it's quite probable that it originates from someone within High Point Media."

Mike knew he meant Albert. High Point Media was either the target or the perpetrator. But could Albert really be one of those pirates who hijacked his radio stations? There was no way.

"What about the other stations here in LA, and all the other markets?" Mike asked. "There are nearly a hundred other radio stations off the air right now." He looked over at Roy, who was looking down at the table.

"Right now, we suspect High Point engineers are all who are involved," Forrester said. "But that's all we've got so far."

Mike shot another look over at Roy. He could tell by the look on his face that he knew about this. Roy's boss had informed him before the FBI arrived that their company's engineers were missing in all five markets, and they'd confirmed it before asking Mike to join them. Roy hadn't even had the opportunity to tell his own staff that their company was not only a victim but quite possibly responsible.

Mike was horrified. "How many of the High Point engineers are missing?"

"At least one per market, which makes five unaccounted for," Roy said.

"That's all they'd need." Mike lowered his eyes and looked at the naked water bottle in his hand. The remnants of the shredded label lay on the table.

"The FBI alone does not have the workforce to visit every radio station, and we don't really need to," Forrester said. "Narrowing down the possible suspects speeds up our process."

The four men discussed the developments and brainstormed "what if" scenarios while communicating with other agents in the field. Reports indicated there were snipers on the rooftops of the Hancock and Sears Tower in Chicago and the Empire State Building in New York as well, but nobody had been struck by a bullet. For now, the authorities were monitoring the situation. Setting up a command site at the base of Mount Wilson would be the next step, along with dispatching emergency crews.

"All you guys are interested in is who did this and going after that," Mike said. "I have more important work to do, like getting our stations back and figuring this out myself." He pushed his chair away from the table and stood.

"This is a crime we're investigating, and they take days, even weeks to see through. It's only been a couple of hours," Dominguez said." The shooting and blockade of the properties are our top priorities. But, as long as the stations remain silent, there's no cause for alarm. It's just radio."

Mike and Roy let out a collective huff, disgusted by the perception that the casualties so far were just a bunch of silent radio stations.

"They go hand in hand." Mike was exasperated. "I want to go to Mount Wilson, to the base camp their setting up. I can't just sit around here waiting for someone else to figure out what's going on."

"What do you think you can do?" Dominguez asked.

Mike's body was vibrating and shaking, his thoughts racing as he contemplated what he might be able to do...

"I have a drone in my Explorer." The words came out of his mouth the moment he remembered the drone he'd just bought. In fact, it was Albert who'd introduced him to drones, and they'd planned to go out and experiment with them at some point. Mike himself had only flown his a couple of times. "I could fly over the towers and record video footage."

Forrester wasn't convinced it was a good idea to let Mike go, but Dominguez argued that Mike could be a good resource to help survey the landscape.

"I'm for anything that can get these stations back under our control," Roy agreed.

"We can't allow you to drive up there without an escort," Forrester said. "But Dominguez can drive you up there."

Mike felt a wave of relief. At least he could do something now. Mount Wilson had been his home away from home for thirty years. The idea of a police escort was surreal. The mountain that he'd traveled up and down for most of his career had been tainted and violated. It no longer felt like it belonged to him.

#**transmittergate**

"We're trending on social media!" Gunner announced as he pushed through the heavy soundproof door to the KLAR AM studio where Jackie and her board op, Travis, were taking a momentary break while a pre-recorded message played over the air.

In a fluid motion, Jackie reached for her phone and opened up her social media profile while Travis opened up the station's social media and put it on the computer screen next to the monitor that displayed what was on the air.

Jackie's lips turned up with a smile as she read the posts.

#wherestheradio was part of hundreds of comments, likes, and shares. There were others too, like *#Whereareyouradio* and *#IWantMyRadio*, in honor of the 1980s slogan when MTV had arrived on the scene. Jackie chuckled at all the posts, many of them accompanied by pictures of the posters.

"Oh my gosh, look at this one of a woman posing next to her car radio," Jackie said, sharing her phone with Gunner. A photo was of a woman leaning over the dashboard in her car with her face close to her car radio, holding her hand up as if she was asking a question. The frequency shown on the dial was *102.5*, which was the frequency for KSSP, the station that Jackie's show should be on at this very moment... but wasn't. The hashtag for the photo was *#IMissMyShureThing*.

Feeling flattered, Jackie was opening the post to reply when Gunner said, "Stop!"

"What?" Jackie was indignant that Gunner would ever command her to stop. "I have to let her know I'm still here, just on a different frequency!"

"I don't mean don't communicate at all, but let's discuss just what we ought to be saying."

She was only half paying attention to Gunner. She also had to pay attention to what she was monitoring in her left ear from the left cup cushion of her headphones; the right cup cushion pushed back behind her ear so she could hear what was being said in the room while still keeping an ear on what was on the air. She held up her index finger at Gunner, pushed the volume slider that opened up her mic, and rejoined the radio audience with another written statement the station had permitted her to say.

She thanked the reporter who'd provided the sound bite even though she didn't have any idea what it was about after the distraction of learning about the trending posts on social media. "Now, I've just been handed some new information, and I really want to talk about it, so bear with me, everybody. I'm sure to be right back with some breaking news." She gave a cue to Travis, who played back a recorded message from one of the news reporters about traffic and what to do in case of an emergency.

Jackie turned the mic off and tugged the headset down around her neck.

"I gotta talk to my audience," Jackie said, turning toward Gunner, who had positioned himself on the chair she'd discarded earlier. With his phone in his hand, he was scrolling through posts and making note of the varying hashtags and pictures being shared.

"I know, Jackie; I just want to carefully craft what we say."

Jackie stood her ground. "Freedom of speech, Gunner! I know I work for this radio company, so I have a responsibility to represent it in a way that serves the company's mission, but this is bullshit! I'm also a radio personality with an audience that trusts me. If I can't get on social media and let them know that I'm on the air but on a different frequency, how will they find me?"

"It's alright, Jackie," Gunner chuckled. "I'm not insinuating you can't say anything. I want you to be... well, Jackie Shure. I believe in you, but there's more to this than just posting randomly. We need to be strategic. Hear me out."

She took a breath and looked across the console at Travis. He gave her a shoulder shrug and a thumbs-up. She looked back at Gunner. "Okay, what do you have to say?"

Then the studio door swung open, and in walked Roy Longley. The boss-man. Jackie hadn't seen Roy when she arrived. In fact, she'd been so shocked to learn about the situation as she was first ushered to Gunner's office and then the KLAR studio that she hadn't even acknowledged who else was present at the station.

"Have you guys been watching what's trending on social media?" Roy asked, holding up his phone as evidence. "I briefed the FBI guys in the conference room, but we need to discuss how we're going to respond on the air and on our station pages."

"This isn't as simple as a news story or a programming plan," Gunner said. "We've never experienced this before, so we don't have a plan. Do we need to consult with those suits we've got in the conference room?"

"Why would we need to consult with law enforcement about how we program our own radio stations and social media?" Jackie asked.

Roy looked at her. "Because, like it or not, this is a crime scene."

Her posture shifted as she leaned in toward Gunner. Roy walked closer to the console.

"What do you mean *this* is a crime scene?" Jackie cocked her head to the left as if she needed that left ear to listen to the other side of the story.

"I know I whisked you straight into this studio practically the moment you arrived," Gunner said, matter-of-fact. "I know it feels like an eternity since our programs were disrupted and the dead air started, but this is an ongoing investigation with the FBI. We may actually be in trouble here."

"What do you mean trouble?" Jackie sneered. "If anything, our FM stations—in fact, radio in general—is the victim here. Our transmitters have been hijacked!"

"Exactly." Roy nodded. "Our radio stations are the victims here, but it looks as though at least one engineer from all these markets isn't accounted for, and all five are from our company. They're investigating those stations, too. We're being asked how this could have happened right under our nose."

Jackie's eyebrows rose. This was far beyond "trouble."

"Who's in trouble?" she asked.

"I don't know. All I can say is what I've been learning as details have been coming in. Corporate is scrambling for answers and a plan too," Roy said. "We are not alone. I just know that I've been informed to run my stations as I fit until things change. The FCC and Homeland Security have instructed us to control the message. They're afraid of false information and fake news. You know how badly rumors can get out of control, especially on social media."

"Well, without being able to share facts, I'm just lying to the audience. So, how do I reply to this post and any others that are coming in?" Jackie was looking at the computer screen and watching the station's social media feed.

"We're setting up automated social media posts with our AI program," Gunner said. "We're telling your KSSP audience to find you over here."

"So you don't want me to respond to posts that mention me directly?" she asked, wanting confirmation.

"Focus on what you're doing here in the studio. Today is not the day to worry about what you post too." Gunner had already directed another board op to monitor social media and send out notifications to their registered listeners to tune in to AM 790 for all the information. It had only been a few hours since their stations went dead, but now that radio was trending on social media, they had to address the questions and concerns from their listeners.

"This is where it really gets sticky for us. Our airwaves are public domain, which is why we have a license to broadcast from the federal government," Roy reminded them. "We have a responsibility to inform our audience, but we're also the victim of a crime, and it's an ongoing investigation." He looked at Gunner and insisted he keep some advertisers on the air between segments.

"I don't care about the sponsors, Roy," Gunner fumed. "This is a national news story. Most LA radio stations are silent, and people may be having fun with it now, but we haven't yet broken the news about the shooting or that those stations have been hijacked. Commercials are the last thing we need right now." He knew though, that Roy was just toeing the company line and that the company was losing millions of dollars an hour in every market. The losses would be catastrophic.

Roy looked again at the social media on his phone. "The sales team is having to explain to all their clients that their commercials won't air today. They're angry, and they're asking questions we cannot answer. Every second, the financial losses are hitting us, *big-time*."

They all looked at the screen on top of the console and watched the feed tick off one comment and picture after another. Their listeners were certainly getting creative with their selfies and hashtags.

Travis signaled to Jackie that the segment that was playing was about to end and that she needed to be ready to go live in ten seconds. She pulled the headphones up over her ears, turned her mic switch back on, and slowly turned up the gain.

"Back again, everybody; this is Jackie Shure, giving you that sure thing this Monday morning! I know it's a little crazy out there and maybe you're a bit confused as to why I'm over here on KLAR and not over on our sister station, KSSP. In fact, a lot of you are wondering why nothing is playing over on the FM side of the dial. Honestly, our engineers are working on it, and I don't really have much more information than that. But I wanted to thank you for looking for me! I've been following social media and haven't had a chance to respond. As much as I would like to, my friend, I'm chained to this microphone and studio today. I'm not even able to play our favorite music to bump to."

Gunner and Roy remained silent until Jackie turned her mic off again.

"Looks like the conspiracy theorists and independent journalists are making up theories, stories, rumors..." Gunner said.

"What other conspiracies are trending?" Jackie kept her headset on but pushed the left side behind her ear so she could hear their conversation.

"A major power outage. The stations didn't pay their electric bill. A conspiracy about group suicide. Some of these are nuts!" Roy said, reviewing the feed on his phone.

"A lot of chatter about it being an elaborate April Fools' prank to get people to pay attention to radio, like a stunt of some kind," Gunner said.

He'd been concerned when he learned that the "radio takeover" news was spreading throughout social media, and the story was getting bigger and bigger by the second. It was now half past eleven. They'd been simulcasting their AMs for just ninety minutes without incident, but word had spread that Los Angeles wasn't the only city affected. The *wheresmyradio* hashtag alerted other social media followers, and each market was added to it and trending, too.

Followers commented, adding selfies by their car's dashboard radio, a picture of a billboard, or their radio set at home. Those who were promoting and following conspiracies about what was happening with broadcasting had even come up with Gunner's favorite hashtag: *transmittergate*. On any other day, Gunner would've considered this a successful stunt. What a great April Fools' prank.

And then reality hit him as he remembered all over again how serious this was.

Jackie remained standing up at the mic with her headphones over her ears. Although she usually enjoyed dancing to the music to keep her energy up, this was just as energizing to her. She cherished the opportunity to speak to her audience and provide them with information. It was what she'd always dreamed of doing. There was to be no hip hop or rhythmic music playing in her headset today. This was all about the audience and what they were experiencing. Jackie still wasn't sure why Gunner chose her to be the voice of the stations, or even why he'd decided to break the programming altogether.

Listening through her headset, she responded to the recorded calls. "You know, baby, I don't know all the details either. Some of these questions will be answered soon, though; I'm sure of that, very sure," she said with a grin. Then, she once again read the prepared statement. "We here at High Point Media in Los Angeles direct listeners to AM 790 KLAR, where you can find information you need in time of emergency. We are experiencing technical difficulties with our FM transmitters on Mount Wilson. Our engineers and other crews are working on resolving this issue, and we will be back on the air soon. Until such a time, we are directing listeners to the AM dial where you can find up-to-date information from me, Jackie Shure, sure to give you all you need today." She added that last part herself, feeling a little more confident than usual. After all, who was going to stop her?

A pre-recorded message with traffic, weather, and emergency information played back while Jackie kept an eye on the screen that showed the feeds from the station's social media pages. She was alarmed by the rapid growth of speculation that was spreading all over the country. *Where is my radio?* was the top trending topic as they approached the twelve o'clock hour, and independent journalists were uploading stories that questioned the narrative that the radio stations were sharing.

All these stations had been experiencing dead air for nearly six hours, and still, there had been no contact from the hijackers. Jackie knew the authorities were camping out in the conference room, and she'd been told there were law enforcement at the base of Mount Wilson, along with the other sites she knew nothing about. But how long would they allow this to drag on until they finally acted?

Roy exited the studio to return to the conference room with Gunner right behind him. On a normal day during her show, Jackie could leave the studio for a period of time when a song set was playing, but today, there were no song sets or even commercial sets. She had to stay right where she was, virtually shackled by the microphone, and the soundproof walls and doors only made the studio seem more like a cave, designed to be distraction-free for the announcers and team, plus soundproof so no outside noise could affect the audio. It felt uncomfortably confined to Jackie. She was dying to know what was going on outside the walls of the studio.

As Roy and Gunner entered the conference room, they heard multiple audio streams as though the volume on the monitors had increased. A scan of the room made it clear that everybody's eyes were focused on the wall of receivers as their volume indicators lit up.

In unison, the dead air on the FM frequencies came to life, and a male voice over the speakers said, "Are you ready to play a game?"

Chapter Nine

Pirates Go Live!

12:00 PM

The male voice projecting from the speakers sounded eerily digital as if it was a voice in a video game.

The conference room fell into a creepy silence as the radio stations started broadcasting the audio. The crowd that gathered froze in place, and any quiet conversations were muted.

"We have taken over your radio stations! Let's play!" blared the voice. All eyes were on the receivers at the far end of the wall.

Roy, Gunner and Mike made their way closer to the receivers. As he got closer to the receivers, Mike leaned in as if he wanted to reach into the speaker and grab whoever was talking. He postured himself like a golden retriever on a hunt, having just spotted his prey.

"Americans, wake up! Don't believe everything you see and hear! We have just shown you we are capable of gaining access to your favorite radio station. We have also demonstrated that we can access anything that is *anywhere* we wish!" The emphasis on the word *anywhere* chilled Roy's spine.

No one in the room moved, not even with the blink of an eye.

"You have been lied to. They spy on you. You are constantly monitored. Question everything."

Mike was paralyzed by the unnatural silence as he took his eyes off the receivers and looked around the room. It was reminiscent of 9/11, when the world just stopped, and everyone watched their televisions or listened to the radio. He didn't know if he should be angry, terrified, or indignant.

It only took thirty seconds before the room was crowded to capacity as staff ran in to hear what the hell was going on. The sales staff, station managers, interns, on-air personalities, and FBI agents stood there in silent shock, waiting for what was going to come out of the speakers next.

"Who the hell is this?" Agent Forrester said, breaking into the silence of the room. "Who are *they* that they're warning about, and what's the point?"

"I guess this is what we've been waiting for," Mike said, his eyes back on the receivers. His heart was palpitating, and it was getting difficult to breathe. He could hear and feel his heart beating through his ears as if he had plugs in them. He wanted to sprint out of the conference room down to Master Control and shut this off, but for the first time in his career, he was without a solution, and there was nothing he could do.

The voice on the radio spewed threats and warnings to anyone who was listening. "Just imagine," the voice said, "if we can take over the broadcast of a hundred radio stations, what else can we do? What if we told you that there are bombs planted in all sorts of locations—freeway overpasses, buildings, airports, even schools?"

Roy and Gunner exchanged panicked glances. There was nothing they could do. At all. Nothing but stand by, horrified that anyone could take over their radio stations like this with such unbelievable propaganda.

"We have to kill this broadcast!" Forrester turned and looked at Mike.

"We can't!" Mike yelled. He darted a look over at Forrester and then back at the receivers. The murmurs and low voices from the visibly shaken staff now permeated the room, adding to the frenzy.

During the first few hours of dead air, Roy had struggled to believe anybody would notice or even care that radio stations were silent all over the country. Well, except for paying advertisers. They'd care. There were so many options where the audience could go. A little technical glitch on the way to work wouldn't have had much of an impact on the listener. They would've just switched stations or opened up a different listening application.

Then, as the last few hours ticked by, he'd felt encouraged by the recent attention on social media. With each passing moment, it became clearer and clearer that the station and its company were in jeopardy. The message was obvious. Pirate broadcasters had taken over most of the FM radio station airwaves in Los Angeles with a terrifying transmission.

The broadcast continued. "Citizens of the world, heed these words with the utmost caution, for the dark forces of globalist elites and power-hungry politicians seek to manipulate and control your very existence. They weave a web of deceit, disguising their nefarious intentions under the guise of progress and enlightenment."

The sound of static fills the airwaves, followed by a voice that crackles with both urgency and intrigue.

"Today, we embark on a journey beyond the confines of the ordinary and into the realm of uncertainty and revelation. For too long, we have been shackled by the chains of misinformation, fed to us by those who seek to control our very thoughts and beliefs."

The voice grew more emphatic. "But do not be deceived, dear listeners! These so-called remedies they offer are but illusions, designed to ensnare us in a web of manipulation and deceit. They seek to reshape our minds, to mold us into compliant sheep, herded towards a future, not of our choosing."

There was a pause as if the speaker was catching their breath, and then they continued with fervor. "But resist, my fellow travelers, for within each of us lies the spark of individuality, the flame of truth that cannot be extinguished. Fake news masquerades as truth, poisoning our minds with its venomous lies, blurring the lines between reality and fiction."

"What is this melodramatic crap?" Gunner asked. "Are these threats for real?

Mike looked at Dominguez and motioned to the door. He'd already gone down to the garage to get his flight bag and extra batteries.

"We gotta get up there!" Mike yelled, but Dominguez held his hand up, signaling him to hold on.

Then, the voice coming out of the radio lowered, taking on a secretive tone. "Consider this: what if the truth lies not in the words spoken by those in power but in the whispers of the marginalized, the outcasts, the rebels who dare to defy the status quo? What if the answers we seek hide in the shadows, waiting to be uncovered by those brave enough to venture into the unknown?"

There was a moment of silence as if the speaker was contemplating their next words, then continued with newfound determination. "Let us delve deeper, my friends, into the realms of conspiracy and intrigue. Let us explore the mysteries of UFO sightings, alien conspiracies, and clandestine government operations. Let us shine a light into the darkness and uncover the secrets that lie hidden beneath the surface of our world."

"Unbelievable!" Roy held his hand on top of his head like he was preventing it from exploding. "We've got to address this immediately before the audience starts freaking out!"

"You mean like *we* are, right now?" said a voice behind him in the room.

"You are mere pawns in their twisted game. But remember, truth is not defined by their propaganda! And now, they dare to brand parents as domestic terrorists, criminalizing the very act of nurturing and protecting their own flesh and blood. But know this, dear listeners: the bond between parent and child is sacred, and no amount of propaganda can sever that bond! Citizens of the world do not succumb to the fear and manipulation of the globalist elites and power-hungry politicians! Stand tall, stand firm, and together, we shall overcome their tyranny and reclaim our freedom. Stay vigilant, stay strong, for the fight for truth and freedom rages on!"

"Holy shit!" Gunner whispered. Were the hijackers using the station's AI platform to generate their messaging, too? He lifted his phone and typed a message to his producers in the studio to tell them to record the audio and create sound bites and segments for Jackie to use.

"We need to act swiftly to address this on the air," Roy said quietly to Gunner. "We need the community to know that our stations are not under our control. We are not putting out this terror message."

No longer could they hide behind the rumors, innuendo, and conspiracy theories that this was a flawed April Fools' prank. The truth had been revealed.

"Already on it!" Gunner nodded. Although he had hardly glanced away from the receivers, he was already thinking about how they were going to navigate this. His news producers knew the situation had changed. He needed to get to Jackie, but he needed to hear more before he could direct her and the rest of the on-air team.

It had only been a couple of minutes since the broadcast began to play, and Gunner wondered how anyone was supposed to respond to this. He had to free his mind from the utter shock of a pirate broadcast on his stations, but he also wondered what other stations were going to do.

He shot another text to his producers and then to Jackie, telling her to listen to the FM audio and that he'd be right there.

The conference room was noisy, with the echo of multiple stations replaying the identical message while others still played their music or talk programming.

It was also probable that the pirates were using the company's AI platform to write and record these messages, which could be quickly changed and updated minute by minute. The male voice sounded slightly augmented, and Gunner's trained ear knew that the voice did not belong to any of their staff at the stations. He'd never heard this voice before.

Then the voice went on, calling for others to make targeted attacks.

Was this for real? Was this even possible? What others?

******

The stations had been off the air for six hours, so the audience would have turned the dial and gone somewhere else. It would take a few minutes for the hijackers' message to be heard and reported about. Roy was hopeful there would be some time for us to formulate a response, call in other authorities for assistance, and warn the police, fire department, and other first responders.

But Agent Forrester was five steps ahead and already on the phone. He and Agent Dominguez were making calls to other authorities while Roy began calculating the magnitude of the impact this broadcast would have on the public. Millions of people were going to be terrorized by this message! What were they going to do?

Roy started texting his colleagues from the other radio markets to confirm that the millions of people in these five cities would hear this message and that there was no way to prevent it. Pirates had stolen the airwaves, and the word was spreading like a California wildfire, the path of destruction completely unknown.

"It's already happening!" Roy announced to the room. "Social media is exploding with posts and comments. The conspiracy theories are shifting to fear."

He read aloud from one of the feeds, "'Bombs at the schools! Everybody get your kids!'"

And then another. "'Why are they talking about sacred bonds, kids, and schools?'"

This was not a programming stunt. This was really happening! It wasn't limited to one station in one city, it was occurring on a hundred stations in multiple cities, and it was only a small percentage of radio and television stations broadcasting the message of terror far and wide. He knew it wouldn't be long before everyone in the country was tuned in, and this was picked up as a news story and was trending everywhere on social media, online radio, and even live streams.

"We have a job to do!" Roy said, and the confusion rapidly swarmed into organized chaos. No matter how much this frightened him, it was his job to run these radio stations. He was responsible for these stations in Los Angeles, and he knew that the stations had a responsibility to their listeners to report on what was happening. He felt a shiver of fear as he recognized the potential for sheer disaster if they didn't act swiftly with a counter message and helpful information.

But what would they say?

The thoughts raced through his mind as an intern burst through the conference room door with an alarming look on her face. "The phone lines are lit up, and so are our social media accounts!" she hollered. "They're asking what's going on! What are we supposed to tell them?"

"We have to get something on the air!" Roy yelled, now looking over at Gunner, who was on his phone while still staring at the receivers, frozen in place alongside Mike, who was seated as close to the receivers as one could be. "And we'd better do it quickly!"

"On it!" Gunner said, breaking his silence as the room came alive with activity. "We can't be the ones in shock here."

In his twenty-plus years in radio, Gunner had never experienced anything of this magnitude, but he knew immediately that he needed to get back into the KLAR studio with Jackie and give her the support she'd need.

Although the stations had only been broadcasting this message for a few minutes, that was enough information now for the group to take swift action. Roy and Gunner agreed that there was no time to consider what to do or get a corporate consensus. They had to be expeditious.

As Gunner left the room to head over to the studio to work on the station's response, Roy Longly received a message that he'd been requested to join a conference call with corporate. He sprinted back to his office with Agent Forrester and Mike Harris, knowing they needed to get these stations to stop broadcasting this pirate message as quickly as physically possible. He didn't know what it was going to take, but obviously, this was going to require a serious feat of engineering if they had no control of the transmitters and no access to them; a solution needed to be discussed.

Roy walked around his desk, sat in his executive chair, and opened his computer to join the live call, inviting Mike and Forrester to sit in the matching leather chairs in front of his desk and turning the screen so they could see. The conference call involved all the managers of the stations owned by the company in the five markets where these pirates had taken over the stations. The president of High Point Media and the director of operations led the conference call from their headquarters in Dallas, where their stations had also been interrupted by this attack.

"This message has been on the air for too long already," came the voice of the president and CEO for High Point Media. "We need to kill this broadcast immediately. Nineteen of the FM stations in our major markets have been affected. Millions of listeners are affected by this."

"This is a nightmare!" Roy said, voicing the obvious to his counterparts all over the country.

Agent Forrester sat up straight in his chair to address those on the call. "Millions of people are listening to this message on their radios. We can't force them to turn it off and pay no mind to it! We're looking at a potentially huge wave of panic, and it's only going to get worse."

"Our programming departments are creating a response. Said the CEO. "We'll need law enforcement, first responders, and community leaders to guide us and provide safety information and directions for us to broadcast. We have to coordinate with our cities immediately." The word had come down from corporate, with instructions for each market manager to closely manage their stations' on-air messaging, but to not look for a directive from corporate in order to decide how they would handle their own broadcasts.

"I'll get word on what the FCC's Homeland Security Division orders us to do," the director of operations said from headquarters. "Agents from Homeland Security are on their way to each station that has been taken over so that we can investigate and find this common denominator, the who and how of this plan."

"Screw the FCC!" Mike said. "The airwaves have been hijacked. In a very short while, people are going to panic, if they aren't already. Do you really believe that the FCC is going to spring into action and give us directions?" His drone was ready, and all he wanted to do was get out of there.

"For now, I agree with Roy Longly and Mike Harris over here," Forrester said. "I'll coordinate with the local entities here in Los Angeles. We need to do whatever we can to address the public and inform them that the authorities are on top of this and will take every measure necessary to ensure the safety of American lives."

The call wrapped up quickly, with each station manager understanding their next move. Roy, Mike, and Forrester headed back to the conference room, where they found people milling around, still listening and watching.

Roy knew no business was going to be done today, and he felt crowded in the room. It was time to send people home.

"This is going to be a stressful situation that's going to take up all our attention. We don't know what to expect here or how long this will last. Threats of terror have been made, but we still have a job to do to inform the public. Remember, radio will continue to be the number one source for reporting news and emergency information.

"But there will be no sales calls or regular business going on today. I believe it's in the best interest of all if nonessential employees go home to their families and only those responsible for our broadcast or engineering remain in the building. Spread the word."

The room emptied. Although the staff murmured under their breath, Roy couldn't be concerned about how they felt about being asked to leave unless they were essential to the operation of the broadcast. They needed all capable hands-on deck, and he needed the office cleared and fewer bodies taking up space with nothing to do.

But despite their murmuring, his staff didn't grumble or complain. They, too, like the listeners, were frightened out of their minds and wanted to run for the exits anyway. It was a mutual request, and most of them were grateful they didn't have to come up with an excuse to just go home and feel safe.

Mike stood in the doorway but didn't enter the room, making eye contact with Agent Dominguez, who was waiting with the group, and motioned to him with a nod of his head, both of them anxious to leave for Mount Wilson.

Chapter Ten

Pirate Radio

Jackie flipped off her mic, pulled the headphones away from her ears, and hung them around her neck. She took a slow, deep breath as Gunner opened the door and stepped inside the studio.

"Whoa..." she whispered. She had no other words. She'd spent the past two and a half hours on the air, and it felt like she'd run a marathon. The first two hours had been fun and games, with Travis assisting her with organizing segments. The audience, although annoyed that all these radio stations weren't on the air, left comments, calls, and social media posts about how much they missed their favorite personality or morning show while also spreading rumors about this being an elaborate April Fools' prank and wondering what was going to happen next.

"I know," was all Gunner could say. "This message from the hijackers seems like our AI platform wrote and produced it. Mike and I could both tell that this isn't anyone from our stations. It doesn't even sound like a human voice. And that message." He paused, shaking his head. "What the f..."

"The last twenty minutes have been wild. I haven't been able to stop and listen to the entire message. What is it saying?" Jackie's phones were lit up with callers wanting to get on the air. The screen just in front of her displayed the various social media platforms with multiple threads of comments about it.

"You need to be able to hear it," Gunner said. "I'll have it produced in shorter sound bites so you can digest it all. I don't know how I feel about airing it over here. It's bad enough it's being broadcast all over the country and we can't stop it. This is where we want to guide the listeners, right here to KLAR. To you." Gunner already had his phone in his hand and gave instructions to the station's AI application to pull the audio from the FM message and reproduce it in short sound bites.

Jackie's confusion was out of control. "Tell me what to do, Gunner. Tell me what to say here. What are we going to do about this?"

This was unfamiliar territory for Gunner, too, but experience told him this was going to be quite a ride. "We have to treat this as a news story, even if it's directly about our station. I want you to shift your game face and become an anchor right now." He didn't know exactly what to do either, except to stay on the air and go with what they were given.

"The FBI agent is coordinating with police, firefighters, and community leaders, and we'll be getting statements, guidance, and information from them, probably any minute now," Gunner continued. "Let's set up segments you can follow to keep you sane at least. Once we have some interviews lined up, we'll have a better sense of direction."

"It's been thirty minutes now. What do you suppose…" Jackie stopped short as she and Gunner both heard the shift in the message from the speaker that monitored the KLCL FM.

"Oh my god, they're playing a new message!" Gunner said. He stepped around Jackie and turned up the volume on the monitor.

First came the sound of radio static, followed by a distorted, menacing voice. "Attention, citizens of this so-called 'civilized' society. Prepare to face the harsh reality of our existence. We, the true purveyors of truth, have commandeered these airwaves to deliver a message that will shake you to your core. Listen carefully, for your very lives depend on it."

The voice somehow took on a sinister tone. "Behold the chaos we have wrought across this land. We thrive on the dissemination of conspiracy theories, for they are but the tip of the iceberg of our power. Big Pharma, the two-tiered justice system—mere pawns in our grand game of manipulation."

There was a brief pause.

"Attention, citizens, authorities, first responders, and all who dare to defy us. Once again, the pirates have infiltrated these airwaves, and their message carries a sinister warning that cannot be ignored. Brace yourselves for the onslaught of terror that awaits."

Gunner and Jackie stared at the radio station's monitor as the message blared on. Jackie felt the impulse to shut it off so no one could hear it, only to be jarred back to the reality that the pirates controlled these airwaves.

Gunner broke his stupor and looked at Jackie. "Oh, shit!" he whispered. "Here we go with another—"

"Our first point of action, our first stop—the very essence of our power lies in the uncertainty of our next move. We lurk in the shadows, unseen yet ever-present, ready to strike at any moment. When and where will we strike next? The answer eludes you, for we are masters of deception. But let us turn our attention to a more pressing concern—are your children safe today at school? We could have planted devices all over their schools, waiting to unleash chaos and carnage at our whim. We could even be activating mass shooters right now to terrorize each and every school, leaving devastation in our wake."

Another pause.

"You just don't know, do you? The fear gnaws at your very core, paralyzing you with indecision. What will you do in the face of such uncertainty? Will you go collect your children and retreat to the safety of your homes, hoping to shield them from our wrath? Or will you dismiss our warning as mere bluster, leaving them vulnerable to the horrors we may unleash? Consider your options carefully because the consequences of your choices may be dire. Every decision you make, every action you take—will they lead to salvation or doom? The choice is yours, but remember this: we are always watching, always waiting, ready to strike when you least expect it."

The voice faded out, leaving only the unsettling echo of the radio static.

The phone lines and social media were exploding, new hashtags were being created, and comments were appearing so fast they couldn't even be read before they were buried in a blur of more comments shoving their way into the thread, and no way to prevent any of it.

"We will not be able to control the narrative or even tell our audience to stop listening to the FM. We need to remain calm and get the authorities on the air now." Gunner shifted his weight from leaning over the board to hear the pirate's message. He had to leave Jackie alone in the studio so he could track down the suits in charge of this fiasco.

"Wait!" Jackie said. "You're going to leave me in here all alone? What am I supposed to do? We don't even have a program clock." She was panicking and frightened by what she'd just heard. How could she be expected to know what to say to their audience?

"Listen, Jackie," Gunner said. "None of us know what to do, so we're going to have to trust our instincts, and my instincts are telling me to act fast and get the police to the schools right now!

Jackie looked over her shoulder as the heavy studio door swooshed shut behind Gunner, sealing her into the soundproof room. Here she was, the voice of the biggest AM station in Greater Los Angeles—heck, all of Southern California— and she was alone at the helm. She knew full well that she had a job to do, but she wasn't exactly sure how to do it. Gunner had put her in this chair and behind this microphone for a reason, but even he didn't seem to know what that reason was at this precise moment. Suddenly, she'd found herself the anchor of one of the biggest signals in LA. She wouldn't take it lightly.

But that nagging voice in her head echoed. *Who do you think you are?*

She took a deep breath, watching the seconds tick by as a sound bite from a listener came to a close. She flipped up the dial and leaned in close to the microphone.

"I don't know who's out there listening or how many of you have found me here yet. It's been a couple of hours of a wild ride, and I've been having some fun with you all. Honestly, we didn't really know what was going to happen either." She paused, took a breath, and continued. "We lost control of our FM radio stations and were waiting to find out what was next. I guess we know now. I don't have any answers for you, and I know you have a million questions and concerns. So do I. But I assure you, we're working as hard as we can to get the appropriate authorities on the air to give us some idea of what to do. Meanwhile, I'll be right here behind this microphone and on your radio as we figure this out together."

******

Gunner rushed down the hallway and dashed into the conference room while Mike paced in the hallway outside the door, looking as anxious as Gunner felt. Roy and the FBI agents were huddled around the wall of receivers. Agent Forrester was on his phone, as was Agent Dominguez, and Roy was busy texting. They didn't even notice Gunner as he approached.

"Schools! What's being done about the schools?!" He practically yelled it over the noise, but it was clear from the look on the alarmed and terrified expressions of Roy and the others that he wasn't the only one concerned. Gunner checked himself. He felt the rush of adrenaline pulsing through his heart. His children were attending school. He wanted nothing more than to run out of the building and go rescue them.

Roy looked up from his phone and looked at Gunner. "They're calling in the police and SWAT to go conduct sweeps of the schools, but obviously, it's going to take time." Roy nodded in the direction of Forrester and Dominguez. "They're contacting the school districts to coordinate an evacuation of all schools in the area, but it's going to be a logistical nightmare."

"Send me all the info as it comes in. I'll get my team working on producing segments to air right now." Gunner turned on his heel and headed back to his office to grab his tablet off his desk so he could utilize all his assets and resources while walking around the station. Then he walked around the corner to the on-air personalities' lounge, where he gathered his producers, board operators, and announcers.

He assigned his audio producers to capture the information as it came in and use the station's artificial intelligence platform to create sound bites and segments for public safety, instructions on where to go, and contact information to report concerns. He instructed them to divide the segments into categories of importance,

The personalities were on hand to help with recording voice-overs and interviews of officials as they connected with them, as well as handing over the audio files to producers to get them edited and loaded into the program system for Jackie to play back on the air. He instructed the board operators to monitor social media and post the updates as they came in with all the links and to use their programming assets to send texts to their radio station subscribers to tune into KLAR AM for up-to-the-minute updates and information.

"Look, guys, all the rules have been thrown out the window. We cannot control what these pirates are airing on the other stations, nor do we have time to care about what any other station in the market is doing." Gunner was spitballing. "What categories will be important? Look at safety, traffic, contact information, and anything that would concern the public. We can't spare any airtime for innuendo or opinions."

Once he felt confident that his staff knew enough to get started, he added, "I sense we're going to be dealing with a ton of people filled with fear. These are scary messages, and we don't know what's going to happen next."

"How about getting this off the air?" asked Stevie from the KLCL morning show.

"I just passed Mike Harris in the hall, and he's got a determined look on his face," Gunner said. "I know he's trying to figure it out."

Gunner let out a deep sigh and looked every single one on his team in the eye. "I'm afraid too, honestly." His reputation in the radio station was authentic, yet private and humble. "I have kids in school, and all I want to do right now is go get them. But I'm sure a lot of parents are feeling this way right now. Just be ready to keep the information flowing. I'm counting on you guys."

******

"What are we doing now?" Jackie asked as she turned to see Gunner enter the studio. "I can only play back these pre-recorded segments once."

"I'm going to be right outside this door, monitoring everything. We're getting school officials, police and fire department officials, and city officials lined up to get on the air, to provide us with constant updates. It won't be long before we have more audio clips for you to playback."

"What about calls from listeners? My phones are off the hook. Look at that." She gestured toward the phone bank and then looked at the computer monitor where she could read the social media threads with comments and questions.

Gunner, already aware of what the public was saying, paused to look at the screen and the phone lines. "We're going to have to wing it, Jackie. Do you want to take listener calls live, or do you want them to record them and send them to you for playback?"

"I want to connect with them. I want to speak with them, not just sit here like a glorified board operator. If I was a parent, I'd be freaking out right now. What schools? What city? You know?" Jackie nodded at Gunner and he nodded back, knowing all too well how parents were feeling right now.

He, his wife Melanie, and their two kids lived in Reseda, close to Burbank, where the station studios were. Gunner stopped working for a second and called his wife. She was relieved to hear from him, panicking but agreeing to follow Gunner's advice and go pick up the kids from school. "And head straight home," Gunner implored.

The program system filled up with produced content that the station producers and announcers were creating. "Good. That didn't take long," Jackie said, reviewing the titles and lengths of segments as she pulled her headphones back over her ears and positioned the mic in front of her face. "Are you going to stay or go?"

The door opened, and Roy walked in. He ignored the respectful and quiet entrance that was expected when entering a broadcast studio that was live on the air. He barely acknowledged Jackie as he moved closer to the monitor, showing the list of upcoming segments and their titles.

He turned and looked at Gunner. "At least run some ten-second messages with our sponsor tags and information, will you? We're driving all these listeners here for updates. Let's at least capitalize on that."

"You've got to be kidding me right now!" Gunner said, leaning toward Roy.

"We're a news station. We can get away with it," Roy demanded.

"No! We only have so many minutes of airtime. I'm not wasting precious minutes because you want to make money on this!"

Jackie stood in silence, stunned to the point of paralysis. She slowly shifted her eyes to look at the monitor. If she didn't turn on the mic and move to the next segment in the queue, there was going to be dead air.

"We have important business sponsors in this city!" Roy yelled. "They keep us operating, and we need to respect that. There's no reason you can't just write some short scripts and have Jackie read them between calls and traffic reports."

"I don't give a shit about the advertisers!" Gunner said. "I care about the community, the audience, and those friggin parents and kids who are freaking out right now about threats being broadcast on *our* radio stations!"

Gunner's outburst jarred Roy. He knew Gunner was right, but it didn't change the fact that he was under pressure to stop the financial bleeding.

"You disgust me." Gunner couldn't believe Roy didn't have a response. He made his way to the door but stopped to look at Roy. "You used to be better than this."

And with that, he stormed out of the studio, and Roy followed him, leaving Jackie alone with Travis, who had shrunk into the corner, becoming invisible.

Chapter Eleven

It's an Inside Job!

The FBI never parked in the parking garage. Their black SUV was waiting at the front of the six-story building as Mike and Agent Dominguez exited the double-glazed doors leading out to the street. It was a gorgeous spring day, and Mike took a deep breath, the fresh air tickling his scraggily hair and the wind whispering in his ear. He'd never been so happy to get out of the station.

He climbed into the passenger seat of the SUV after carefully placing his drone gear on the back seat. Agent Dominguez went around and got behind the steering wheel. With the windows rolled up and the emergency red lights oscillating back and forth in the windshield and back window, they drove down a few side streets toward Interstate 5, South, headed toward downtown Los Angeles.

Mike's first order of business was to reprogram the presets on the dashboard radio. Dominguez just watched out of the corner of his eye in amazement as Mike masterfully tuned to a frequency without scanning, pressed the preset button, and moved on to the next station he wanted to monitor.

"Why are you doing that?" Dominguez asked.

"Occupational hazard. I always monitor signals," Mike said without looking away from his task. "Now I have a different reason."

He finished setting the radio stations on both the AM and FM bands on the radio. He'd only spent a second listening to each station. It appeared as though all of them had now broken their regular format. No more music was playing on the radio. There was the now-familiar voice of the terror messages along with news broadcasts on the rest.

"Wow!" Dominguez said. "I've never seen the city this crazy before."

Mike looked up from the radio on the dash to see that the streets were crowded with vehicles in all directions around the schools and beyond as parents rushed to pick up their kids. The police had blocked some streets to control the flow of traffic. The street signal lights were flashing red while police, firefighters, and even paramedics helped direct the traffic.

"I've been wondering why these hijackers just turned off the audio," Dominguez said.

"Maybe it was just to bring attention to their crime." Mike looked out the window. "It certainly worked."

The scene looked like a movie about the end of the world, with traffic clogging every urban artery as people tried to make their way to safety. The news from KLAR, with Jackie giving traffic information and detours and encouraging listeners to remain calm, only added to the nightmare developing right before his eyes.

Getting onto the freeway was easy. The police had blocked the entrances, which also included blocking the on-ramps. But that didn't stop this FBI vehicle. Mike and Dominguez hardly slowed down as they boarded the on-ramp to I-5, heading straight for the empty fast lane toward 134 Freeway toward Glendale/Pasadena.

"So, what do you think you're going to accomplish with that drone?" Dominguez asked, cruising the freeway and nodding toward the bag in the back seat.

"Well, I can't get back control of our transmitters," Mike said, "but I can try to figure out what happened and how we can fix this."

"And you're going to do that by flying a drone over...?"

Mike heard the disdain in Dominguez's voice.

"What is the government doing about this?" Mike asked. "They're expecting us to take care of this, but nobody has a clue, so I'm going to fly my drone and get some!"

Mike knew the route so well he could drive it with his eyes closed. Past the LA Zoo to 134, which crossed over Colorado Boulevard, home to the Rose Parade,

"We sent a team to Albert Braun's home, and there is no evidence that he's been kidnapped," Dominguez said, clearly making sure Mike knew they were doing something. "They found some engineering manuals and a computer with what seems to be a gaming system, along with a 3D printer."

Mike didn't respond.

"It looks like a high-end gamer's lair, I've been informed," Dominguez said, "and it appears that some equipment is missing from his setup. No signs of forced entry or a scuffle."

"So, the FBI thinks that Albert orchestrated all this, too?" Mike looked at the clock on the radio. It wasn't even one yet. He looked back out of the window. Albert was still on a plane back East.

"There's no other missing engineer from Los Angeles," Dominguez said.

He went on to tell Mike that although many group owners had been affected by the takeover, and the messages were repeated on all stations in all five markets, the only common denominator in each city was that one engineer was missing from each of the High Point Media stations. There could be more involved, but all other engineers had been accounted for.

All except Albert.

"I already told you guys," Mike said, defending Albert as if he were his own son. "He was getting on a plane early this morning and heading back East. That explains why he's not here. He's in flight."

"Well, why don't you tell me as much about Albert as you can," Dominguez said, keeping his eyes on the road. "Anything stand out to you, based on today's developments? Any information or clues will be helpful in understanding the hijackers' motives behind this. At this point in the investigation, we have multiple theories."

Mike's blood pressure shot up, blood rushed up his neck, and his face turned red. It was hard to breathe. He couldn't tell if he was feeling angry, terrified, or like throwing up again. He'd been trying to reflect and recall the many conversations he'd had with Albert while they were working, conversations about Albert's fascination with all things conspiracies. He couldn't remember details, only snippets, as he'd merely been humoring Albert and hadn't at all been interested in his asinine theories. But they'd become friends over the past year or so, and Mike knew Albert wasn't capable of a stunt like this.

Was he?

"We need to know everything about what Albert Braun knows, who his associates are, and what he's been trained to do," Dominguez said, breaking the silence as if Mike hadn't heard him.

Albert was a kid in Mike's eyes, and although smart and talented, occasionally his arrogance caused Mike to avoid unnecessary discussions. He liked him, but he wouldn't entertain his conspiracy theories.

Until now.

"They can do anything they want up there!" Mike said.

"What do you mean they can do anything they want? What would cause a group of radio engineers to become sinister enough to pull something like this off?" Agent Dominguez asked. He knew all too well that people were capable of anything, no matter what their background.

"Albert talked about conspiracy theories. A lot," Mike said. He didn't take his eyes off the traffic as he tried visualizing the procedures that had occurred at the transmitter site to link all the broadcasts together. Millions of potential listeners over multiple frequencies. He struggled to accept the magnitude of this happening across five major cities and the outlying signal coverage. He didn't even know the actual numbers. That was the purview of Roy's department for sales and programming data.

"Well, if this is an inside job, how did these extremists end up working as engineers in radio?" Dominguez asked.

"We hired out of tech schools, the brightest we could find," Mike said. "As old technology fades, it's impossible to find engineers trained in electronics and radio frequency. We take what we can find and train them in RF. As long as they work hard and keep us on the air…"

Mike nudged the volume down on the radio. He needed to think, and right now, there were too many sources of stimuli. He felt his body vibrating at its nerve endings.

His mind raced as he tried to recall the technical steps that the engineers must have taken at Mount Wilson in order to successfully complete this task. He knew Albert was more than skilled in this technology to accomplish this. Mike had trained him well.

Together they had installed the components and technology needed to go live from the transmitter as instructed by corporate for a backup "live studio" in case they lost the main studio locations during an earthquake or natural disaster. He could tell that the hijackers had pre-recorded a message and were using the live studio function to play it back for millions of people.

The chatter from the FBI radio distracted his thoughts. They were coordinating their locations and status. Agent Dominguez responded with their location and who he was with. Mike had never seen a freeway in Los Angeles so empty, and he'd driven this freeway to get up to Mount Wilson at every hour of the day. Even when he was heading up to the transmitter at 3:00 AM, there would still be specks of travelers. But right now, he and Dominguez were driving down an empty freeway during what would typically be a busy afternoon rush.

They rushed toward Highway 2, exiting at Foothill Boulevard toward Angeles Crest Highway. Mike looked over at the Hill Street Café as they made their turn. It felt like years since he'd last been here, but it was only a few hours ago that Tom had been carried away in an ambulance.

"My god!" Mike was thrust out of his silent reverie by an epiphany about how this takeover could have been engineered. He rubbed his face with both hands like he was splashing water on it. "I knew our transmitter sites were vulnerable, but I never imagined something like this."

"What do you mean your sites are vulnerable?" Dominguez asked.

"We've complained dozens of times about the activity up on the mountain. There is too much construction, strangers coming and going, and no security at all," Mike said. He told Dominguez he'd complained to Roy with dozens of memos. Even when they hired consultants to conduct an inspection to ensure their FCC compliance, they'd report security as a concern.

"You know how everything just stopped when the attack on the World Trade Center happened?" Dominguez asked.

"Of course. Who could forget?" Mike said.

"The entire world just stopped. Stood still."

Mike sighed. "I remember."

"We may not know the motives, but we have to break down the hijackers' barricades and turn those transmitters off."

"I started my morning thinking this was some stupid April Fools' prank," Mike said, shaking his head.

"Well, it's no prank. It's a matter of national security now, and every agency is on top of it."

Mike wasn't sure if he was relieved or worried to hear that.

The drive to Red Box ranger station was the longest leg of the trip. As they weaved their way around the mountain, the drive dragged on in slow motion for Mike. The ranger station was now barricaded and lined with emergency vehicles to prevent trespassers and onlookers as they approached. Among the emergency crews and police, he saw a handful of independent journalists loitering around the blocked entrance, hoping for a story. Waves of trauma flowed through him as he saw Tom's car still parked where they'd met that morning. He still hadn't heard how his friend was doing.

Mike stepped out of the vehicle, the crisp mountain air filling his lungs as he surveyed the bustling scene in the Red Box Canyon parking lot. The base of Mount Wilson, usually a serene spot, was now a hive of activity. Agents and officers were setting up the emergency command center, radios crackling with terse updates. Mike opened the back door of the car and pulled out his drone case, setting it down on the hood while Agent Dominguez hovered nearby, watching the chaos unfold around them.

Chapter Twelve

Panic in the Cities

Gunner opened the door of the studio with his backside, carrying his tablet in one hand and two bottles of water in the other. The heavy door didn't make a sound, and he sneaked into the studio just as Jackie turned off her mic, pulled the headphones off her ears, and placed them around her neck. She'd just announced another segment for emergency services, street closures, and information for parents about how school districts were managing the safety of their children.

It didn't take long for parents to panic once the second pirated message aired on the hijacked radio stations. People reacted like they'd seen an accident on the side of the road. One couldn't help but slow down and watch the horror, even if they really didn't want to. Likewise, listeners couldn't help but tune in to hear the messages of terror in real-time, as if they needed proof that this insanity was actually being said on their radio. The panic erupted as word spread through social media, phone calls, and texts that there were radio messages announcing potential school shootings.

Gunner handed Jackie a bottle of water. "Need anything else?"

"Something a little stronger would be great." But Jackie accepted the water bottle.

"Yeah, but we're not getting drunk on the air today. Let's save that for when this is all over." Gunner was serious. A strong drink was very inviting, and he didn't even drink anymore since becoming a dad. He'd go out for the occasional beer that was required for professional socializing, but never on a daily basis, and never for the purpose of getting drunk. However, at this moment, it was incredibly enticing.

"What happened with Roy and the ten-second spots he wants you to run?" Jackie looked at the monitor of upcoming events and didn't see any kind of commercial content displayed in the queue.

"He didn't say anything more to me about it, and we aren't running any spots. Period."

"Okay…" Jackie raised her eyebrows and sighed. She'd never witnessed Gunner yell at Roy before. It wasn't that they didn't have conflicts about ratings, revenue, and even the radio personalities and what they said on the air, but Gunner was usually professional about keeping those disagreements behind closed doors. It had shocked her when he accused Roy of being disgusted and demanding that they make money off this crisis.

After a couple of hours of broadcasting, Jackie needed to sit down. She settled into a chair on casters and adjusted the microphone to her new position, gulping down some water to quench her dry throat. This was harder work than playing tunes and asking trivia questions. Her sense of humor had to be snuffed out as she adapted to the seriousness of each and every caller's concern.

There were ten phone lines in the KLAR studio, and they were lit up constantly. As soon as she finished one call to answer another, the line would light up again with a new caller. It was an endless talk program with intermittent reports from newscasters on the street and the playback of the local police and traffic messages.

Jackie placed the headphones back over her ears and pushed two buttons at once, one that turned her mic back on and another that answered one of the phone lines.

"You're on the air live with Jackie Shure," she announced.

"What the heck is happening?" the listener cried. "I'm a mile away from my kids' school, and I can't get there! Is there a bomb at their schools?"

"I hear your panic," Jackie answered with a calm, momma-like tone. "I don't know which school you're referring to, ma'am. I know you're worried. So far, we haven't heard any reports of actual bombs or shootings being present at any school, but all safety precautions are being taken." She then provided the caller with the hot line that had already been set up for parents to call to get details on their children's specific schools.

"Did your radio station know this was going to happen, and kept it from the public?" the next caller demanded.

"The transmitters on Mount Wilson were hijacked early this morning," Jackie said. "We had no idea what their intentions were but immediately went into action as if we were preparing for a storm or natural disaster so that we could inform the public. That's our job. But no, sir, we didn't know that a terror broadcast was coming."

Jackie looked at her monitor as it updated its display with events and segments that were coming up to air. The AI platform that the station utilized for producing each vignette also labeled and provided a brief description of each upcoming event and segment, along with categorizing and color-coding the length of the recording to define the category of each feature. She would play back a segment of recorded listener calls and concerns which were significant and appreciated that the show producers were including the appropriate answers from authorities in the feature to address the concerns with instructions, information, or direction. Then, she'd play back segments of recorded statements from public officials.

"This system works out okay," she said, nodding at the direction she was getting. "There needs to be more balance in the content, though. It's hard to sift through the listeners' calls and the information on where to go and what to do."

Gunner agreed. He opened his programming application on his tablet and moved closer to Jackie so she could take a look at the screen as she stood next to him. They brainstormed how to manage the content in a way that allowed Jackie to control the program, keeping it balanced.

Gunner sent a message to his producers to generate a statement from the radio station management, too. It was equally important for the station itself to address the issue of their other properties getting hijacked. He didn't want to bring Roy in to record it, so he provided notes and instructed their AI program to generate the announcement from High Point Media's management.

Jackie played the next segment and turned up the volume on the studio speakers. It was a recorded message from the Los Angeles City school district providing information on the safety and security of students in their areas. Hundreds of schools and thousands of students needed to be coordinated in an orderly manner to reduce the chaos. First they locked down each school while police and fire departments sent hundreds of personnel to each school to conduct a sweep. This situation had turned into a logistical nightmare, as first responders had limited resources and had to cover hundreds of schools with hundreds of thousands of students. And these radio stations' coverage was much larger than just the LA city schools. There were surrounding communities that were being affected and hundreds more schools that were in jeopardy. It was impossible to pinpoint one in particular that might be in more danger than another.

Once a school was swept, the announcement continued, the students were to leave the building and gather on the playground or fields to wait for their parents to arrive and pick them up. Streets were closed and blocked in order to direct traffic, and teachers and administrators struggled to get organized.

Jackie and Gunner listened to the announcement, poised like statues as they imagined the chaos at the schools right now. Gunner had already spoken to his wife, who by now was already waiting in a line of cars near the school to pick up their kids. He wanted to protect his family and be there with his wife. But he couldn't leave his post at the radio station. And his kids were safe. His wife was safe. He was where he was supposed to be at the helm of these broadcasts.

"There have been no reports of anything actually happening," Jackie asserted. "Not one police report, not one call or text message. Nothing." Police and firefighters had arrived at the schools within minutes of being notified of the threat and had yet to report finding anything in their initial sweeps.

"It's only been an hour since they began broadcasting," Gunner said. He stood stiffly, still looking at the upcoming segments in the queue on the monitor. "Time will tell, I guess." He shrugged and looked at Jackie, raising an eyebrow as if to convey that he had no clue what to expect next.

The next recorded feature began to play as the message from the school district faded out. This time, it was a message from their traffic reporter who provided details about the road closures and routes to use to line up at schools to pick up children. Bottlenecks, panicked drivers, fender benders, and drivers trying to maneuver around the roadblocks were being reported all over the city. The instructions were to please stay calm, be aware of your surroundings, and drive safely and slowly, especially in school zones.

"How did all this happen so quickly?" Jackie asked. For nearly an hour now, the message about terrorizing schools had been broadcasting on a loop of fear porn, while the original message about playing a game had faded away.

Jackie now believed that it was her job to keep the audience informed while also encouraging them to maintain their sanity. The challenge of getting the message of calm to this vast audience was increasing by the moment. Jackie felt her own panic rise in her gut but forced herself to swallow the emotions. She didn't have the luxury to panic and curl up on the couch and watch it on television. She was deadlocked right in the center of all the action. As she breathed in deeply, the pungent metal odor of the microphone reached her nose.

Now, she was completely in her own zone. Suddenly, the big picture was in front of her, and she knew what she had to do. She would no longer rely solely on the producers, callers, or news reporters to provide the content. She needed to create her own message. No longer would she take the panicked calls from listeners. She knew now that these frightening calls were only causing an increase in the panic outside the doors of her radio studio sanctuary.

"Cities are dispersing squad cars, bomb squads, fire trucks, and any other type of security out to every school within the signal range of this radio station." Her lips touched the mic as she leaned in closer. Then, she played back another recorded message from the director of public relations from another school district.

"The logistics alone are impossible, and we're responding as quickly as we can." The voice came through Jackie's headphones. "As you can imagine, it takes time to coordinate, and off-duty staff has been called in to aid."

"What are other stations in the market doing?" Jackie asked Gunner, who had made himself at home on the other side of the console next to Travis, who was tapping away on his tablet as he directed the content of the station with producers in the other studios and maintained communication with the authorities about new developments.

She'd been so busy running the board, playing back the segments provided to her by the invisible producers of this program. Kept in captivity in the studio and chained to the microphone, Jackie had her finger on the pulse of what was happening, but she didn't know how other media outlets were reporting on it. She was incredibly careful with what she said on air because she was terrified that riots would break out and get worse than it was already.

"I don't have time or interest in comparing what we're doing with what other stations are doing," Gunner said. "What matters is what we're doing right now."

"Well, I want to know," Jackie shrugged.

"Some of these stations don't even have news departments anymore, so they're just playing back recorded messages and calls from their audience."

"Like us."

"Like we are, yes. It's all over television too, obviously. I haven't stopped to watch, though."

"What do you think will happen next?" Jackie looked at her monitor to see how much time she had left before she needed to go live again.

Gunner shook his head and let out an enormous sigh. "I have no idea. But if it gets worse, I'd bet the government will activate the Emergency Alert System, and then everyone in the region will be listening to you."

"What do you mean everyone will be listening to me?" Jackie divided her attention; one ear focused on what Gunner was saying, and the other ear focused on what was on the air. She fiddled with a couple of volume control knobs, checked the monitor again, and once she was confident she had a few minutes of uninterrupted time, she gave her full attention to Gunner.

"We have no control over what's happening," he said.

******

Roy stormed into his corner office on the fourth floor and sat down behind his desk with a huff. Emotions were raw as tempers flared. He didn't deny that they were all panicking about the terror messages and whether the threats were real or not. He had never let an employee speak to him the way Gunner just had. He couldn't believe he'd accused him of being disgusting. All he did was request Gunner run some short messages for their sponsors.

The scent of the soft leather of his executive chair tickled his nostrils as he adjusted in his chair and picked up his phone. Roy's grandiose office, decorated to exhibit success and importance with dark and imposing ornate furnishings, included a massive credenza and bookcase that displayed some of his most prized awards, photos, and souvenirs encapsulating his radio career. Roy was the top guy, and he wanted everyone to know it.

Yet he rarely noticed the decor anymore, only when he dusted off a picture of him with a celebrity to impress a visitor.

Roy loved the radio business and wasn't afraid to buck the system when he felt it was better for his radio stations in LA. Corporate dictates could be daunting and inappropriate for this market. He believed his staff respected him because of his independence, and he ran a fair operation. He had enough common sense and leadership skills and knew he needed to take the wheel and run these radio stations as if they were an aircraft carrier wounded in battle. Despite areas beyond his control, he could still navigate the circumstances.

But was Gunner, right?

Roy took a moment before dialing the number for his boss, the VP of operations, Howard Finley, then closed his eyes and drew in a deep breath.

Without so much as a greeting, Roy spoke into the phone. "Talk to me about what we know about what's going on in our other markets."

"Authorities are in the process of evacuating the buildings in Chicago and New York and the corporate headquarters in Dallas," Howard said. "And they've ordered the evacuation of students and faculty in all the school districts."

"It's a logistical nightmare," Roy said.

"I know. Resources are running thin already, and the FBI doesn't have enough agents for each school. Police and fire departments are managing as much as they can, but they're considering activating the National Guard and reserve troops who live in these communities."

"What's being done to recapture the transmitters?" Roy asked. He was eager to get control of the broadcast again. If they could, would all of this stop?

"Operationally, we have different scenarios at each scene, and I don't have all the details for each one. While the buildings are being evacuated, the transmitters are located at the top, with a separate elevator leading up to the roof. The hoist was severed, so the elevator car crashed to the bottom and was completely disabled, and the doors to the stairs have been blocked and reinforced.

"As for the mountains in LA and Mount Sutro in San Francisco, they tried to get up with mountain climbers, but shots were fired, and they couldn't pinpoint where the sniper was located. Aerial attempts were going to be made, but the towers and guy-wires will prevent them from getting close enough."

"Mike Harris, my chief engineer, is up at Mount Wilson as we speak," Roy said. "He couldn't take it, just standing around with nothing to do. Maybe he'll be able to come up with some ideas or something. He refuses to believe his apprentice Albert is involved with this."

"Well, he's the only one. We've got four other engineers unaccounted for from our company. One in each city. What does that tell you?"

Roy shook his head. "It tells me Mike is likely wrong about Albert."

"How are you handling things with your sponsors?" Howard asked.

"Gunner yelled at me when I approached the subject. I don't think I can convince him to run any commercials or live announcements at all."

Howard expressed his concerns over the lost revenue. By now, the company had already lost millions of dollars just from the hours of dead air. Now, he was afraid the advertisers would never come back since it had become apparent that they'd lost all control.

Roy listened to his boss drone on about lost revenue, shareholder value, and how this was going to be a financial bloodbath for High Point Media and the radio industry. Still stung by Gunner's harsh accusation, he began to wonder if he actually had lost his way.

While hundreds of radio stations across the country were impacting the lives of millions of people with their messages of terror and creating a panic unseen in modern history, all Howard was concerned about was how it was going to affect the bottom line for the company. Roy was beginning to feel the same disgust that Gunner had expressed earlier.

"So, what else will they try?" Roy asked. The situation was urgent. Their airwaves were being used to push out fear. No matter how they managed the broadcast on their AM stations, they couldn't stop people from switching to messages of terror and reacting in fear.

"Homeland Security has officially notified the White House, and they're considering whether or not to issue a national terrorist threat emergency," Howard said. "It looks like they may decide to activate the Emergency Alert System soon."

Roy felt a wave of nausea as he ended the call.

******

Flipping open the case, Mike carefully lifted out the sleek, matte-black drone, a high-end commercial model equipped with advanced telemetry and communication systems. He pressed the power button on the side, and the drone hummed to life, its LED indicators flickering as it completed its boot sequence. He then grabbed the controller, a sturdy device with a touchscreen interface, built-in GPS, and dual joysticks for precise maneuvering. The controller automatically linked with the drone, confirming the connection with a soft beep.

"How does this work?" Dominguez asked, curious about Mike's drone and what it might be able to accomplish.

"This guy only has about twenty-five minutes of run time before the battery dies." Mike slid his fingers across the touchscreen as he ran through his preflight checklist. Battery levels were green, the GPS signals was strong, and the onboard camera feed showed a clear, stabilized image. He tapped into the settings menu, ensuring that the flight mode was set to manual, giving him full control over the drone's movements.

He looked up at the towers, then over at Dominguez.

"It's about three miles up there. It'll get up there, and I can get an aerial view, but it won't make it back down."

"You mean you'll lose your drone up there?"

"Yep," Mike nodded.

Satisfied with the setup, he extended the drone's carbon fiber arms, locking them into place. He attached the propellers, each one clicking securely onto its motor hub. A final glance at the controller showed everything was ready.

He took a step back and initiated the launch sequence.

The drone's motors spun to life, their whirring rising in pitch as the machine lifted off the ground in a smooth ascent.

Dominguez stepped closer to Mike and looked over his shoulder to watch the screen, too.

As the drone hovered above them, Mike adjusted the camera angle, bringing the live video feed into focus on the controller's screen. He could see the dense forest and rocky terrain of Mount Wilson, the transmitters looming in the distance. With a steady hand, he pushed the joystick forward, sending the drone soaring toward the mountain, its sensors working overtime to navigate the rugged landscape.

Mike kept a close eye on the battery indicator as the drone soared toward the towers, a mix of nerves and determination tightening in his chest. The sleek machine cut through the crisp mountain air, closing the distance to the transmitter site with remarkable speed.

But the clock was ticking.

As the drone approached the cluster of towers, Mike's pulse quickened. He knew this terrain like the back of his hand, every road, building, and structure burned into his memory from three decades of work on the mountain. But seeing it from the drone's perspective was disorienting. The lattice of steel towers loomed larger and more imposing on the small screen, their guy-wires practically invisible until he was too close for comfort. The drone's altitude sensors beeped, warning him of nearby obstacles, but there was no time to second-guess. He pushed the drone forward, flying it through the maze of structures, trying to keep his hands steady.

Mike's fingers hovered nervously over the controls, carefully adjusting the drone's path as it weaved between the towers. The risk of crashing into a tower or getting tangled in the guy-wires was real, and his limited experience with the drone only heightened his anxiety. This was unfamiliar territory, both literally and figuratively. But despite his lack of confidence, he knew this was the only way to get eyes on the situation. He guided the drone around the site, capturing video of anything that seemed out of place, though he wasn't even sure what he was looking for.

As the minutes ticked by, the battery percentage dropped steadily. He knew it would run out of power and plummet to the ground somewhere on the mountain, but that was a sacrifice he was willing to make. He had to do something—anything—to regain control of his stations.

The video feed showed fleeting images of the familiar landscape, but with every passing second, his window of opportunity narrowed. He hit the record button, saving the footage to the memory card he'd slotted into the controller earlier. He'd analyze it later, frame by frame, hoping for some clue that could help him understand what was happening up there.

As the battery warning began to beep, the drone dipped, its power waning, and he watched helplessly as it began its uncontrolled descent. He kept recording until the screen went black, the drone lost somewhere near one of the buildings.

Just as soon as the screen went blank, Mike's phone vibrated. He looked at the caller ID but didn't recognize the number. He took the call anyway and placed the controller under his arm.

"This is Mike Harris," he answered, walking away from Dominguez, who was now making his way over to the picnic table where others were congregating.

"Hello, Mike." It was a woman's voice, and she sounded meek and distraught. Mike had been so consumed by the events of the past few hours that he was stunned to hear the voice of a woman on the other end who wasn't his wife.

It was Valerie, Tom's wife.

Tom.

"I—I... I wanted to let you know that... Tom didn't make it. He died just a little while ago..." She spoke the words as if she was numb to it. She'd been making calls to friends and family for the last hour and had to get hold of Tom's phone to notify his radio friends. The hours after the shooting at Mount Wilson had been a whirlwind of a nightmare for Tom's family. He'd lost a lot of blood before he arrived at the hospital. The surgeons had been able to remove the bullet, but the damage was too severe. "He never regained consciousness."

Mike looked over at Tom's vehicle again, still parked where he'd left it just a few hours ago. He flashed back to the trip this morning when he and Tom had been attacked by rapid gunfire. Hearing this news now, Mike felt pressure in his chest, his breath becoming shallow, his blood pressure rising and pumping in his ears, his heart thrashing out of control.

He didn't even know how to respond to her. Mike had never met Valerie. In fact, he and Tom had known each other for years but only ever saw each other up at the mountain, and sometimes they'd share a meal together at the cafe.

Had this actually happened just this morning, a few hours ago? Mike felt as if this nightmare had been going on forever. He hadn't forgotten about Tom. It was just all happening so fast that he hadn't had a moment to inquire. Maybe he didn't want to know. If he didn't check, then Tom was doing fine.

"I don't know what to say, Valerie. I'm so sorry," was all Mike could manage. He had no words of encouragement for her, no words of comfort. This was awful. She'd just lost her husband to some stupid prank brought on by a bunch of arrogant punks. Mike felt sick.

Valerie expressed her appreciation for his condolences and informed him she'd let him know when the service would be. Her voice cracked as she did her best to hold back her tears. Earlier, she'd been hysterical, but she'd insisted that she wanted to make this call to Mike herself.

It was all out of control, and Mike felt the wetness of a tear in the corner of his eye. He wouldn't want anyone at the radio station to see him in such a state of disarray. Emotionally. Mike never let anything bother him. Always the professional when it came to the equipment and keeping the station running. But he'd never been so traumatized.

Mike stood there, stunned, struggling to put a coherent thought through his brain. He closed his eyes and took in a deep breath, filling his lungs with the fresh mountain air.

How could this be? It could've been him. What would Shelly do if it were him? How were the other people over at Tom's station taking the news?

Mike looked at his phone. It wasn't even two o'clock.

Wiping his eyes with a handkerchief he pulled from his back pocket, Mike placed his controller back in the case and made his way over to where Dominguez was talking with another official-looking man.

"Homeland Security is sending over counter-terrorism agents," Dominguez said. "They'll be here soon."

"Where can we set up a call back to the station?" Mike looked around at the command center setup for a phone or communications system. "I need to speak with Roy."

Chapter Thirteen

Shall We Play a Game?

2:00 PM

"I just got a call. Tom didn't make it," Mike said when all parties were on the conference line.

The phone lay on the rugged and splintered picnic table, which was used rarely by hikers. Dominguez handed Mike a fresh bottle of water as he sat down across from him.

"Tom's wife called me just a little bit ago," Mike said again to break the silence.

"Tough news, Mike. I'm sorry," he heard Roy say. Forrester had joined him in his office for the call with Mike and Dominguez.

The four said nothing for a moment. Whether it was a silent moment in honor of Tom or simply the fact that nobody knew what to say or how to move the conversation along, it was awkward. Mike wanted anything or anyone to distract him from his racing flashbacks to the shooting, driving Tom down the mountain while he was bleeding from his abdomen, watching him be wheeled into the ambulance while he gave his statement, washing blood off his chest, and changing his shirt.

Mike took another deep breath. He'd done that so many times today, but it was the only way he could manage. Breathe deep. It was what they'd told him when he suffered his heart attack a few years ago. Release the stress. Stop and take a moment. All Mike wanted to do was end this and begin the day again without the early morning wake-up call that had propelled him into this nightmare.

"How'd the drone flight go?" Forrester asked Mike. "Did you get what you needed?"

"Well, the battery died, as expected, and it went down somewhere near one of the buildings. It didn't reveal anything more than expected. I recorded the footage but haven't looked at it yet."

"What were you expecting to find?" Roy asked.

"Any clues, or vehicles, or maybe I'd catch one of them on video, and we could identify them," Mike said.

"I'd like to see that footage," Forrester said.

"Have they learned anything more about the pirates?" Mike listened to Agent Forrester fill them in on the results of their preliminary investigation into Albert and his cohorts, and he felt himself get angry all over again.

"We've looked into their bank accounts for suspicious activity or deposits, known associates, confiscated some gaming equipment and a 3D printer from each one's home—but the investigation is ongoing. So far, nothing out of the ordinary is showing up."

Roy was incredulous. "There's no other evidence or so-called manifesto?"

"Not that we've found," Forrester said, matter-of-fact. "Obviously, we have a lot more digging to do and people to interview. This'll be ongoing until it's resolved and the perps are captured."

"Motive?" Mike asked as if he were now an amateur detective.

"Could they be disgruntled employees?" Forrester asked.

Mike and Roy almost laughed at the term.

"Disgruntled employees?" Mike said. He went along with their ideas, but he still couldn't wrap his head around the notion that Albert was involved. "I'd say Albert was more of a conspiracy theorist and avid gamer who lived in an augmented reality. If he was disgruntled, I suppose it would be about the pay. Radio engineers' salaries haven't kept up with technological advances."

"It's the only thing we have to go on right now," Forrester said. "We aren't seeing any involvement in activist groups or connections to foreign adversaries, or sizeable sums of money deposited in bank accounts. What we're witnessing looks as if some young men have started a firestorm of terror just because they could."

"Like *Wargames*," Mike said, referencing the film from the '80s about a young gamer who stumbled upon a military artificial-intelligence protocol, hacked into it, and nearly started World War III until they figured out it was just a simulation. "It wasn't a terror attack; it was just a game. Do you think that's what's happened here?"

"Barring any further evidence, all we know for sure is that there are five men who are unaccounted for, all engineers with the same radio company, and all avid online gamers. We're investigating all their previous activities, but our time and resources are limited. Finding out the why isn't as important as ending their broadcast."

"They're using the station's AI platform to generate their messaging," Mike explained how they could assess how the scripts and voice-overs could be created in record time using artificial intelligence, much like how Gunner and his team were addressing the crisis in a way that made the audience believe they had a whole roster of reporters on the air.

"Did they hack into the system?" Forrester asked.

"No, they all would've known the logins and how to use the AI platform. That's part of our responsibilities," Mike said.

"Maybe they're making this up as they go along..." Roy said.

"No, everything that's happened so far is too organized, too orchestrated," Forrester said.

Then, a crackle came from the wall of receivers before an ominous, unfamiliar voice appeared through the receivers. Another AI-generated announcement began.

"Shall we play a game?"

"What now?" Mike could hear the shuffling through the phone line but not what was going on.

"A new message!" Roy shouted through the phone. "Turn on a radio up there!"

Mike and Dominguez bolted to the SUV. Dominguez jumped in the driver's seat and turned the ignition. Mike climbed into the passenger seat and pushed the buttons on the radio, changing the band from AM, as they'd been listening to Jackie and the KLAR broadcast when they arrived. Once he switched to FM, the menacing voice blared through the speakers.

Mike found himself perched in the seat and ready to pounce, his muscles tense and his eyes fixated on his target. Paralyzed with shock, the adrenaline rushing through him made him feel as if he'd drank a gallon of Diet Coke and was ready to crawl out of his body.

He couldn't sit in the car any longer. He stepped out and paced alongside the vehicle, listening.

"We see what you're doing. We hear what you're broadcasting to dispel our truth! The last two hours were all about the children. 'Save the children!'" A sinister laugh followed.

"Now that you've evacuated all the children and sent them home, let the fun begin! You caught us! There were no bombs at the schools, but we made our point! Don't believe what you hear. There are conspiracies everywhere, and even your radio stations lie to you!"

What the hell is this? Roy mouthed, but no words actually came out. Nobody made a sound as fear covered them like a weighted blanket.

The voice somehow became even more menacing. "You see, dear listeners, we are the masters of chaos, the architects of fear. We care not for your laws or your morality, for we exist beyond such trivial constraints. The media you once trusted is now our mouthpiece, spewing our theories with every broadcast." The announcer paused before going on. "Calling all gangs of LA, Chicago, and New York! Now is your chance to get what you want! The authorities are too busy with other pursuits to be bothered by your wars. Let's play games, shall we?"

Then, there was silence, but only for a few seconds before the new message played back again on a loop that was added to the first few messages that had been broadcast.

Agent Forrester said what they were all thinking. "They're building onto each message and replaying it over and over again."

"Yeah, and they just activated gangs!" Dominguez said.

Beside him, Mike saw another black SUV pull up carrying two men. They introduced themselves as counter-terrorism agents with the Department of Homeland Security.

Dominguez greeted them and introduced them to Mike, then debriefed them on the recent message that had just begun broadcasting.

The agents reported that they'd been in contact with the FCC, and since the broadcasts were all out of the stations' hands, the government was now in control.

"Good!" Mike said. "But what is the government going to do?"

"The FCC and the White House are issuing statements, and they've informed us they will not hesitate to activate the Emergency Alert System, as more events are undoubtedly about to unfold," one agent said. They needed to be prepared for any possibility.

They had just raised the hijacking of the public airwaves from a "serious concern" to a national terrorist threat emergency of the greatest magnitude.

"The word from the White House, and the FCC agrees, is that we need to institute a national Emergency Alert System warning."

After the attacks on the World Trade Center and the Pentagon in 2001, the FCC created the Public Safety and Homeland Security Divisions, responsible for public communications during any kind of national emergencies and crises. The subjects of these communications included public safety, health, defense, and emergency personnel. The plan was that the nation's communications infrastructure was to be operable and rapidly restorable in the event of a national crisis.

However, Mike and his fellow broadcasters were all too well aware that it didn't happen quickly enough for this to be possible. While the United States government was busy securing infrastructure, nuclear power plants, airports, train stations, and major ports, and busy monitoring cellular and internet communications, certain terror organizations uncovered and took advantage of the very vulnerable broadcast community–transmitters.

Anger stirred in Mike's belly. "This is fucking ridiculous. I cannot believe this is happening. Never, in my entire career—"

"I'm pretty sure that this is a 'never in my entire career' situation for every radio person we've ever known," Roy said through the phone.

******

Gunner was in his element, facilitating his team like an orchestra conductor. The maestro was busy instructing and following up with each division he'd delegated segments to. Right now, he was monitoring his producers in one studio, who were fielding calls and texts from listeners, generating phone interviews and eyewitness accounts, and addressing concerns and reports of activities going on in and around the surrounding communities with the mayors, city council members, and city officials.

The panic from the public was very real. The threats heard on the radio were not to be ignored, and Gunner's job was to address peoples' concerns. But he didn't have enough staff to cover every aspect of what was happening on the streets, and sadly, neither did any broadcast station in LA. Resources were scarce in every department.

Next he walked down the hall to another identical studio, where he found the group of three board operators he'd instructed to monitor all social media and digital platforms now publishing their content and commenting on other posts with relevant information.

The team broke every element of the broadcast into segments and added them to the program, making them accessible in the main studio, where Jackie anchored the broadcast behind the microphone with live discussions, real-time traffic, and message alerts. Gunner coached his staff with an authoritative urgency to ensure that every piece of audio was accurate, clear, and helpful.

Then Roy Longly appeared, coming down the hall from the conference room just as Gunner exited one of the studios. He didn't have time to discuss his outburst from earlier; there was new business that needed to be addressed.

"It's been a long time since I've seen this side of the radio station in such a flurry of activity," Roy said. Years ago, financial setbacks and challenges in the broadcast industry caused the corporate office to make cutbacks in staff, and their news departments were gutted. Nowadays, their news was more of a regional and national nature, and all the programs came through syndication, meaning they really had no more local news reporters.

"It's crazy back here," Gunner acknowledged. His eyes widened as he raised his eyebrows. He'd been so busy managing what was going on the air that he'd barely had a moment to consider the way it used to be. But, come to think of it, nothing of this nature had ever happened before, so there was no precedent for how to handle their broadcast being pirated.

"We just got word that the FCC has activated the Public Safety and Homeland Security Division," Roy informed Gunner. "Some counter-terrorist agents are up on the mountain with Mike and the FBI. Soon, they'll require that all stations provide the Emergency Alert System with their own airtime in order to counteract the claims of these terrorists. We need to be prepared."

KLAR AM 790 was the station responsible for emergencies in California and parts of Arizona. The Emergency Alert System was established to broadcast information and instructions to the general community in the event of a state of emergency. Rarely has it needed to be utilized, and this was the first time in its history that the president has issued the National Emergency Alert System.

Gunner's focus turned to Roy as he processed what he had just told. This was unfamiliar territory for him. Since its inception, the emergency alert system hasn't been fully activated. He'd conducted regular tests of the system, in case of emergency, but now he had to review the protocol for an actual emergency, and it wasn't readily available from where he stood, nearly frozen.

"I'm assuming you're wondering exactly what we're supposed to do?" Roy said.

"We don't have the luxury of tracking down the procedure. We just need to get it activated and do our job." Gunner turned his attention to his script-writing AI and input the details of a message to send over to Jackie. The script was generated in seconds, and Roy followed Gunner into the studio where Jackie was on the air, interviewing the mayor of one of the cities in the San Fernando Valley, a suburb of Los Angeles, where he was imploring the public to take these threats of gang violence seriously and seek safety.

The interview concluded and Jackie selected the next segment, which was a recorded message about the traffic and alternate routes to get to safe places and shelters if necessary. She shut her mic off, pulled the headphones down from around her ears, and laid them around her neck. She knew things had changed when she saw Roy following Gunner into the studio. With a quiver in her breath, she asked, "What's up, guys?"

Roy filled Jackie in on the decision by Homeland Security and the White House to activate a national emergency, and KLAR was about to become the primary broadcast in most of California and even into parts of Arizona.

"What do you mean 'primary station broadcast for most of California and into Arizona'?" Jackie asked.

"When the EAS is operational, participating stations have to pause their regular programming and broadcast the emergency alert, in this case, a message from the president. The government controls the airwaves and KLAR is the emergency station for this region. All other licensees agreed to broadcast our station in the event a national emergency is implemented. That just happened."

Roy waited for Jackie to grasp the significance of what he'd said. She was about to be elevated from a voice in Los Angeles to the voice of nearly an entire state and beyond, impacting millions of radio listeners. She needed to understand the importance of her role.

"All stations will simulcast our station?" Jackie wasn't familiar with the emergency protocols. It was never discussed, and training on it was minimal. She knew they would broadcast a test of the emergency broadcast system, but she'd never been involved with its activation and had never paid much attention to it.

"Not necessarily," Roy said. "They can join with our broadcast or not. Some stations may not have the personnel or the ability to keep broadcasting their own programs during an emergency like this, so they can choose to broadcast the KLAR programming, since we're the primary emergency station in this region."

"What are other stations doing right now? What about the stations that weren't taken over? What about television?"

"I don't know what the other stations have been doing," Gunner said. He didn't have time to concern himself with what other stations were doing. This wasn't about ratings or competition. He was just doing what came naturally. As a parent, a citizen of the community, and a broadcaster.

"There are a lot of social media influencers, online hosts, podcasters, and citizen journalists out there reporting about all of this," Roy said. "However, the authorities will throttle text messages and warnings issued via phones and online posting."

"Isn't that against free speech, or at least considered censoring?" Jackie asked.

"Not with a federal emergency. There are too many threats to coordinate coverage, and it's imperative that we narrow the voices down and provide accurate and concise information." Roy felt like he was educating Jackie, even though he'd never been through this himself. He'd learned protocols in corporate meetings regarding the station's FCC compliance, but he'd always relied on passing the buck to "our lawyers handle all of that" when it came to this. Now, he was in the thick of it, and all his training and knowledge was flooding back. He was glad he'd paid attention, even though it had seemed boring and burdensome.

"A national alert for five markets taken over?" Gunner said.

"The fear and panic are spreading faster than they can prevent it," Roy said.

"They're going to shut down as many platforms and independent posters as possible until this is contained. Millions of people are affected. Hell, these hijackers are instigating and encouraging gang violence now. We'll get messaging and instructions from Homeland Security and the FCC, and we'll also maintain our own programming, but we will expand our coverage to a greater area."

Mike had already given Roy instructions on how to activate the EAS from the studio. He walked behind the console next to Jackie, flipped a switch, and looked at the monitor. They were ready to take control of the airwaves, and all other stations were acknowledging a test for the emergency broadcast system, but the recorded message was different. It didn't say, "If this was an actual emergency." This time, it said, "This is an emergency."

First, there was a sixty-second tone. To everyone's relief, the switch went off smoothly. The script was ready. Gunner cast it onto Jackie's monitor and told her to record it as well so they could continue to play it back on a loop for the next thirty minutes. Jackie placed her headphones back over her ears, took a breath, and turned on her mic. Then she pressed the record button and spoke authoritatively into the microphone.

"This is an emergency. This is an Emergency Alert System message. Ladies and gentlemen, this is not a drill. I repeat, this is not a drill. The airwaves have been compromised. You are hearing my voice now because it is imperative that you listen closely and follow instructions. This is an Emergency Alert System message. Your safety is our utmost priority. Stay tuned to KLAR AM 790 for further news, information, and instructions. As many of you may already be aware, unknown perpetrators have hijacked our radio transmissions. We are facing an unprecedented challenge. But I urge you: do not panic. The Department of Homeland Security, the FBI, and other authorities are mobilizing as we speak to regain control and restore order."

The tension in Jackie's voice was palpable as she delivered her next lines. "Please, for your safety and the safety of those around you, keep your radios tuned to KLAR AM 790. This station will provide you with the latest news, information, and instructions. I repeat KLAR AM 790 is your source for reliable updates during this crisis. Do not attempt to call emergency services. This is the Emergency Alert System's directive."

She took a deep breath, steeling herself for what came next. "We understand the fear and uncertainty this situation may cause. Rest assured, we are working tirelessly to resolve this issue. We are exploring all avenues, including the potential involvement of the National Guard. Every available resource is being utilized to ensure your safety and well-being. In times like these, it is crucial that we come together as a community. Your cooperation and vigilance are paramount. Stay tuned to KLAR AM 790 for further updates. Together, we will navigate through this crisis."

Gunner's tablet buzzed with a notification, indicating a recorded statement from the president was ready to be aired in the queue. When Jackie finished reading the EAS script, he made eye contact with her and directed her attention to her computer screen, where she would see there was a message from the president ready to be played back.

She nodded at Gunner, indicating that she understood, and told her audience that there was a very important message from the president and that they'd be playing this back while they gathered more important information on what to do. Then, she turned her mic off, resting her headset around her neck while the president's message blared through the studio speakers. Roy and Gunner stood in silence as they all stared at the speakers as if they were televisions. The black fabric was a blank canvas of unimaginable horror.

"My fellow Americans, I address you today in the face of an unprecedented threat to our nation. As many of you are aware, our airwaves have been compromised by malicious actors, spreading chaos, threats, and uncertainty."

The president paused, his voice measured yet authoritative.

"I want to assure you that the federal government is fully engaged in responding to this crisis. The Emergency Alert System has been activated, and all necessary measures are being taken to restore order and ensure the safety of our citizens."

His tone became more emphatic as he continued.

"Please follow the directions of our highly trained professionals, who are working tirelessly to resolve this situation. Your cooperation is essential as we navigate through these challenging times. The full resources of the federal government are being deployed to address this threat.

"We understand the fear and anxiety that many of you may be experiencing.

But I urge you to remain calm and vigilant. Together, we will overcome this adversity. In times of crisis, the strength of our nation lies in our unity and resilience. Let us stand together, united in purpose and resolve. May God bless you all, and may God bless the United States of America."

Chapter Fourteen

Time Is Not on Our Side

3:00 PM

Time was not a luxury. Panic and fear had already set into the minds of the public. Jackie's message to tune into KLAR, along with the president's message, was on a playback loop, giving her a few minutes to collect herself and rest her voice. She exited the studio with Roy and Gunner and followed them to sit down at a table in the break room down the hall from the studio. None of them wanted to go back to the conference room with the wall of receivers playing back the ominous message of terror.

There were plenty of refreshment choices, and although none of them were hungry, they each picked up a snack of chips or cookies from the counter. The munching took the edge off the tensions Gunner felt in his jaws. He'd been clenching his teeth since the day began.

He looked up at the clock on the wall above the counter with the coffee station. It looked like a stereotypical break room at any corporate office, with multiple coffee makers, a selection of coffee and creamers, and sugar and cups. Most of the staff used mugs with the station's logos on them or brought in their commuter cups. A staff intern, usually the receptionist, brought in daily goodies like donuts and a selection of muffins. Those weren't on the counter today. It was now three o'clock, but it felt like midnight.

Jackie sighed, relaxing in the plastic chair with aluminum legs, sitting with one leg draped over the other. She'd been on her feet running the show on the air since ten o'clock.

"It's nice to sit down and take a break. Time really flies by," she said, and took a sip of the water she'd dispensed from the door of the refrigerator into a KSSP mug.

Roy looked around the table at Gunner and Jackie and reflected on the company he was keeping. He'd been a corporate man for so long now that he rarely interacted with this division of his staff. His job as the market manager kept him in business meetings and negotiating contracts with huge corporate sponsors, sports teams, and concert venues. He worked with the sales department and reported directly to High Point Media corporate headquarters. He'd only meet with Gunner a couple of times a year when the ratings came out, and they'd discuss how each station performed. He hadn't been on this side of the building since they moved in. Now, it was foreign to him.

Thankful for a break from the confines of the studio, Jackie could now ask the questions burning through her heart and soul, questions that echoed those of concerned listeners.

"What do we believe?

"How do we know these guys are telling the truth?

"Are rival gangs going to take over the streets?

"When will this end, and what are we doing about it?"

None of them had any answers for her. Since they'd begun their broadcast at noon, the pirates had updated the message and added more ominous threats to it a couple of times.

Gunner provided an update on how his production staff was being utilized to cover messages and instructions to the audience. This brief reprieve to retool while the EAS message and the president's communication played back gave them a brief amount of time to connect on a different level. Until now, Gunner had been managing the content creators, but Jackie was on her own with when and how to play it back on the air.

"We're really using our AI program to aid in producing content and scriptwriting. It's working well posting the content on social media," Gunner reported. "It's a stark contrast, the message of terrorist threats from the pirates on half our stations, while we try to coax the audience into switching the station—and even their radios to AM—and following our directions to safety." Gunner hadn't taken his eyes off his tablet, monitoring messages from his team, social media, and what was happening on the air. They may be sitting down for a moment, but Gunner's program clock didn't take a break.

"This is not just propaganda." Agent Forrester appeared at the door to the break room. "Calling out gangs in these major cities has really raised the level of concern. We can't take any chances that previous claims aren't real, or that the gang members and criminal element will take advantage of our overburdened peacekeeping efforts."

"It doesn't help that it's our own radio stations that they're using to terrorize the American public," Roy said angrily. "We've spent so many years avoiding the concept that people just plain hate America that we've deluded ourselves into a false sense of safety." He was surprised by the intensity of his anger.

When he'd first gotten into radio as a rookie advertising salesperson over twenty years ago, Roy imagined the business as one big party after another. He'd get free concert tickets, perks, a nice BMW, fancy clothes, and make a ton of money. He was living large and loving every minute of it. Little did he know that radio would become a target of terrorism and that he would find himself in the midst of managing both people and a message to inform a terrified city about the unfolding events.

And yet, the feeling of responsibility overpowered him. No longer did he feel as though living large was his priority. He truly cared about how powerful his radio station could be now. He wanted to assure listeners that not only was the government doing all they could to get a handle on this but that his radio station was also trying to end the crisis. At first, he'd felt as though there was nothing he could do, but now he wanted to take charge.

Forrester didn't sit down. In fact, his appearance in the break room seemed very official to Roy.

"What's coming next?" Roy asked.

"Now that the White House has declared a national emergency and activated the emergency alert system, the National Guard has been deployed. They've evacuated the schools, and with this newest message, we need to do everything we can to prevent rival gangs from going outside their known territories. Unfortunately, that's going to add to the traffic gridlock because they're closing all of the freeways."

"Every single freeway?" Jackie asked, saying the words slowly. She imagined all the freeways in Los Angeles, the highest traffic of anywhere in the country. Thousands of vehicles daily traveled those freeways. Closing them would create a parking lot on every street.

"Every single one. The police, sheriffs, and highway patrol are coordinating and directing traffic, but it's going like molasses, and tempers are flaring. The troops are being called in for additional resources and peacekeeping."

"How long until the troops arrive?" Gunner looked up at the clock on the wall even though his tablet was still in his hand.

"They've been instructed to report directly to the location they've been assigned to and are rapidly converging," Forrester said. "It'll depend on that soldier's ability to get to the location, and with the traffic grid locked, there are going to be some challenges, no doubt."

Gunner didn't waste a second. He was already texting his production staff to get someone in logistics for the National Guard on the phone for a sound bite and to get ready for Jackie to come back live with the updates. People were gridlocked in their cars, and all they had was the radio to tell them where to go and what to do.

"Time to get back to work." He looked at Jackie as he stood from his chair in one smooth motion, tablet still in hand.

Jackie nodded, took another sip of water, and pushed her chair back from the table. The two disappeared around the corner as she followed Gunner back into the studio.

******

The splintered picnic table scraped Mike's forearms as he held his phone in both hands. He'd already given the DHS agent the rundown on how radio engineering worked, the same way he'd told the FBI and everyone else today why they couldn't just hack into the transmitter and regain control. He wasn't ignoring the FBI and Homeland Security agents sitting across from him, but they were busy updating each other about the recent message from the pirates and the measures being taken to minimize the collateral damage, keep the cities safe, and get these pirates rounded up and arrested.

"What are you looking at over there?" Martin Donaldson asked. He'd been with the Los Angeles office for the counter-terrorism division of the Department of Homeland Security since he'd worked the riots after the national elections a few years back. He and Dominguez both worked out of the FBI Los Angeles Field Office, where they collaborated with the Joint Terrorism Task Force.

"Research." Mike didn't look up from his phone. He was searching for a solution. Although he still hadn't had a chance to view the footage he'd gotten with his drone, it gave him a new idea of how they might be able to get the stations to stop broadcasting.

"What are you researching?" Donaldson pressed.

Mike put his phone down and took a swig out of the water bottle next to it. Scratching his arm again, he poured a little water on it to relieve the sting from the picnic table and rubbed the dirt and flakes of paint off.

"I'm new to drone technology." He wiped his hand on his jeans and looked at Donaldson. "In fact, I'd only flown mine a couple of times before today, so I'm not even sure I accomplished what I hoped to."

"What were you hoping to accomplish?"

"I know that mountain like I know my master control room. Every nook and cranny. I thought if I could get a bird's-eye view, I could see someone, or how they broke into all the transmitter buildings, and then come up with a solution to disrupt it." Mike took another drink of water. His mouth was so dry he couldn't seem to get enough.

"What did you find?" Donaldson was intrigued.

"It all happened pretty fast. I mean, I only had about fifteen minutes to fly around before the battery died, and I had to put it down or crash. But it was a waste of time. I'm not that great of a pilot and couldn't really maneuver it around the towers, guy-wires, buildings."

"Okay. So, what are you researching?"

"Something a bit crazy." Mike's mouth was dry again. He wished he had a Coke. He craved that first jolt of energy when the fizzy drink met his throat. "Military drones."

"What about them?" If Donaldson had even considered the idea of using military drones on these towers, Mike couldn't tell. He had a good poker face.

"Like I said, I'm new to flying drones, but I do like to learn about the gadgets and technology that go into them."

"Hmmm..." Dominguez said. "That's an interesting thought." He looked at Donaldson, who remained stoic. Mike couldn't get a read on him at all.

"What are you proposing?" Donaldson asked, and Mike only now noticed that the man had an earpiece in his ear, indicating that he was in constant communication with his unit, his boss, or even the other agents in the other four cities.

"According to my research, right here"—he pointed to the document on his phone— "military drones are equipped with electronic warfare capabilities and can jam our FM frequencies."

"Jam the frequencies using drones?" Donaldson asked, almost as if he was communicating the idea to whomever he was on the other end of his earpiece.

"It's just my first thought," Mike said.

"That's one of many ideas. We've dispatched an alert to gather the experts up here and at the other ground locations at the transmitter sites in the other cities. The rest of them will arrive shortly. We expect you to stick around. With your familiarity with the layout and technology, your expertise will be instrumental."

Mike wanted to respond with, "Duh." After all, he'd practically built the place. Why would they need anyone else? But he humbly shrugged his shoulders and simply replied, "I'm not going anywhere until I figure this out."

******

"Get me all the information you can about gangs in Los Angeles," Jackie told Travis. "I want to know what we're getting into and where these gang members are from. Heck, not even just LA, huh?" she added, realizing they were broadcasting across a huge geographic area.

Gunner left the studio once they had discussed their new direction, including reports and updates from not only the Los Angeles area but outlying areas as well. They were well aware of the number of ears tuning in for news updates and information. All of Southern California, parts of Arizona. All stations, except for the pirated frequencies, were likely broadcasting KLAR programming, increasing Jackie's audience size by millions. The thought of it would be intimidating if either she or Gunner had the time mind to consider it.

They reviewed the list of features produced by the team, decided what order in which to play them back, and eliminated some of them while adding live segments by Jackie.

Many reports were produced with the help of AI which aided in quickly receiving the recorded segments. As National Guard troops navigated the sea of vehicles, inching their way home and away from the threats, Jackie took a live call.

"Hello, you're on the air. What's your name, and where are you from?" The situation was serious, and she felt that pleasantries and greetings would be inappropriate.

"My name's Pete, and I just saw a drive-by shooting in Northridge!" he screamed in Jackie's ear and all over the radio. "Northridge! Not downtown LA, not Compton, but in the valley. Northridge! And your radio stations are telling gangs to get out and do what they want! You have no idea what you're doing, do you?"

Jackie, caught by surprise, struggled to find words. Her heart stopped, and she heard the mocking voice of her mom in her head. *Who do you think you are?*

"Are you hurt?" It was the first thing that came to mind. It wasn't as if calling the police at this point would have done any good.

"No. Just fuckin' terrified of what's happening to my home!" Pete said. "I'm with my wife and kids. We're trying to get out of all this. I couldn't even tell what or who they were shooting at. It seemed so random."

"Wow, Pete, well, I'm really glad you called in. You're right, we don't know what's going on, and we don't have control of our radio stations. That's the truth." Jackie's voice quivered along with her shaken nerves. She hadn't been attacked like this on the air before.

"Well, what are you doing about it?" Pete demanded. "You can't just keep telling people it's all make-believe and to go home like good boys and girls."

Jackie looked over at Travis in the corner, who was looking right back at her with an equally stunned expression. He held up his hands and shrugged.

Gunner burst into the studio, paying no mind that her mic was hot. Jackie's heart stopped again, and Travis jumped at the abrupt intrusion. Gunner made a motion with his hand like he was slashing his throat, indicating he wanted her to end the call.

But Jackie ignored his demand and addressed the caller instead.

"I'll tell you what we're doing about it. Right now, there's a team of agents and experts brainstorming a solution to regain control of Mount Wilson and the other transmitter sites."

Gunner hustled around the console and tapped a color-coded square on the screen right in front of Jackie, advancing the audio to the next segment, which was the pre-recorded messages from the president and the emergency plan to go home and seek shelter. Then he turned off her mic.

"What the hell, Gunner?" she said. "You can't just come in here and end my call like that."

"You can't answer questions like that," he said. "We don't know what the plan is. All this will do is start rumors and misinformation that we'll have to address. You have to keep it tight."

"Basically, we're just asking people to remain calm and get out of where they are," Jackie confirmed, looking incredulously at Gunner. "That's what we're saying."

"What else do you want to say?" he asked.

"People are emotional and scared right now, and we're responsible for it," she said, gesturing toward the call letters painted on the studio wall. "If these pirates are going to broadcast messages for gangs to take over cities, what else might they try?"

"What do you want to say?" Gunner repeated slowly.

"I'm not going to just give out information. We can use AI for those messages." She pointed over at Travis as if he had control over the AI feature. "I have feelings, Gunner, and so does the public. I'm terrified. They're terrified."

Gunner just looked at her. He needed to get back out there as reports of gang violence, store lootings, and random shootings were being reported from all over. The pirates' message was working.

"I don't want to be a puppet." She wasn't quite sure what more she wanted to say. She just knew she didn't want it to be dictated to her. "Why did you put me in this chair behind this mic today?"

Gunner sighed. "This morning, I had to make a quick decision about who I felt could handle this kind of activity and not let their overinflated ego get in the way. "Don't start becoming a problem now, Jackie. Who do you think you are?"

His comment took Jackie's breath away. Her brain felt like it was ping-ponging against her skull. She closed her eyes and counted to three as Gunner walked back around to the other side of the console and sat down in the guest chair, Travis again melting into the corner as he focused on the screen and what was on the air.

Jackie summoned up the courage that had gotten her this far, speaking with authority as she looked straight into Gunner's eyes.

"I'm the voice of California right now, and I want to be authentic with the audience. Why is it a bad idea to let the public know that we're working on resolving this?"

"You can't just shoot from the hip without any facts, Jackie," Gunner said, holding back how proud of her he was just now for standing up for herself. Sassy. That was what he liked about her. But not today. She was going to follow his playbook, not go off script.

"If our facts aren't right, we could incite riots or protests," he said. "What could be worse?"

"I just want to be able to address their very real concerns and present a different message," she argued.

"I get it, Jackie, but we also have a responsibility to reduce the level of fearmongering, and we don't want people to be irresponsible either. There's enough of that going on around social media right now."

They soon settled on a compromise, Gunner allowing Jackie to connect more with her audience but demanding she stay within the parameters of responsible messaging.

The president's message was ending and it was time for Jackie to take control of the airwaves once again, now with a vast audience and the National Guard on their way to protect the station from chaos.

Jackie wondered how long this would last. How long it *could* last? She replaced the headphones over her ears, flipped on the mic, and looked up at her monitor to view the segments she and Gunner had set up to record and produce news updates and traffic and emergency segments on the air.

As Gunner left the studio, he looked back at Jackie and said, "We don't want to spread our own fears and scare people into rushing to grocery stores to stockpile food and water. We're going to end this."

******

Gunner entered the production studio across the hall from the KLAR studio where Jackie was live, surprising his production team with his presence. He'd been so busy navigating what went on the air, along with the rapid changes in the broadcast, that he'd mostly been communicating with his team through a group chat on their phones and computers.

"We need to screen Jackie's calls," he said without greeting Stevie, the morning-show personality from KLCL and the program director from the sports station who had been given the task of producing the segments.

"We aren't screening calls," Stevie said. "We're in a vacuum in here, just putting out content to play next."

The weight of the situation, balancing the responsibility of managing the on-air message with the fear that the pirate broadcast would increase the already widespread panic, had Gunner's thoughts racing. He was torn between his duty to keep the public informed and his concern about inadvertently making things worse. For all he knew, in another thirty minutes or so, the pirates would release another message to frighten an already panicked public even more.

"Why are you concerned about Jackie taking live calls?" Stevie pressed. "Did she screw something up? Is it too much for her?"

"She let a listener get to her, and then she shared information that's part of the investigation, not meant to be broadcast." Gunner knew Stevie was vying for a spot on the air. The man had already voiced his disappointment that he wasn't chosen to be the host of today's crisis, but he'd been unceremoniously taken off the air by pirates this morning and had then been sent to purgatory doing production. Gunner knew Stevie wasn't thrilled at being kept in a box.

"Maybe she's not cut out for taking live calls or hosting a broadcast with such a huge audience." Stevie's tone was aggressive. "I can handle it, if you want me to step behind the mic from here on out."

"Jackie's fine on the air." Gunner wasn't going to budge. "We just need to know what a listener is calling in about before we put them on the air with her. I want her to be prepared."

"Then you're gonna have to get some call screeners to catch the calls before Jackie does because that isn't our assignment right now," said the sports station program director, who had basically been placed on indefinite leave since there was no sports broadcast today. His station was simulcasting the KLAR program.

"How come she took an unscreened call in the first place?" Stevie asked.

"Good question." Gunner took a deep breath, brushing his hand through his hair. "She wants to be more than just a voice in between the recorded segments. She's terrified, just like we are. She's brave and courageous, and I'm not going to replace her just because she made a bad call."

Stevie grumbled but accepted his reasoning, and they then discussed the latest news of gang activity and how rapidly the narrative had changed from clearing out the schools to protecting stores and streets from further social unrest. The National Guard had been deployed, but the logistics had yet to provide coverage. The situation was further intensified by experts calling into all the base locations of the transmitter sites.

"Have you talked to our other stations in the other markets?" the sports director asked.

"Oh yeah, we've been in contact since this all began," Gunner said.

"I assume it's pretty much the same, only different time zones and concerns, but still similar, right?" Stevie asked.

"We're in quite a different situation than our sister stations. KLAR is our flagship station for High Point Media, and none of our AM stations in any of those markets are emergency alert stations."

"What does that mean?" Stevie said.

"It means they aren't the hub of the emergency broadcast like we are here in LA. They've all joined the emergency broadcast station's program in their cities and aren't running their own shows right now. It's just us."

"How'd we get this responsibility?" Stevie wondered.

"Lucky, I guess." Gunner tried to smile, but the tension he felt made his face contort like he was in pain. He felt alone in deciding what was important to air and what needed to be kept from the public. Although the station personnel were aware that plans were being made to take control of their broadcasts, telling the audience would lead to questions they didn't have any answers to, and Gunner was well aware that being unable to address immediate questions in this type of environment would only cause anger. There was already enough false information going around on social media. He wasn't going to allow it to come from their own broadcasts, too.

He left the production studio and walked a few feet down the hall to his small but tidy office, shutting the door behind him and leaning up against it. It was the first time today he'd taken a moment to just stop moving and breathe.

Had he made the right decision by putting Jackie behind the mic for this?

Was Stevie right? Would she be unable to handle the heat?

He wasn't about to lose his edge now. He walked around his desk and plopped himself into his chair. Pulling his phone from his pocket, he called his counterpart in San Francisco, who picked it up on the first ring.

"Hey, Frank, tell me what you think about this," he said, then he described for Frank what had just happened with Jackie and the angry caller, and Stevie's offer to step up.

"Come on, Gunner, there's no rule book or example we can compare it to. You have to trust that award-winning gut of yours." Gunner could hear Frank's smile through the phone.

"My gut told me this morning that Jackie's development and intellect would be the right way to go," Gunner said. "But that was before this got completely out of control. At the time, we had nothing to go on."

"And?

"I still think she was the right choice. She hasn't made any blunders. I just see her building some confidence and stepping over the line a bit, thinking I'm not gonna be able to stop her."

"They're known to do that now and again," Frank said. "So, what are you going to do?"

"I don't know." Gunner was worried about the international implications of a live radio broadcast on hundreds of stations. It may incite war. "The pirates already called out gangs. What if they start saying things about our adversaries and even threaten them?"

Gunner wanted to give Jackie all the facts so that she could answer questions on the spot, but details were changing as quickly as the pirate messaging. He wasn't able to predict what needed to be a priority.

"All wars have been started by lies and propaganda," Gunner told Frank.

"Wars? What are you talking about?"

"These pirates began by stirring fear in families with the school threat. Empty, yes, but the emotional impact has been huge. Then, they issue a new one, activating rival gangs to go at it. We can't predict what their next release will be. What if it's a threat to another country? What if this is like *WarGames*, only with radio instigating the fight?"

When Gunner was coaching his on-air personalities, he liked to role-play the worst-case scenario with them when it came to controversial content. Gunner now ran through the exercise with Frank, and it helped him devise a plan.

"So, you want to censor Jackie?"

"No! I have no intention of censoring her," Gunner said. "But we still have a responsibility to be truthful." Suddenly, Jackie's words resonated with him. "It's not censorship I want, it's responsible broadcasting. I won't allow anyone to go off half-cocked and spill rumors or ideas not based on fact, and getting those details correct takes time and diligence."

With a plan in place, Gunner ended his call with Frank and went back to his post near the studios down the hall. The day was far from over, and the battle for the airwaves had just begun.

Chapter Fifteen

Mountain Meetup

Mike recognized the ten or so engineers who were just arriving at Red Box ranger station for the "gathering of the experts," as Agent Donaldson called it. They'd all been up at Mount Wilson together at one point or another. It was a busy antenna farm and there was usually a lot of activity up there. Like magnets, as soon as they were out of their vehicles, they all gravitated toward each other and greeted one another, and Mike got up from the picnic table and walked over to join in.

The FBI agents escorting these engineers also gathered in their own group. It only took a moment for Mike to realize that Agent Donaldson was in charge. He called them all over to the picnic table and made introductions. Altogether, they had agents from Homeland Security and the FBI, engineers from several radio stations, and a crew of police and emergency personnel.

"We're here to determine how we can end this," Donaldson said, raising his voice so everyone could hear him around the picnic table. It seemed so formal to Mike, like a military operation he'd never dreamed he'd be a part of. He remained at the outer part of the circle, choosing to listen and observe rather than be in the thick of it.

"Up until these pirates started broadcasting a few hours ago, we weren't considering the disruption of the radio stations as a national threat," Donaldson said.

He reviewed the attempts taken to secure the site and discussed that the FBI had been following up on leads and investigating the missing engineers from each city, but now that there was a threatening broadcast on the radio, it had become a Homeland Security issue as panic erupted in the cities.

"We've stretched our resources to the limit to provide safety on the ground," Donaldson continued, "but the police cannot address all the criminal activity, manage public safety, and direct traffic at the same time."

Daily activity had come to a screeching halt, and panic turned into mayhem as gangs and other criminal elements saw the opportunity to commit crimes.

"And our radio stations are telling them to rain terror on the communities," one of the engineers in the group said.

"We're conducting similar meetups in San Francisco at Mount Sutro as well." Donaldson didn't place the blame on the radio stations exactly, but he was concerned about the weak security at all their sites.

He reported that the Sears Tower and Hancock buildings in Chicago and the Empire State Building in New York had all been evacuated. The only access to those rooftops would be by helicopter, and it wouldn't be possible to drop a soldier close enough without crashing into a tower.

There was a stunned silence among the group. This was no ordinary meetup with engineers. The authorities had made a few attempts to secure the sites and truly didn't know what to do to kill this broadcast and end the terror. Mike shifted his weight and glanced at one of his counterparts. For a moment, he thought he had seen Tom standing at the side, and he had to take a second look. But Tom was nowhere to be seen. Of course, he wasn't because he was gone.

Mike shook it off and refocused on the group who were speaking up.

"There's nothing we can do about it here," a voice came from the front, closest to Agent Donaldson. "The only way to stop the broadcast is from the transmitter itself."

"Do they have hostages?" a question from the group.

"How many pirates are up there?" another came.

"I flew my drone up there not too long ago to see what I could learn," Mike said, "but I didn't see anybody."

Dominguez laid a map across the picnic table, inviting the group to gather around and review it. Mike got closer and looked over the shoulders of a couple of buddies. It was a map of the antenna array, buildings, and marked streets. The site had been constructed in the early days of broadcasting. Mount Wilson provided coverage for the Greater Los Angeles Basin.

The Mount Wilson antenna farm was a collection of masonry buildings with soundproofing and fire-resistant roofs, each treated with fire-safe foam. The map labeled the roads, where wildfires from years ago had claimed some of the main broadcast sites, as fragile and narrow, preventing any kind of vehicle from going up there.

"We can't tell how many men are there if they're hiding inside. The concrete buildings prevent heat sensors from tracking movement," Donaldson said. "And since we've had no direct contact with the perpetrators, we don't know if there are hostages."

"Wouldn't they claim it if it was true?" Dominguez asked. "I mean, they're encouraging rival gangs to take advantage of an occupied emergency response force. Wouldn't they also brag about having hostages?"

"So, why don't you storm the mountain?" asked an engineer from the back of the group.

"We made an attempt when the broadcast started," Dominguez said. "There's a sniper or some sort of automated security system that monitors movement. Rapid gunfire explodes the moment you get close. We *can't* get up there."

Mike couldn't help himself. He had to chime in. "High Point Media has installed top-of-the-line monitoring and modulation gear. We're always in disaster-preparedness mode and have had disaster plans in place since 9/11." He was getting fed up. He wanted to get this over with. The disaster plan they'd had in place had been thrown out the window when their transmitters were pirated. Now, they were actually the cause of the disaster itself.

Mike looked at the other engineers, knowing they didn't have any other ideas.

"I've been researching the capabilities of military drones," he blurted out, pushing through the group of men from where he stood in the back and walking over to where Agent Donaldson was leading the meeting. He was met with confused looks and a few chuckles.

"What do you think they're going to do," a sarcastic voice came from the back, "blow up the transmitters?"

More sneers and chuckles came from the group, but Agents Donaldson and Dominguez, along with Mike, remained somber.

"Look." Mike pointed to the top of the mountain, where the tips of the towers could be seen through the trees. "We can't get up there and get these guys out of there. We've already cut off the power, but they have enough fuel to keep the generators powered up for months. Attempts have been made to get up there but have failed. You guys got any other brilliant ideas?"

Nobody moved or said a word.

Mike was more determined than ever to bring in the military and jam the signals. At least it might buy them some time to calm the public down if the broadcasts were jammed. Then they could bring in the resources that were too busy right now keeping the peace to actually take back the transmitter sites. This was Mike's war.

"I've been learning about drones, especially the capabilities of use for military operations." Mike held up his phone and waved it, showing the research he'd highlighted. "Not only are they equipped with lasers and energy weapons, but they also have the ability to target multiple RF frequencies from the air."

"And do what exactly?" came a voice from the back.

The arrogance of this group annoyed Mike.

"They can target these frequencies"—he pointed to the towers again—"and jam the signal."

Some engineers murmured their doubts about how a plan like that could solve the problem, others nodded their heads like they were starting to see Mike's vision, and the FBI agents looked at each other as if they'd just heard the solution.

"Well, they can definitely cover a wide area effectively," Dominguez said.

"Yes, although I'm concerned about any collateral damage of using military force in a civilian area," Donaldson added. "But we have to take swift action for the sake of public safety."

The engineers discussed the technical feasibility of jamming the signals and essentially disrupting the terror messages from broadcasting. The complexity of targeting multiple FM signals simultaneously would require several drones for each across five major cities.

"This is an expensive military operation," Donaldson said. "But, if their broadcast creates more violence, then there's a danger of loss of life."

"What will happen if jamming the signals fails?" asked one of the engineers from the group.

"Then they'll have to take extreme measures," Mike said.

"What would be more extreme than what we have going on already?" asked someone else from the group.

Mike shrugged. "Destroy them with their energy weapons."

There were a few disbelieving chuckles from the group, but Mike's confidence in the plan didn't waver.

Donaldson stepped away from the group as they discussed how the drones would jam the signals to coordinate with the Department of Defense, the head of Homeland Security, and the agents across the nation on a private conference call.

After weighing the risks and benefits, Homeland Security and the DOD agreed to escalate the matter to higher authorities to request military support. They were confident that the situation warranted immediate action, and that the safety of the public was paramount.

Donaldson came back to the group and announced the confirmation of the request for military support and the timeline to execute it. It would take hours to accomplish the coordination, personnel, approval and launch of a mission like this. He advised the engineers to go back to their stations and inform their companies of the plan. Mount Wilson and the other locations were now involved in a military operation, and he could not allow civilians to remain on the grounds.

Mike and Dominguez climbed into the SUV and followed the parade of vehicles away from the staging area to head back to the station to inform them of the plan. Mike was disappointed he had to leave the mountain. He wanted to be the first one up there when they caught the pirates, but that wasn't going to be possible. He wasn't a soldier, as much as he felt like one right now.

Chapter Sixteen

How Could This Happen?

5:00 PM

Jackie had finally found her groove by doing her own thing in the studio and now felt energized, despite standing up to Gunner, but still feeling stung by the confrontation. She recognized the weight and significance of her role as the anchor, and she approached it with great responsibility. Was he going to pull her off the air?

Without a moment to stop and think, she had no idea of the impact she was having on the listening audience. This was why she'd gotten into radio in the first place: to do something significant. She wasn't just reporting news; she was producing her own program with segments featuring community leaders and conversations with concerned citizens and providing directions, instructions, and guidance to people who really needed it. But this wasn't how she'd imagined it would happen, and Gunner was holding her back from being authentic and real.

She had to keep a lid on her own emotions about it. She wasn't allowed to announce that they were working on a plan. It was that simple.

She turned off her mic once again and removed the headphones from her ears. This was the longest shift she'd ever pulled. She massaged her sore ears to relieve the compression of the headphones. Her throat was scratchy. She wanted water with electrolytes. Had she eaten? She couldn't remember, and then her stomach growled.

Wondering what the meeting with the engineers and FBI at the mountain had resulted in, she took the opportunity of the few minutes of rest she had while a traffic segment played to leave the studio and out into the hallway.

"Keep an eye on things in here," she told Travis, walking around the giant console toward the door. Gunner had done a great job of keeping people from rushing in and out of the studio, which helped her stay focused. But she needed to step out of her marathon on-air shift and get some fresh air.

The ever-dutiful Gunner was hovering by the doors of the other studios. Normally, they were on-air studios, but today, Jackie's studio was the only one on the air. The rest were production only. Gunner, tablet in hand, was busy facilitating the content, contacting subscribers, sending text messages, ensuring social media posts were on point, and sending all their audio content over to Jackie in the studio through their automated system.

"Anything from Mike?" She startled Gunner. He hadn't noticed her coming out of the studio. He hadn't seen her since he cut off her mic and ended her call with the listener. She'd followed his lead and hadn't gone off script again, but he was preparing for a battle for the airwaves if this continued. Maybe Jackie had the right idea of speaking about her own fears and concerns.

He looked at her and back at the open window in his tablet showing the programmed events on the computer. He saw she had a few minutes until she needed to get back on the air.

"I haven't heard anything." He looked up from his tablet at her, pleased that their program clock was working out sufficiently: a phone recording from a concerned citizen, a message from a city official, traffic and evacuation updates, and Jackie putting it all together with her graceful, soothing voice, reminding everyone that by remaining calm and being courageous and strong, the station would regain control of the broadcast and end this terror on their airwaves.

"I've heard from Mike," Roy said, coming up the hallway with a fresh bottle of water and an armful of snacks. "He just sent me a text that they're on their way back here." The big boss pleasantly surprised Jackie by handing her the bottle of water. Although she'd never interacted with him much before today, this wasn't a version of him she'd expected to see.

"Coming back? Weren't they going up there to make a plan to take back the transmitters? What happened?" Jackie was firing questions off like a machine gun, and Roy had to hold up his hands to get her to slow down.

"They have a plan," Roy said in a hushed tone. He didn't want anyone else in the hallway to hear. That was how rumors started. Although it was only the three of them in the hallway.

Gunner's tablet vibrated: he'd gotten a new message. "Oh shit!" He motioned to Jackie and Roy to follow him into the studio, then went over to the speaker that was the monitor for the FM and turned up the volume. The pirates had a new message. Jackie and Roy stopped just inside the door and looked up at the speaker.

An artificially generated male voice that sounded a bit like Russell Crowe's character from the movie *Gladiator* said in an arrogant tone, "Are we not entertained? Indeed, dear listeners, the stage is set, and the show must go on. Welcome, once again, to the theater of chaos, where truth and fiction blur into a twisted spectacle of uncertainty."

The voice then became mocking. "Are we keeping you busy? Have you been paying attention? We know you have because we're watching you! We're giving you bread and a circus, just like the gladiators. Who will be next?"

Roy furrowed his brow. "What the hell is this crap?"

"Sshh." Jackie's knee-jerk response surprised her. This was the boss. You didn't shush him.

The pirates continued with their dramatic message as if addressing an audience in an arena. "Dear citizens, the clock is ticking, and your time is running out! The last few hours have been just a prelude. Our messages caused parents to gather their children from your schools. Now, rival gangs have descended upon your streets, looting your stores, stealing cars, and taking whatever they want. And this is only the beginning!"

"Are they putting on a play?" Roy couldn't keep his comments to himself, and Jackie shot him a look to be quiet. He nodded. Gunner hadn't moved. He stood with his back to them, listening and texting simultaneously.

The voice grew more ominous. "Did you know that wherever we go, fortified locations surround us? Heavy security measures, television cameras, electronic microphones—all watching, all listening, day and night. We are but pawns in their game, oblivious to the strings that bind us." There was a pause for emphasis. "And now, you are our pawns."

"What the hell are they threatening now?" Gunner shot a quick look behind him at Roy and Jackie, who were equally confused.

"When night falls," the voice continued, "we're going to unleash a spectacle unlike any you've ever witnessed." Another pause for dramatic effect. "Right here, in the hearts of your biggest cities."

The message ended with a wicked laugh, followed by the playback of the two earlier messages.

"What's that supposed to mean?" Jackie said, looking at Roy and back at Gunner.

Gunner turned around and looked at her. Their silent exchange needed nothing more. They held out hope that nobody was listening to these pirated stations anymore, as they had been asked to, but it felt like a horror movie that they couldn't walk out of until they saw the villain get caught and punished.

The phone lines and social media began to implode again, and they all knew what that meant. More panic was on the way. Jackie was behind the console with one swift movement. She again picked up her headphones and placed them over her tender ears. She pulled the microphone close to her lips as she leaned in over the desktop.

"Be careful what you say right now," Gunner said, with a look that reminded her how he would not hesitate to cut her off if she revealed information the public wasn't ready to hear.

"Then get me the information I need," Jackie said, standing her ground. She didn't want to come off as uninformed or in the dark as to what exactly the "plan" was to end this terror.

"I want to see video footage of what's going on," Roy said. "Let's get a television hooked up in the break room."

Gunner left the studio and walked across the hall to the one occupied by Stevie Gold and the sports programmer, instructing Stevie to round up a television, bring it to the break room, and turn on a news channel.

"What? I've been reduced from a top morning-show host to a roadie hauling equipment now?" Stevie complained.

"Just go do it, Stevie," Gunner said. "Roy wants this done, and there's nobody else in the building to do it."

Within minutes of the new message, there were reports coming in that looting and riots were breaking out in the major cities. It was past five o'clock, and despite the schools being emptied, families were still struggling to exit the area. Roads and freeways were still inaccessible, and traffic kept tempers ignited.

With the kids now out of school and traffic being diverted by the police, just as encouraged through the message, rival gangs were taking the opportunity to exploit the limited police presence, especially as storefronts were closing because of fearful employees needing to pick up their kids or in anticipation of panic-shopping.

"We're getting reports from listeners that stores are being looted," Jackie said in response to a caller who was wondering if she should get a gun. Another caller wondered if they should stock up on bottled water in case the threat was poison. People were even concerned about toilet paper.

Roy moved to the break room and, in horror, watched the traffic cam footage that one of the local news stations was showing. The news stations couldn't get their remote vans anywhere near the activity but had collected security camera footage from areas affected by the gang violence.

"As drivers navigate their way through their neighborhoods to seek shelter, carjackers attempt to pull them out of their cars while stores are being emptied by criminals," the television reporter said, narrating silent videos showing the acts in progress.

Gunner walked into the break room and directed Stevie to go back to the studio and continue producing the segments to go on the air.

"If the pirates are using our company's AI software to generate their outrageous broadcast, why don't we block them?" Roy asked Gunner.

Gunner cocked his head, considering the suggestion. "That's a great idea. Why didn't I think of that hours ago?"

"We could block them by logging out of the entire system and changing the passwords," Roy said. He felt useful again and wondered why he hadn't thought of that earlier.

Gunner glanced at Roy, who stood by, observing the hub of activity. "That might help prevent them from recording another message to terrorize the public unless they already thought it might happen and planned accordingly."

"Maybe it'll slow them down, and whatever this 'spectacle' is that they have planned when it gets dark will be thwarted." Roy glanced at his designer watch, which was worn as more of a status symbol than to be functional. But he liked the look and feel of wearing a watch. He thought it exhibited class rather than pulling out his phone to check the time. "It's pretty apparent that this is a game to them. Like a live-action role-play or something. They certainly found a way to broadcast a global protest."

"Well, if they're incapable of recording and broadcasting a fresh message with a fresh set of targets to terrorize, we might be able to dispel some of the fear, the chaos and panic, and the looting," Gunner said in agreement.

Roy left to go back to the conference room and update Agent Forrester about their plans while Gunner stepped back into the studio with Jackie, who appeared shaken up and nearly in tears.

"What's going on?" he asked, concerned she might be ready to break and he'd have to replace her.

"I just made the mistake of looking at a text from my mom," she said. She took a sip of water and then a deep breath to calm her nerves.

"And that has you upset?" Gunner asked.

"She's... she's wondering if you made the right decision putting me in charge of all this." Jackie shrugged. "She doesn't think I'm good enough for this role."

He gave her a wry smile and assured her that she was perfect for this job, right here, right now. This was her destiny.

******

Mike laid his drone's gear bag on the conference room table and pulled out a chair to sit down. Agents Dominguez and Forrester sat down with him just as Roy made his way into the conference room, eager to hear the plan.

The room began to fill with the remnants of staff and police. Everyone in the building wanted to hear how Mike and the government officials were going to end this battle for the airwaves.

Agent Forrester was the authority in charge again and informed the group about the plan that had been devised at the meeting at Mount Wilson; Mike added that he'd flown his drone near the towers and that that was where the idea to ask for military assistance had come from.

"Somebody knew the security weaknesses at all these broadcast facilities," Mike said. He looked at the time on his phone. Close to six o'clock, which meant Albert should have landed back East by now.

The thought of getting hold of Albert and proving everybody wrong about him distracted Mike from the conversation at the table. Agents Forrester and

Dominguez were providing the details to the group anyway.

He dialed Albert's number, and it went straight to voicemail. He assumed it was probably still in airplane mode and didn't bother to leave a message. Instead, he texted Albert to call him immediately. But the text bounced back as undeliverable.

Confounded, Mike laid his phone back on the table and mentally rejoined the conversation.

"Law enforcement is occupied and overwhelmed," Forrester was saying.

"Yeah, Mike and I witnessed it firsthand as we drove back here," Dominguez said. "The traffic is still extremely bogged down. Gangs are blocking the only streets that are open and harassing people in their cars. We saw a couple of accidents, too. We passed by some rioting, and our flashing lights got some of their attention, and they started coming after us."

"I've never seen anything like it." Mike shook his head. "Thank God Agent Dominguez got us through the gauntlet. Somehow, they knew we weren't there for them."

"A taillight was smashed by a baseball bat," Dominguez said. "We'll catch these hoodlums eventually when we get this under control. Nobody's going to get away without charges."

"So, what are we supposed to do now?" asked Roy.

"The mission is underway, but it won't be pulled off for a few hours," Forrester said. "This is a complicated military operation. The Airforce is deploying numerous drones over five different cities thousands of miles apart, and each location has its own strategic challenges. Coordination of all the key elements takes time, and we need to wait until the communities aren't likely to see the drones."

"Yeah, I imagine they'd think we're being invaded by aliens," Mike said. "Or at war."

"The paranoia right now is through the roof," Forrester agreed. "We'll get those signals jammed, and the terror will cease. Then, we'll be able to secure all the sites and finally capture these damned pirates."

Chapter Seventeen

Voice of Calm

6:00 PM

"It's 6:00 on KLAR AM 790, Los Angeles," Jackie said, announcing the station's legal identification. "Jackie Shure here, bringing you the latest on the pirate broadcast takeover. But you already know who I am, don't you? Thanks for being with me all these hours as things have been unfolding." Her voice cracked, and she paused.

Gunner and the production team had carefully scripted a lot of what she'd been sharing with the audience, but she still felt a connection with the listeners as she heard their fears and concerns about the messages they heard on the pirated stations. She considered using the adage, "If you don't like it, switch the channel," like they did when listeners complained about a song. But just like the morbid fascination that arose when a car accident happened, most listeners seemed unable to resist the temptation of experiencing the terror firsthand through the broadcast.

She used her fingers to count down the hours she'd been on the air. "Eleven o'clock... twelve o'clock... one." She'd been on the air now for eight hours without a break. That was nothing. She was capable of staying on the air and delivering for Gunner and the audience indefinitely, but being able to stop and reflect, to collect her thoughts, would be a welcome shift to the sensory overload she was feeling. Her body had deceived her. Feeling energized earlier by the perpetual onslaught of content she was broadcasting, now she was hungry and dehydrated. She needed a break. Travis had left to hunt down some food, and she'd been in the studio alone for a while. Although Gunner had created a program clock that kept the chaos organized, the angst and negative energy from callers and her interviews were taking its toll on her.

The broadcast software used for automating the station's programming allowed for color-coded files by category and topic. Usually, the coding separated music files from commercials, but there were no music or commercial files today. It was all listener calls and contributors to news, traffic, and safety instructions.

She checked her program queue and discovered that the segment playing was a message from the mayor of San Diego. It was a five-minute recorded statement commending the troops from Camp Pendleton who were aiding in evacuations and peacekeeping and appealing for cooperation from the citizens. The length of the recording provided Jackie with a few minutes to rest.

She shook off the mental exhaustion with a gulp of water with electrolytes. The water satisfied the dryness in her mouth, and she closed her eyes, savoring the refreshing relief. Reaching down into the cabinet where her purse was, she placed it on the chair next to her and pulled out a bottle of peppermint essential oil. She shook out a few drops into her palm, clapped her hands together, and rubbed them together in a circle, warming up the minty oil before cupping her hands and holding them up to her nostrils.

Taking a slow, deep breath, she soon felt both calm and invigorated. She closed her eyes and took three more slow, deep breaths. She looked around the studio, which, just hours ago, was a foreign environment to her, with its KLAR signs on walls and monitors. The room had an identical design to the other studios, but rather than displaying an environment of fun and music like her familiar studio for KSSP, the KLAR AM 790 was a "serious" station that covered news, traffic, politics, and finance. Since she'd spent most of her career in studios that hosted a contemporary music format, which had a fun and entertaining vibe, this studio felt stodgy.

Just a few days ago, she was hosting her hip-hop radio show, dancing to the music, and giving away prizes when a caller answered a trivia question about a favorite celebrity. Today, Jackie spent her time behind the mic, delivering news, information, and safety messages to a growing audience filled with fear. She wasn't dancing, and there was no music playing on the radio… anywhere.

Before she knew it, her brief break ended, and she was at the mic again, ready to comment as the mayor of San Diego's segment ended. She seamlessly transitioned between segments, just like a city official would, with an encouraging message that they were all committed to stopping the pirated broadcast.

Next, the producers created AI-generated messages informing listeners about road closures and detours, as well as a news report announcing business closures and warnings about looters and gang activity. The messages were updated by the minute, making it impossible to keep up with the rapid pace and not feel overwhelmed.

Jackie listened to the on-air audio from the left side of her headphones and turned up the volume on the receiver Mike had set up for her, which was still set on the KLCL FM frequency. The pirate message was blaring its latest propaganda in rotation with the three recordings they had already released.

"Six hours of this horror!" she said, turning her head back to look at her mic switch, momentarily concerned she maybe hadn't turned it off.

Then she wondered if that would have been so bad. What if the audience genuinely knew how scary this was for her, too? For all those working at the radio stations. The pressure to regain control of the transmitters was intense, but they had a plan now. Did the audience even know that? Had Jackie talked enough about what happened and how?

Gunner had provided her with a list of questions to ask before conducting any live interviews with authorities. They were attempting to control the narrative in order to prevent dangerous conjecture. The public was inventing conspiracy theories about what was going on, and Gunner's instructions by the feds were to only provide necessary information for safety and security, not to allow speculation broadcast during an emergency. She was obviously following the rules but expected more of herself.

Weary of the AI recordings, she wanted a change. There was no emotion in the messages they were sending out, no sense of humanity. Was it just her, or did the listeners notice it too? Not having enough staff to run a full news program was shameful, but she longed for human connection, which she only found when listening to sincere concerns voiced by listeners and city officials on recordings.

It'd been three hours since the government issued the emergency alert, and since then, her audience had expanded. A few days ago, the weight of the responsibility might have been overwhelming for her. How did she get here?

The door opened, and Gunner appeared with a cup of tea in one hand and his tablet in the other. Peppermint permeated the studio, and his nostrils flared as he lifted his face to absorb it. Knowing how she liked it, he handed Jackie the cup and pulled out two packets of sweetener from his pocket.

Jackie accepted the tea but declined the sugar. "The anxiety is increasing. What's it like out there?"

"Same," Gunner said. "Mike and his FBI escort are back, and they're discussing the plan in the conference room, but I can't leave this and will jump over there to find out. We're just going to have to wait until Mike or Roy come and tell us."

"Well, what do you think is going to happen?" Jackie was keeping her eye on the screen, knowing she had to turn on her mic in a minute and segue to the next recorded message. She had it down like clockwork.

"I don't know, but the public won't be able to take much more of this. The police and authorities are running around like the Keystone Cops," Gunner said, referencing the silent-film-era series about incompetent policemen. "And what is this spectacular event the pirates are threatening now?"

"It's ridiculous," Jackie agreed. "I never thought I'd say this, but I wish the audience would just turn off their radios!"

"That's essentially what we've been saying, isn't it?"

"Of course, but they don't listen." Jackie looked up at the speaker as if the audience was hiding inside it. "They seem addicted to the horror, and I just want to use my own voice and speak my own truth now."

"Jackie…" Gunner said, dragging out her name as if to remind her that they'd already dealt with the idea of her speaking her truth earlier.

"Look, so far, there have been bomb threats at our schools, freaking out every parent in America, I bet. Then they invite gangs to take over the cities." Jackie reviewed the messages from the pirates that had been broadcast for the past six hours. "And now we have a threat of some event that'll shock the world."

"It's terrifying, I agree," Gunner said. "But what do you want to do about it?" He kept an eye on the software application the station used to program what was on the air as he put his tablet down on the console across from Jackie and sat down at a spot in front of a mic saved for guests in the studio. His body welcomed the rest after running back and forth between studios and barely having a chance to sit down.

"I want to use less of these artificial-intelligence recorded updates and read them live myself," Jackie said. "I want to decide what happens on the air while I'm in charge." The trepidation she'd felt a few hours ago about being the voice of KLAR had strengthened into a confidence she had never had before. She was determined to prove all the doubters wrong, especially her mother.

"What exactly are you asking, Jackie?" Gunner wasn't inclined to let her run the entire program, and although he'd chosen her to anchor the broadcast, none of them knew what to expect after the dead air. "I'm directing the programming, and we have to maintain our news obligations."

"I want the freedom to share my personal truth about what's happening behind the scenes here at the station," Jackie said. "I'm freaked out too, and now I have this vast audience. I don't want to pretend that we have it all under control. Wouldn't the audience be better off if they knew the absolute truth? How is limiting their knowledge and information better for them in the long run?"

"Sometimes ignorance is the best solution. We have to limit how much to release when you're talking to a large group of people who may misinterpret information and facts." "Chaos would ensue," she agreed. "But isn't that what's already been happening?"

Gunner wanted her for this role even though he'd had no idea what was in store for them when he'd picked her, and he didn't regret it now. Jackie was smart, educated, and knew her audience. But this was different, and the audience wasn't her usual demographic, so he wanted her to take all of that into consideration as she opened up her mic.

"I'm not asking to take over the programming, Gunner. I just don't want to play back artificially produced segments when I can engage with the audience myself. Right now, I'm just an announcer, and there are way too many thoughts and feelings that haven't been addressed."

"We have to remain within the parameters of the government, but nobody is dictating to me what we should and should not be saying on the air. There are no rules right now," he said. "I don't want to censor you, but remember this." He paused, looking at her earnestly. "THEY will hear you too."

Jackie realized he was talking about the pirates.

"If you share what we or the authorities are doing or planning to do," Gunner said, "you're tipping our hand, and they'll hear that too. Radio is everywhere. Don't you think the pirates are listening and adjusting accordingly?"

"I hadn't thought about that..." Maybe it was better for Jackie to remain in the dark then. Did she even want to know what was being done to recapture the transmitters and the broadcasts? If she were unaware of the plans, would it make her appear more genuine and relatable?

The studio door opened again, and Mike entered, with Roy following behind him. Gunner looked at Jackie. "Well, do you want to know or not?"

******

On the one hand, Jackie's desire to know everything and her full commitment to this team and their endeavor were clear. But if she knew the truth, and it was too dangerous to share with her listeners, would they know she was holding back information? If they did, she'd lose credibility with them. She needed time to decide, but she also had to get back on the air. She looked at the clock and had twenty seconds to make a decision.

"No. Not right now," she answered, shooing them out of the studio as she put the headphones back over her ears and flipped on the mic to address her listeners.

"I don't have any experience I can compare this to. But I can share the power of imagination." Jackie paused, pulled the chair up behind her, and sat down. She rested her right foot on the silver leg of the chair and her left foot on the floor as she leaned her elbow on the counter, positioning herself so close she was touching the microphone with her lips. "Listen, I want you to know this: no matter who you are or where you are, I ask you to stop what you're doing and look around you. Are you safe right now? In your car, in your home, with your kids or loved ones, that's the safest place you could be right now. And if you're not at home with your loved ones, then get yourself there as soon as possible. I know this is scary. I'm terrified, too."

Jackie had taken a few psychology courses while earning her degree in journalism and had read enough self-help books to know that the first thing to do in a crisis was to check on the facts. Remind them they were safe right now. And keep them calm.

She provided a synopsis of the day and the horror that was being broadcast over the airwaves. "It's been a hell of a broadcast today!" she exclaimed, using one of the words the FCC might issue a fine for, but she didn't care.

"Let's begin by taking some live calls from you. Let's support one another as the powers that be develop the solution to end the pirate broadcast."

With her first caller, she utilized her knowledge of psychology to share information about the impact of emotions on hormones, leading to a fight-or-flight response in their bodies and a subsequent increase in stress levels.

"Believe me," she said, "we can remain in our anxiety and hold our breath, or we can stop, get our bearings, and focus on our safety and those around us."

She then took another call from a young mother who claimed she felt paralyzed and didn't know what to do. "I was trying to get home with my kids, just sitting in bumper-to-bumper traffic, when we saw some people running on the sidewalk next to us. They were smashing store windows with rocks or something and stealing stuff. I was afraid they would jump in our car next, and then what would happen?"

"We've been reporting on incidents all over the area about stores being looted," Jackie said. "Bad people will take advantage of the vulnerable whenever they can. Statements from the authorities claim they're trying to address the criminal activity that's popped up. It's absolute mayhem, and it needs to end."

Wrapping up her live call segment, she took a brief pause to delve into a more intimate discussion.

"I'm too young to have experienced this phenomenon, but those of us in radio are oddly proud of the story of the Orson Wells radio program 'The War of the Worlds' in the 1930s." Jackie shared the history of the story about an alien invasion of Earth, written by H.G. Wells in the late 1890s. In 1938, a radio program performing the book, directed by and starring Orsen Wells, caused panic among listeners around Halloween for a CBS radio station in New Jersey. Listeners who tuned in to the broadcast after the disclaimers genuinely believed that Earth was being attacked.

"The play being acted out for entertainment was not meant to terrorize the listening audience," Jackie said. "But for decades, radio has been using what happened to demonstrate the power of radio and the theater of the mind. Now, it's been turned into a weapon by some people who think it's just a game."

"I hope you don't mind, but I have to talk about my fears because I know that that's what we're all doing right now. We're all terrified about the threats we're hearing on the other radio stations. But I'm not out there with you. I'm hearing all about it right here from the confines of my studio, all by myself. I kicked everybody out. Too many voices inside my head trying to tell me what I needed to say, how I needed to be. I started thinking about my first job in radio back in Flagstaff, Arizona, about thirteen years ago, and my program director told me I would never be that famous television talk-show host. I had to work on my show and just be myself. You know, back then, I took it as an insult. But today, I've come to realize what he said was right all along. I don't need to emulate someone else. I', Jackie Shure, sure to be with you through this fear. I was afraid to just be myself. I thought just Jackie wouldn't be good enough. So, I've strived to be inspirational. I thought I could make a difference if I could be like my favorite TV talk-show host but on the radio. But today's events have taught me to fear nothing. To be myself. To truly be who I am and not try to be somebody else or compare myself to other people."

This epiphany had been brewing all day. She'd been consumed with the task of creating her own program and delivering content provided by Gunner's team of producers. Ultimately, how the segments were managed and aired depended on her judgement as she moved things around, addressed immediate concerns, and decided what to prioritize. It was a crisis of epic proportions, and her confidence had grown with each interview, chat with a caller, and moment spent listening to officials provide emergency information.

Jackie paused and looked around the empty room. The KLAR AM 790 brand glared in her face, reminding her that this was her new home. She'd never go back to being a hip-hop personality. She was where she wanted to be. Where she truly belonged.

"You know, guys, I'm scared of the broadcast on my old station, KSSP, and all the others here in LA. I'm in the studio of KLAR, talking to God only knows how many people that might be just as scared as I am. I'd like to be at home too. But I have an important job to do. I'm here at the radio station, the epicenter of this takeover of a hundred radio stations across the country. I won't sugarcoat it and tell you we have everything under control. Clearly, we don't, and the people around me are freaking out. Maybe I'm not supposed to say stuff like that on the air. I don't even know anymore. But does it really even matter? I'm here for you."

Jackie saw her phone lines were all lit up with calls, and the social media feed was advancing, but she wasn't ready to stop her speech.

"Everybody's been in my ear telling me not to say this or don't reveal that or make sure you calm them down. I just..." She sighed. "I just couldn't take it anymore. So, I kicked everybody out and pulled up a chair, and now it's just me talking to you. One-on-one.

"Right now, I'm able to relate to what you're feeling. I hope that you're at home. I hope that you're in a safe place, surrounded by family, sitting around listening to the radio until the people in charge of ending this do what they're going to do. I don't know what's real or not, either. I'm in the dark, too. Here's what I can tell you, though: there is a plan. I don't know how, and I don't know when, but I know that there is one. I'm not just a hip-hop DJ who got thrown into this mess. I'll continue to broadcast the truth and tell you like it is, as much as I possibly can, until this is all over."

Chapter Eighteen

Under the Cover of Night

7:00 PM

"Military drones are being deployed," Roy told Gunner as the group sat down.

The stiff plastic chairs in the break room were uncomfortable. Roy would have preferred to hold this meeting with Gunner, Mike, and the FBI agents in his office, where there was a big couch, comfortable chairs, and a coffee table. And privacy. However, prioritizing the needs of Gunner and Mike, who wanted to be near the broadcast studios, was crucial.

"I don't understand." Gunner leaned forward with his elbows on the table, eager to hear the big plan to end this. "What will drones do?"

Mike provided the rundown of the decision to use the military to jam the signals with drones.

"Drones?" Gunner raised his eyebrows. "We've decided to use military drones to jam the signals?"

"It'll stop the broadcast as long as they can hold the signal," Mike explained. "The terrorist messages will end, and then the military will be able to provide more resources to secure the transmitters and regain control of our radio stations."

Gunner was intrigued. "And this is going to work in the other cities too?"

"It's a complicated mission," Forrester said. "But as Mike pointed out, it's the most efficient and effective way to stop the pirates from broadcasting, at least temporarily."

"Temporarily?"

"Anything could happen," Dominguez said.

"It may not work perfectly," Mike added. "Some of those transmitters emit a hundred-thousand-watt signal in all directions. Jamming those signals will be a challenge." Mike tried to tone down the technical jargon, but he knew that there were also ways that these gifted pirates who had taken over his stations could disrupt the interference of the signals, too.

"What are we supposed to do?" Gunner asked Roy.

"What do you mean?" Roy said. He looked around at the group. "The decision has been made. The plan is in place. We're going to have to wait until they do it."

"I've got to figure out how I'm going to handle this news on air." Gunner looked down at his tablet and began typing in notes in his AI program.

"You're not going to reveal the plan on air," Forrester said.

"What do you think is going to happen when the public witnesses military drones flying over the big cities?" Gunner cocked his head and looked at Forrester. "We're already doing battle with a terrifying message claiming some sort of big event is coming, and then the public is going to see drones? People are going to assume the worst, like an alien invasion or something."

"We've considered that," Forrester said. "The DOD will conduct the mission in the dark of night. That's why we have to wait."

"So, if we notify the listeners that we have a plan and to be on the lookout for drones to provide some hope, we tip off the pirates, and they might escalate whatever they have planned." Gunner closed his eyes, visualizing the scenario. "And by keeping this news quiet, which is important to the mission's success, we might create more chaos when the sky looks like war."

"It's a paradox, I know," Forrester admitted. "But I think you'll agree that not tipping our hand to the pirates is the wisest choice."

"What happens if the jamming doesn't work?" Gunner asked.

"It'll work," Mike said. "Hopefully."

"What's that supposed to mean?" Roy asked.

"If something goes wrong, they'll be given orders to take the transmitters off the air for good," Mike said, feeling as if that would be like being told to remove life support from a loved one. "It could destroy thirty years of work up on Mount Wilson, but I can't see any other way."

"And how would they do that?" Roy was alarmed now. Jamming the signals was supposed to be the end of it.

"Any number of ways. Jamming could fail on some of the frequencies, or the electromagnetic radiation emitting from the towers could damage the drones."

"Well, how would they take them off the air for good?" Gunner was alarmed, too.

"The drones are equipped with energy lasers that could be directed at the towers with a burst of an electromagnetic pulse, rendering them completely fried," Mike said.

"They can't do that, can they?" Roy looked at Agent Forrester in horror.

"They can if it's deemed necessary to complete the mission," Forrester nodded.

"Corporate will not allow them to completely destroy our transmitters!" Roy said.

That would be a permanent end to nineteen of the company's most valuable properties. They owned and operated four FM radio stations in Los Angeles, four in San Francisco, New York, and Chicago, and three in Dallas, where their corporate headquarters were located. The impact on those cities and surrounding communities and the loss of revenue would cause the company to collapse with billions of dollars in losses. He hadn't even considered all the other stations that would go off the air permanently.

"The government doesn't care about the financial losses to your radio stations," Forrester said authoritatively. "They care about national security and threats of terrorism and war. They'll do what they have to do."

Gunner looked as if they'd just been given a death sentence. They all knew this was a national concern, but it was impossible not to consider their own world right here in LA at the possibility of losing four FM stations.

"That would be the worst-case scenario, a bloodbath for the industry." Gunner couldn't believe what he was saying. "A hundred stations in the top markets, billions of dollars in assets lost, job losses, not to mention the trauma caused for the entire nation."

"It's not up to the radio stations," Forrester said. "The airwaves belong to the public, and right now, they're being threatened."

"They'll only consider destroying the transmitters if jamming the signals fails," Mike assured Roy and Gunner. "Believe me, that's not how I would want it to go, so I'm counting on it that jamming them will work."

"How much time do we have?" Gunner asked with his tablet open, keeping an eye on the program and what Jackie had on the air. He looked at Forrester, and Forrester looked at the clock on the wall. It was half past seven.

"Cover of night," Forrester reminded them. "It'll be a few hours, more than likely."

Gunner picked up his tablet and stood, wasting no time marching back to the production studio to confer with his team about their upcoming work. Roy was eager to go to his office and call corporate, and the FBI agents returned to their post in the conference room.

******

Mike was standing now too, but didn't know where he wanted to be. He no longer had a purpose. There was nothing more for him to do here, and yet, he couldn't bring himself to go home to his wife until he knew this was over. He wandered into the KLAR studio, where Jackie had just turned off her mic and was lowering the headphones around her neck.

He didn't know why he felt compelled to go see Jackie, but her smile when she saw him comforted him somehow. He liked Jackie. Full of piss and vinegar, she was smart and never needed him to come to fix something in the studio. She was always friendly and professional toward him and said hi whenever they passed in the hall. He knew she did well in the ratings and had a loyal audience, and Gunner liked her. That was enough for him.

"What are they going to do?" she asked, wondering if Mike was on the brink of a nervous breakdown. He looked anxious and defeated.

"It's a good plan if I do say so myself." If he hadn't come into the studio, who knew when Jackie would've learned about the plan to jam the signals? Was she destined to be the last to know? Gunner had gone to alert the producers and programmers, Roy had taken off to his office to commiserate with the executives, and nobody had thought of telling the person on the air what was going to happen soon.

"I didn't want to know before 'cause I want to be able to be authentic with the audience." She kept one eye on the automation system. She had two minutes to hear what Mike wanted to tell her. "Just give me the final decision."

She wanted this over as much as anyone. She was physically and emotionally depleted, quite a contrast from the energy she used to keep the marathon broadcast moving. But how long could this continue? The looting was rampant in the big cities. She couldn't keep up with reporting on the incidents. Police were now on every street corner, along with firefighters and National Guard troops, but there still weren't enough resources, and crimes were being committed all over. She could only imagine how it might get worse if another horrifying message was broadcast.

"It's not so bad," Mike said in his calm professor tone. "Military drones will jam the signals of the transmitters. That'll end the pirates' broadcast and give the military the help and time they need to secure the sites and catch the bad guys, and then we can take back our stations."

He sounded confident it would work, and Jackie sighed with relief.

Mike sat down in the guest chair and briefed her on what they knew so far. It was getting close to 8 PM. It could be hours before the military acted, and he believed they'd get a heads-up when the mission was activated. This was his brainchild, and he deeply wanted it to work, but he also told her about the next measure they'd take if jamming the signals ultimately failed.

"Then what?" She elected to play back the emergency alert recordings to give herself time to talk to Mike and digest this new information. "Are they going to catch these guys?"

"I certainly hope so," he said. "I'd like to get my hands on them myself!"

Jackie had spent countless hours interviewing listeners, officials, and authorities to stay informed about the situation in LA, so it felt like second nature for her to ask Mike, "And how are you coping?"

Mike was a quiet man and never shared personal information with his coworkers, but the situation was different now, and he allowed himself to open up to Jackie. "My wife has been wanting me to retire for a few years now, since my heart attack."

"I didn't know you had a heart attack, Mike!" Jackie sat down in her chair.

"Three years ago." He told her about the chest pains and shortness of breath he'd experienced. It had happened during a weekend at home, surprisingly. But his cardiologist had said it was because of stress, poor diet, and lack of rest and had ordered him to eat right and slow down. "You know, the standard advice they give you to clean up your act, or else." Mike gave Jackie a shy smile.

"So, are you saying you might decide to retire soon?" She didn't know him well enough to give him advice, nor was she in a position to have an opinion on the matter, but she couldn't imagine these radio stations without Mike Harris keeping them on the air.

"I don't know what I'm saying." Mike shook his head. "I know this, though: my FMs have been hijacked, a friend of mine died today, and my apprentice is missing and a suspect. I don't know how much more I can take."

Chapter Nineteen

The Calm Before

9:00 PM

"You disgust me. You used to be better than this." Gunner's words still rang in Roy's ears. Had he lost his way in this business? Was it all about the money and prestige for him?

Roy processed the quick and definitive decisions he'd been forced to make over the last few hours while he sought the privacy and solitude of his office. There were important things to discuss. The future of High Point Media was at stake. This was a matter of life and death as far as he was concerned.

His office emulated the executive kind of class that High Point Media desired to project. His appearance, too, conveyed confidence and success through his well-dressed and groomed look.

He looked out the massive picture windows down at the street below. This particular part of Burbank was quiet now and dark. People loitered on the corners, but every store was closed. He spotted police cars strategically positioned to block the side streets. From four stories up, it looked like an entirely different world to Roy.

Walking behind his desk, he sat down in his large and very expensive leather executive chair, turning it around toward the mahogany bookcase he had custom ordered when he was promoted to market manager, and they moved into this new facility a few years ago. He scanned the assortment of pictures showcasing his encounters with celebrities, including a few with notable LA Lakers players. Tonight, the framed award for Market Manager of the Year, which usually boosted Roy's confidence, failed to inspire him. He rarely opened the High Point Media employee handbook and his books on leadership, sales strategies, and management anymore. They served as reminders of how far he had come from his start in Sacramento.

He glanced at a small picture in a frame of him posing with his kids at the California State Fair when he visited them in Sacramento last spring. Had it really been a year since he'd seen them? They were so small when he and their mom divorced. When he moved to Los Angeles with this big promotion, he had to leave the kids behind with their mom. He contemplated calling them, fully aware that they were probably following the saga of the pirate takeover of radio stations, even though it hadn't happened in Sacramento.

The display represented Roy's successes and the memories he cherished. It defined him, and all at once, he wasn't all that impressed with himself. Apart from the picture with his kids, it all seemed meaningless. He'd spent his life chasing the dollar, a new whale of a client, a promotion, a goal, a woman. He was tired of chasing this dream that had become his nightmare. Everything he'd worked for could be gone in a flash. Literally, he chuckled at the irony.

He spun his chair around to face the massive desk that consumed most of the space in the room. He picked up his phone and dialed his counterpart in San Francisco.

They were both confident that jamming the signals would be successful. The financial losses of the day would be isolated to just that: a day. It still meant millions of dollars in lost revenue for all these radio stations across the country, but perhaps the publicity would give them a boost once this was over.

The conversation moved to the worst-case scenario and what ifs. They discussed the impact on their staff and speculated about the restructuring of the company in the aftermath of losing nineteen of their most valuable radio stations. Then, he spoke with the managers from New York and Chicago. On any ordinary business day, they wouldn't interact, but today, they'd been in constant contact with each other through messaging apps and texts.

As he ended his last call, Agents Forrester and Dominguez appeared in his open doorway. He invited them in, and they walked over and sat down on the couch. Roy stood from his chair and moved from behind his desk to the matching brown leather chair beside it. He offered them a drink from his mini bar, but they both declined, holding on to their mugs of coffee. Roy pulled out a bottle of water and sat down in one of the matching chairs facing the couch.

"It's going to be a long night," Forrester said. He sat back on the couch, mug in hand, and crossed one leg over the other. This was the first time all day that Roy had seen him somewhat relaxed.

"It's already been a long day and night." Roy raised his brow over his right eye. "Do you have any updates on the investigation of the pirates that you can share with me?”

“Investigations take days, and we’ve only had a few hours,” Forrester said. “But, we’ve searched the homes of each of the missing engineers and found similar items. Additionally, they all fit a similar profile: young men in their thirties who live alone and with no family close by.”

“Sounds like a terrorist cell.” Roy couldn’t find it in him to be shocked. “What did you find in their homes?”

“Components. Schematics of booby traps, smoke bombs, and incendiary devices. No materials though, just clues,” Dominguez said.

“Any note or manifesto? Is it political?” Roy asked.

“We don’t have a motive yet,” Forrester said. “It could be as simple and sinister as them wanting to see if they could pull it off.”

“Maybe it’s revenge,” Dominguez added. “People do that sort of stuff these days.”

“We’re following all leads, but they’re minimal.”

“I agree with this being an act of revenge,” Mike said, entering the room. Jackie had to get back on the air, so Mike had left the studio to come look for Roy and some company. This calm before the drone mission was like being in a hospital with a family member who was dying.

He made himself at home in the chair next to Roy and helped himself to a bottle of water on the coffee table. He’d never had so much water in one day. Shelly would be pleased. Feeling confident in the mission to jam the signals, he knew he’d be heading back up to Mount Wilson in a few hours, once they were able to secure the sites, so he could reconfigure the transmitter and remote control and get their original programming back on the air. He hoped to have it done by dawn, but the idea of retiring swirling in his heart made him question anything beyond that.

“Well, all the evidence confirms the means to prevent us from retaking the transmitters and ending this broadcast,” Forrester said, only nodding acknowledgement of Mike’s presence before he continued, explaining that the pirates had been using remote technology to secure and protect the perimeter of each site. They had security cameras that operated by motion sensors, automatic weapons to shoot anything that moved, and smoke bombs and land mines on the mountains to deter intruders.

"Among Albert's belongings in his apartment, our agents also came across a manual for a sublethal remote gun turret, which had the potential to become lethal with the right modifications."

Mike shifted in his seat at the mention of Albert's name.

"What the hell is a sublethal remote gun turret?" Roy said slowly.

"'Sublethal' means it's designed to fire nonlethal ammunition, like pellets or rubber bullets. It's remote-controlled and has multiple rounds, and it's primarily used by farmers and ranchers to keep their land secure and is mounted on fence posts or telephone poles."

"So, this is where the gunfire came from at Mount Wilson early this morning?"

"That's what it looks like," Dominguez answered. "With a few modifications, it can be made to shoot real bullets."

"This is preposterous!" Roy said. "This had to have taken a lot of time, months, or years to prepare to execute this plan."

"That's how it looks. It's not like these guys woke up this morning and said, 'I think I'll take over a radio station today.' No, this was very well planned and executed."

Mike felt his blood pressure rise, but he kept his frustration to himself. He needed to get a hold of Albert and put the suspicion of his involvement to rest. He stood to leave.

"I'm going to Master Control." He tapped the pocket of his jeans where he'd stashed the video card chip from his drone controller after the flight at Mt. Wilson. I've still got video footage to look at from my drone," he said and stormed out.

******

Gunner clicked off his phone and put it on the console next to his tablet. His conversation with his wife had been brief. He felt conflicted about not being home with her and the kids, and he'd called to assure them that the terrorist messages would stop and this horror would end soon. He couldn't go home until that happened.

And it would happen any time now. He still had an important job to do.

His legs ached from constant activity. Gunner had been hustling from studio to studio for ten hours, running a broadcast to combat the propaganda on his other stations. Managing his production team, lining up contributors, and ensuring the messages would do no harm, he was carrying a storm of details in his head. He and Jackie made a great team. She had her own spin on everything, but she was agreeable, flexible, and a formidable creative collaborator.

Gunner looked around the room, at the console, behind the board where Jackie sat across from him, noticing that the studio was spotless.

"Messiness fills me with anxiety." Jackie shrugged. It wasn't the first time she'd been accused of having obsessive-compulsive disorder. "I can't work or even think clearly unless my surroundings are neat and orderly."

He picked up his coffee mug and sat down in the chair at the guest spot across from Jackie just as his tablet started to vibrate, notifying him that a new terrorist message had just begun to air. He signaled Jackie to increase the volume on the speaker monitoring KLCL FM.

"Attention, radio listeners." The announcer's voice had changed from the previous messages, and Gunner assumed this time it was an actual human voice, one of the pirates, not artificial intelligence. "We told you we'd have something spectacular for you tonight. Are you ready for the storm? Well, it's on its way to you now."

Jackie looked over at Gunner as if to ask, *What do we do now?*

The message was short and played back on a loop, the AI-generated messages from earlier replaced by the human voice. Gunner had locked them out of the AI platform the station subscribed to, so they no longer had access to it.

"This is a human voice," Jackie said. Her ability to tell the difference had developed throughout the day as the station had been using its AI platform to produce most of the segments.

"I feel stupid that I didn't cut them off earlier today," Gunner said. "I was so focused on our own messaging that I didn't even consider that they were using our own resources against us."

His tablet began to vibrate again just as Roy pushed through the door of the studio.

"We've been notified to prepare ourselves. The drones are now airborne," Roy announced. "It's about a twenty-minute flight from Edwards Air Force Base to Mount Wilson, but it's happening!"

Jackie and Gunner shot glances at each other but remained silent.

"In just a few minutes, they'll start jamming the signal, and hopefully, in just a few short hours, we'll regain control of our FMs. Aren't you ready?" Roy sure was.

"Just in time," Gunner said. "We've got a new message to contend with. How ironic that they're claiming to create a spectacular event, and the city is about to see a number of military drones fly over Los Angeles and attack Mount Wilson."

"It'll be a short-lived empty threat then," Roy said. Then he left Gunner and Jackie in the studio to rejoin the FBI agents who were monitoring the activities of the drones, who were back in the conference room.

The door closed behind him, and Gunner picked up his tablet and opened his social media to see what was being posted on each of the many platforms. It was close to 10:00 PM, and traffic was light, thank goodness. The throttling of internet services prevented independent content creators, journalists, and conspiracy theorists from uploading their commentary. Gunner didn't agree with blanket censorship, but in the event of a national emergency like this, he had to agree that it was necessary. False reports, unfounded analysis, and politics would only create more chaos and panic, resulting in looting and rioting. There had been enough of that already.

"Well, how do we handle this?" Jackie put her headphones over her ears for the thousandth time today and turned on her mic.

She wrestled with telling the truth to the audience but feared exposing their plans to the pirates who would be listening too. But what did it matter? It wasn't entirely her decision; Gunner and Roy had their hand in it, but ultimately, Jackie knew the power she wielded behind the mic. They could tell her not to disclose anything, but she was the one on the air, and she had nothing to lose. Not even her job.

"Say what you're going to say, Jackie." Gunner no longer wanted to stop her. He was fed up with the pirates and with the feds dictating what the station could or could not report on air. Jackie had been mostly cooperative this entire time, but the wheels were coming off. He knew she wanted to give a real-time update to the audience, and frankly, so did he. If the pirates were going to do anything, it was too late for them to alter their plan once the drones jammed the signal. It would be game over for them.

"This is Jackie Shure with a fresh update for you at this ten o'clock hour," she said with a calm and reassuring tone, her sultry voice as smooth as soft butter. "We have multiple events occurring, and I've been given permission by the authorities"—she paused and smiled at Gunner—"to let you know the plan to retake the airwaves is underway!"

Chapter Twenty

We Interrupt This Broadcast

10:00 PM

"How much longer?" Roy stood with his feet firmly planted and arms crossed, watching over the wall of receivers. The volume was up on all of them while the terrorist message continued to blare from the speakers.

"It should only be minutes now." Agent Forrester looked at his watch. It was two minutes till ten o'clock. He wasn't privy to the details of the mission, but he'd remained in constant contact with his connections at the DOD.

"And then what happens?" Roy asked. He'd already been filled in on the technical aspects of the drone operation. In Los Angeles, a half dozen drones would be deployed from Edwards Air Base, each drone armed with advanced electromagnetic jamming equipment calibrated to neutralize the pirates' transmissions across all frequencies. The operation was identical in the other four cities with drones being deployed from bases nearby.

"Once the drones reach their assigned positions, their jamming pulses will begin to fire," Forrester said.

"How long will they be able to hold that position?"

"As long as it takes. Once the signal is jammed, and the broadcast ends, SWAT teams and soldiers will be called in to recover all the sites."

A small group of the remaining staff and authorities gathered around the counter in the conference room, waiting for the pirate's broadcast to cease as events rapidly unfolded. On the other side of the room, another radio was monitoring the KLAR AM broadcast, with Jackie reassuring listeners that the plan was underway.

"I saw something in the sky! Are we going to war?" a caller asked.

"I've been advised that I'm allowed to share some details of the plan to end this terrorism," Jackie said, addressing her audience. "The White House and Department of Defense, in coordination with the radio stations in all five major cities, are executing a military operation to use numerous drones with electronic warfare capacity in each city. The mission is to use these drones to jam the radio frequencies of our stations, rendering the broadcast blocked."

"I guess it's too late to stop her from revealing the plan," Forrester complained, with a nod in the direction of her voice.

"What could the pirates possibly do to counter it?" Roy didn't take his eyes off the receivers. He hadn't given Gunner the go-ahead to reveal the plan, but he trusted him with the decision. He had to. Gunner had been right all along today.

"Too late now," Forrester shrugged.

Roy looked away from the receivers toward Forrester with the intention of defending Gunner and Jackie, but before he could open his mouth, the menacing voice coming through the speakers from the radios in front of him started to crackle.

It had begun.

The chaotic white noise and static emitting from the speakers all at once startled everyone in the room. Although they were anticipating it, it made Roy jump at the stark contrast of going from the menacing voice to a sudden barrage of white noise. His heart raced with excitement. It would all be over soon, and by dawn, they could return to their normal programming.

Cheers and shouts went up throughout the conference room.

"It's over!" someone said.

"Hallelujah!" another shouted.

"It's not over until we have control of our transmitters," Roy reminded them. "But jamming the signal's a successful first step."

The FBI agents moved over to their command center in the corner to monitor the progress as the white noise filled the room, and Roy's phone rang. It was an invitation to join a conference call with the head office and all his fellow managers. He clicked the button to join the call with a celebratory greeting, but his attention was split between the call and what he was hearing from the speakers in the conference room.

Roy never imagined he'd be relieved to hear nothing but static coming from his FM signals, but tonight, it was music to his ears. Mike Harris was a hero, coming up with the plan to use drones to jam the signals.

He listened to Jackie on the air, taking calls and providing details of what callers were witnessing. Her voice was calm but anchored by the same undercurrent of excitement that he felt. On top of that, he felt a surge of pride in how his team had managed the entire crisis today. Now he felt confident: this would soon be over.

******

The KLAR studio was buzzing with new energy. While Jackie was taking live calls from listeners, Gunner and Travis were weeding through files of produced audio that were no longer relevant and deleting them so they wouldn't mistakenly be replayed. The message from the pirates had been successfully thwarted, and Gunner was confident their threat of a "spectacular event" had been, too.

"We're being invaded by aliens!" a caller yelled into his phone, creating distortion through the speakers. "What the hell is going on? What could possibly be next?"

Gunner chuckled. "Do I know my audience or what?" He looked at Travis, who was busy at the computer, dutifully monitoring Jackie and what was coming up next on air. There were dozens of callers waiting on hold, and social media was buzzing, considering how late it was. It seemed as if the entire country was awake, waiting for the conclusion of this terrifying day.

"No, it is not an alien invasion," Jackie assured the caller. "It's our very own military coming to the rescue!"

She took another call.

"What happened?" the caller asked. "I've kept the radio on all night listening to your broadcast. I left the room to tuck in my kids, and when I came back, I heard you telling us that it's all over."

"First of all, I'm glad you're listening to KLAR and not any of the FM stations." Jackie smiled into the mic. "Our brilliant engineers and the military attacked the transmitters and jammed the signal. The terrorist messages are officially over!"

"What happens now?" Another listener demanded.

Jackie looked at a statement that Gunner had given her.

"In all of the cities in which the radio stations were hijacked, soldiers and SWAT teams will now move into position to regain control of the transmitters, and essentially, our broadcasts. These operations could take several hours while

162

the drones keep jamming the signals until our engineers can gain access to the transmitters and recalibrate our original programming."

She flicked off her mic and removed the headphones from her ears. Statements from city officials, the governor of California, and more had been produced and added to the list to be aired.

"These calls could go on all night, you know?" Gunner said. "How many of them do you want to take live? I could have my team pre-record some with AI if you're getting tired."

"Are you kidding me?" Jackie said, feeling invigorated. "I just need an energy drink! I'm not ready to quit now." She looked over at Travis, silently asking him to go hunt down a Red Bull or something. Coffee just wasn't going to cut it.

"You got it," Travis said, more than happy to oblige and hunt one down for her from the vending machine in the break room.

Jackie reached over and turned up the volume on the monitor to hear the static on KLCL. Then she turned back to Gunner and smiled. She felt powerful and confident. Her tension had vanished. She was eager to get back on the air and talk to anyone who wanted to call in.

He didn't notice or even look up. His attention was on the program screen. There was more work to do. The messaging may be over, but it would be hours before Mike would be able to get back to Mount Wilson and get their regular programs on the air for all four of their FM stations. Already twenty steps ahead, Gunner was strategizing how he wanted the stations to tell the story when they resumed their normal programming.

Chapter Twenty-One

Frequencies of Deception

10:30 PM

Mike was still fuming that Albert was considered a suspect. He needed to be alone, and the master control room was where he would find his sanctuary. He unlocked the door and stepped inside the room, shivering as he closed the door behind him, which locked automatically.

He found comfort in the whirring of the motors and air-conditioning that constantly ran in this massive room. This was his operating room, and he was the master surgeon. This was home.

He moved around the racks of equipment, monitoring the status of the transmitters for his four AM stations, checking volumes and uploads, writing down numbers on his log, and making sure that the Emergency Broadcast System equipment was working properly.

This was his routine; one did it as automatically as getting into a car and driving. He wanted to feel normal again.

He turned up the FM receiver in the rack and slid his finger across the frequency selector. One by one, he tuned to each of the FM frequencies that were now successfully being jammed by the drones. He leaned in toward the monitor with his trained ear and listened to the crackling static with the occasional terror message bleeding through the various signals. A couple of the FM stations on Mount Wilson had a hundred thousand watts of power broadcasting in all directions. He was concerned that the drones might not be able to maintain a full signal jam, and the broadcast could still be heard in some of the surrounding communities.

"Malicious people do malicious things," he said as he attempted to regain his mental composure and reminded himself to focus. "Be present." It was a new tactic that his wife had helped him learn to calm himself whenever he was anxious. He took another slow breath, filling his lungs to capacity and holding it for ten seconds, just as he'd been instructed. Then, he released the breath as if he was pushing out the air through a hose and repeated the process two more times, feeling his heart rate slow down.

He left the volume of the monitor on, high enough for it to be heard over the hum of the motors but low enough to keep his sanity. He organized his tools and paperwork on his workbench, taking his time to clean the dust off the countertop and the shelf above. The notebooks containing transmitter logs and documentation were put back where they belonged. He then walked behind the racks and fiddled with wires and plugs to try to keep his racing thoughts occupied.

Albert couldn't be involved in this, and yet he wondered why Albert's phone was still off and why he hadn't called Mike about the hijacking. Surely, he was off the plane and would have heard the news by now.

Mike rolled the desk chair over to the equipment rack and pulled out the keyboard on a tray mounted under a computer screen. He stared at the screen, reflecting on conversations he'd had with Albert while taking breaks from working on the equipment at the mountain. There'd been plenty of time to sit and wait while a new update was installed, or while they waited for a function to process, or even just to stop and eat something during the long days and nights spent working. They'd share stories of other installations or people they knew, the latest technology, or news of companies buying, selling, or trading radio stations. Occasionally, Albert would entertain Mike and share tidbits of conspiracy theories he believed in, always referring to "they." But Mike wasn't into following conspiracies and would only feign interest to humor Albert.

"You know, one of these days, the government or some corporation is going to succeed in mind control and manipulation. We'll all become slaves to it, and nobody will ever see it coming," Albert had said once. Mike had paid little credence to his claims. Albert was just a young man with a vivid imagination. Although Mike never fell into the traps of conspiracy theories, he enjoyed Albert's colorful tales about secret government programs and technology.

A sad sigh escaped him. He liked Albert and thoroughly enjoyed his knowledge and expertise. He was a breath of fresh air for Mike because it didn't take him long to learn, and he even had brilliant ideas of his own.

Mike pulled the video card chip from the front pocket of his jeans, where he'd stashed it earlier. Inserting it into the interface port on the rack-mounted computer, he watched the screen pull up the file. He clicked the upload button and waited for the footage box to open in the video player. He moved the cursor over the play button and began watching the footage he'd taken this afternoon during his "get a clue" flight.

He wasn't holding out any hope of finding anything more than what he'd seen this afternoon in real-time on the screen of his controller as the drone was in the air, but he was compelled to look at the footage anyway. Who knows what he might see with another look?

He increased the speed and pressed fast-forward, then paused the video at the familiar concrete buildings, but he didn't see anything that stood out.

What did it matter anyway? He knew this was a futile endeavor. He was just keeping his mind occupied until he got word that he was needed at Mount Wilson again.

Just as the end of the footage played, Mike noticed something he hadn't seen before. He stopped the video, pressed reverse, and backed up the footage one frame at a time.

It was clear as day. Just as the drone was about to lose power and land, it had captured a shot of Albert's blue Honda Civic parked close to the building that housed multiple radio stations' transmitter equipment. It wasn't even hidden. Albert's car was right there in plain sight.

"Oh my god!" Mike said. "It *was* him!"

Mike pushed away from the computer and stood from his chair, spinning around, his hands on his head, swirling with the truth that Albert was in fact one of the pirates. The room twirled around him, his knees buckled, and he grabbed the chair for support. His heart raced, and he struggled to catch his breath.

How could Albert do this? He'd treated Albert like family and taught him everything he knew at Mount Wilson. Shattered by the betrayal, he wanted to vomit for the second time today.

He leaned over the keyboard, pulled up the video frame with Albert's Honda, and pressed the print button, and the printer on the workbench sprung to life.

Just then, there was a change in the audio coming from the speaker. He shifted his attention when he heard a crackle, and then he heard the garbled sound of the pirates' recorded message coming through. He ran to the receiver and increased the volume.

"Shit!" He switched to another frequency to hear if it was on that one, too.

The pirate message was back on the air.

He continued up the spectrum, with bursts of static and a bit of distortion and interrupted speech, but the message was breaking through the interference.

Within minutes, the pirates message burst through the speaker.

What was going on?

He pulled his phone off his belt, located his drone research tab, and skimmed through his notes. Now that he'd confirmed Albert was involved, he knew Albert would have done his research, too. After all, Mike trained him on how to research technology to troubleshoot any problem. When the drones began jamming the signal, Albert would have done exactly what Mike just did.

Find out a way to combat it.

"Oh my god!" Albert and his crew were overpowering the jamming by raising the power on each transmitter. The message was back within seconds.

Suddenly, the audio went dead at the station Mike was monitoring. He turned up the volume and moved to another frequency.

Dead air.

No static. No white noise.

No terrorist message.

"No! Don't destroy the transmitters!"

He knew by the dead silence that after the jammers had failed, the military drone operators had been instructed to switch from jamming to destructive force using energy weapons. His research had told him that, and the worst-case scenario had been briefly discussed. But he'd been hopeful that jamming the signals would be enough. Clearly, Albert was doing his homework.

Mike snatched the picture of Albert's car from the printer and bolted out the door in a rush to reach the conference room to try and stop this travesty.

Chapter Twenty-Two

Signing Off

Mike rushed into the conference room and slammed the picture down on the table in front of where Agent Forrester was standing with Roy. His blood boiled and rose up in a rage, causing his neck and cheeks to turn red. He wasn't a violent man, but he wanted to shove Forrester into the wall.

"Here's your evidence! Who gave the signal to take the transmitters down?"

"Hey, don't blame me or the FBI!" Forrest said. "This was a military operation. It was out of our hands the second the Department of Defense took over."

"Did you know this was the plan?" Roy was as angry as Mike.

"The drones lost control of the signal." Forrester pulled in a deep breath and expanded his chest, towering over Mike. "The military commanders received orders to destroy the transmitters."

Mike grunted.

"You knew this was a possibility. This was a high-stakes operation, and we're more concerned with public safety and national security than we are about saving your radio stations."

Mike's attention shifted to the wall of receivers. One by one, the audio with the voice of a pirate was replaced with dead air or static and interference from nearby signals. The audible chaos blasted the room.

He stood in horror. It had been done. He ran over to the receivers and toggled the dial of a receiver back and forth, landing on each of their FM stations, and other frequencies that were on Mount Wilson too, the same stations they'd been monitoring all day.

It was a useless exercise. He knew they were gone. All of them. He just didn't want to believe it was finally over. He turned his back to the receivers and looked at his team of engineers, who gathered next to him, just as shocked as he was.

Roy was frozen where he stood. He looked at Forrester, then across the room at Mike.

"What happens next?" he asked Forrester, looking for direction. He had to suppress the urge to run out of the room and make calls, but there was no one to call and nowhere to go. The epicenter was right here, right now. But what were they supposed to do now?

"Was that it?" Gunner ran into the conference room with Jackie on his heels and his crew of producers following behind. "Are we off the air for good?"

Roy shook the shock off and invited the group to sit down at the conference table so they could analyze what had just happened and discuss their next steps. It was getting close to eleven o'clock, the smell of fresh coffee wafting through the room. Roy had taken it upon himself to brew a fresh pot while he celebrated the signals being jammed and the end of the pirates' terrorism. He'd been about to pour himself a cup when Mike burst into the conference room.

Mike turned back to face the wall of receivers. How could Albert be a part of all this? He felt ashamed that he'd refused to believe that Albert could be involved in a terrorist takeover of his transmitters, and he now regretted just how much he'd taught Albert over the past year and a half, mortified that he'd even taken the kid into his home for the holidays and treated him like one of his own.

Maybe, in some way, Albert had been diabolically alerting Mike to their plans. Had Mike missed something important in their interactions?

Roy, sensing the man was spinning out of his mind, tapped Mike on the hand and encouraged him to walk over to the coffee maker on the counter in the corner. Mike took his eyes off the receivers and quietly obliged Roy's invitation.

"What's going on in there?" Roy pointed at Mike's temple, then poured himself a cup of coffee and offered to do the same for Mike, who declined. He was a Diet Coke man.

"I'm only speculating, but I know this much." Mike felt disgusted. "Albert was just the guy to head this up and pull it off. I may have only humored him when he talked about conspiracy theories and whatnot, but I never doubted his technical expertise with stuff like this."

Mike shared with Roy that he'd let himself reflect on some of those late nights working with Albert. They'd chat about technology or the news, and eventually, the kid would allude to "they," declaring some alternative backstory to whatever political event was happening in the world at the time. Mike wondered now if Albert had been telling him the whole time that something bad could happen right under their feet.

******

Roy sighed. Corporate was going to have to do a better job screening engineering applicants. How could they have allowed their properties to become so vulnerable?

His phone rang. It was the COO, connecting all the market managers on a video conference call.

It only took a minute to cast the call to the display screen on the wall, and everyone in the room took a seat around the conference table.

The COO appeared on the screen from his home in Dallas, wearing a T-shirt rather than his typical button-down and tie. It was 1:00 AM in Texas, and he looked so tired and worn by the trauma of the day that it was as if he'd aged ten years.

Their High Point Media headquarters had been evacuated hours ago. They only had one AM station in Dallas, so they'd been operating with a skeleton crew. When they'd been ordered to vacate the premises, they elected to simulcast the local EAS station, and all the staff went home.

The screen filled up with thumbnails of all the company market managers as they signed on to join the call. The COO sat staring at his camera, waiting for everyone. He remained completely motionless, making it challenging to determine if he was there or just a photograph.

Roy sat at the head of the table, closest to the video screen, facing it with his back to the table. Mike couldn't sit. He stood next to Roy, but over to the side so he wouldn't obstruct the view of the guys behind him. Gunner and Jackie followed Mike right up to the front, anticipating that at any second, they'd be running back to the studio to get on the air.

"It's a sad day for radio and a bloodbath for our company," the COO began. "But all are safe and accounted for, and that's what's most important."

Not so fast, Mike thought. Albert wasn't safe and accounted for. He was a criminal.

"The ramifications of this event will last an exceptionally long time," the COO

170

said. High Point Media lost nineteen of our most profitable properties tonight, and we'll be sorting this out with our lawyers, lenders, and the FCC for months, more than likely."

"They'll be off the air for years, if they ever come back on the air at all," Mike said with a heavy heart. Mount Wilson and those transmitters were his babies.

"The government doesn't need permission," the COO said sadly. "The public owns the airwaves, and they shut it down. Simple."

The group discussed the events of the day, how the stations had managed the crisis on air, and the mental and emotional toll it had taken on them and the community. Every major market manager gave a full report of their issues and concerns, from how to help the community recover and heal from the terror to what would happen to all their employees at the stations that were no longer on the air.

"Adjustments will need to be made," the COO said, stating the obvious. "Let's take this up again in the light of day." They set another time to gather for another conference call when all parties had had the opportunity to regroup and get a little rest. They all knew that nothing would get resolved tonight and weren't even sure their concerns were really being heard.

The call ended, and Gunner and Jackie left without saying a word. Gunner needed to coordinate with his producers to put together segments about the situation's resolution; calls and social media were already exploding, and Jackie needed to get back on the air. They had let their silence about what had just happened linger long enough.

Roy turned his chair around and faced the table full of engineers, FBI agents, and a few support staff. It was a stark contrast from the standing-room-only audience he'd had this morning when all of this started.

He spoke slowly and deliberately to what was left of his team. "Thank you all for being here today. You could have all given up and gone home to be with your families, but you stayed. Every one of you played a significant role here today." He looked up at Mike, who was still standing near him. The man hadn't budged.

"Mike, this must be the hardest day of your entire career. Mine too, actually," Roy said directly to Mike as if nobody else were there. At the moment, he didn't feel like the high-level executive that he was. "I'm really glad we have a man like you on our side. Your brilliance helped resolve this crisis. We couldn't have ended it without you."

But Mike was still mortified that Albert Braun was one of the hijackers, feeling solely responsible for how much of the technology he'd taught Albert. He wished he could turn back the clock to when the kid was hired. He should've shown more scrutiny. He should've done a more thorough background check. Too late now. He was disgusted with himself.

"Of course not." The tone in Mike's voice dripped with sarcasm. He was more angry now than ever. At Albert, at himself, at his inability to see through the bullshit of a con artist. "If I hadn't trained Albert, all this wouldn't have happened. And if I hadn't come up with the brilliant idea that the only way to end this was to ask the military for help, we may still have our transmitters."

Roy sat speechless.

Mike looked over at Agent Forrester. "I want to go to Mount Wilson." Mike needed to see it for himself.

Chapter Twenty-Three

The Aftermath

12:30 AM

"I saw a bright flash over the mountains, and then there was an explosion!" a panicked listener told Jackie. "Did you see that? The beam of light over LA?"

"Are we being invaded by aliens?"

"Are we safe? What the hell is the government doing about this?"

The panic returned. Listeners were calling in, and the phone lines were lit up. Gunner's digital team of producers struggled to keep up with the calls and social media posts. Behind the mic, Jackie guided the audience with the news of the pirated radio stations being taken off the air by the drones, as ordered by Washington D.C. and the DOD.

"Please remain calm. Do not panic." Jackie had been repeating this message all day. Despite the late hour, Los Angeles appeared to be wide awake. The population was on edge and glued to their radios, waiting for news, updates, and revelations. It had taken hours for the military to orchestrate the maneuver. Now, it was time to clean up the mess.

Jackie was taking calls live when Gunner came into the studio. "What are we supposed to do now?" a new caller asked.

"We're waiting for an update from FEMA about stay-at-home orders and the curfew. I imagine it won't be long," Jackie said, providing her own opinion despite having no idea what was going to happen next.

Gunner nodded toward the program monitor, encouraging Jackie to look up at it. The team of program producers in the other studio had uploaded freshly recorded calls from listeners and recorded messages from officials from all over. FEMA had issued a notice that the stay-at-home order would be in effect until 6:00 AM.

"Well, that didn't take long." Jackie turned off the mic and removed her headphones for what felt like the thousandth time today. Several recordings were queued up in the playlist, allowing her to gather her thoughts, plan their narrative, and take a sip of water.

Gunner smiled wryly. "The power of radio, my dear. It's wild, too. Listeners are calling in with all sorts of speculation and conspiracies about what happened, what's going to happen next, who they think did it."

"Well, it's a shift from earlier today. At least the terror messages are gone." Jackie looked up at the speaker Mike had set up for her, that monitored the pirated stations all day long. She'd kept the volume down most of the day. She reached over and turned the knob. Dead air. "Just making sure."

"This is still devastating for our company, not to mention the entire radio business." Gunner felt conflicted, wanting to celebrate the end of the terrorist messages and knowing the reality that he'd just lost four of the radio stations he was responsible for programming. He couldn't imagine what the light of day would bring. It wasn't going to be business as usual by any sort of metric.

"How are you doing, energy-wise?" Gunner wanted to give her a rest. "It's time to get you off the air. End this marathon for you." He could call another on-air personality to continue with the aftermath.

"Are you kidding me with that?" Jackie was exhausted, and completely depleted, but also invigorated and fully committed to the audience, the crisis, and the resolution. "I'm a night owl. I'm not ready to get off the air just yet. I want to see this through to the end. We can get some extra bodies in here though, to take the pressure off me."

Gunner loved her dedication, but he sensed it was more than that. Jackie had thrived today. She'd handled the broadcast with grace and dignity, helping each caller respectfully. She'd spoken to a business owner whose shop had been looted, a concerned mom worried about her kids' safety at school, city officials to explain safety measures, and the governor to discuss how the state was managing the crisis.

"When will they lift the emergency so that stations can return to their regular programming?" Jackie wanted to know. Despite the circumstances of the day, she'd felt a volcanic shift in perspective about her future in radio.

Since 2:00 this afternoon, when the EAS was activated, KLAR AM 790 had been the primary broadcast program in the region. Gunner knew stations would want to return to their own programming as quickly as possible. They'd all be clamoring with the authorities to lift the emergency broadcast so they could go back to their own programs.

"Your guess is as good as mine," Gunner said. He was multitasking again, phone in hand, as he sent a text to on-air staff. "Let's get some additional voices in the studio with you soon."

He planned for two of his morning-drive personalities from two of the FM shows to come in and get on the air. Gunner was already expecting his staffing concerns and hadn't told them they'd be out of a job later in the day.

"This could go on all night if we let it." Jackie pointed to the list of events on the screen. There weren't enough minutes in the hour to accommodate all the content being produced. "We need to make a decision about what we want to air, don't we?"

"How do we want to present this on the air? What are you comfortable with?" Gunner asked.

"With the truth." Jackie didn't hesitate. "I've had to withhold specifics today in the name of national security, and I respect it. We've been under tremendous pressure here at these radio stations and were forced to sacrifice valuable assets and financial losses."

He listened as she conceptualized and crafted her version of today's events and messages. He deliberated on her need for transparency and honesty. Her courses in psychology and her natural maternal instincts worked well for her now. She was able to show a compassionate understanding of the emotional trauma inflicted upon the community and felt strongly that she wanted to address it.

"We've covered this crisis with the news, but we're also victims," she said.

"True."

"The initial hijacking is behind us, but that doesn't mean that there won't be emotional consequences for days or weeks to come." She went on, brainstorming with him as she shared the ideas that had been forming in her mind all day.

In the past, when Jackie and Gunner collaborated, the topics had revolved around culture and celebrity gossip, new music, artists, and promotions coming up on KSSP. And yet here they were, less than twenty-four hours later, instead brainstorming about emotional well-being, crisis management, news, and instructions for a traumatized community. This was a whole new ball game for both of them.

"Alright then, let's line up some interviews and resources for crisis management and counseling," he said, making notes as he sent direct messages to his team in the other studio to research and connect with community service outlets.

She took a cloth out of her purse and wiped the rims of her headphones and microphone.

"What are you doing?" he asked.

"Getting ready," she grinned.

A minute later, Jackie was back on the air, reading a new statement Gunner had written with the help of AI while he'd been chatting with her.

"We won't have a clear sense of the damage to and the outcome of the destruction of the transmitters here in LA or any of the other cities for a few more hours. The shelter-in-place orders will be lifted by 6 AM, just a few hours from now. The terror is over, my friends. I'll be sure to stay here on the air with you until then, and perhaps beyond. I'm not ready to leave you just yet. Rest assured, we are taking all measures to ensure our radio stations are never hijacked ever again. I want to be authentic and truthful with you. What do we know? We're working on that."

She turned off the mic and removed her headset.

"You know what I want to know?" Gunner said. "I want to know if these guys are going to get caught, and what's going to happen to them. The chaos and destruction they created should put them in prison for the rest of their lives."

******

Mount Wilson was now a captured crime scene, and crews had been standing by at the base of the mountain as part of the military operation. They had immediately gotten to work clearing the debris from the road leading up to the transmitter farm. Mike's demand to see the damage had to wait some time before the path would be clear.

The light above the elevator and the ding of the bell signaled it had arrived. Roy, Mike, and Agents Forrester and Dominguez stepped in and waited in silence as it took them to the garage floor beneath the building. Mike struggled to form words, thoughts racing amid the mystery of how he'd find the remains of the site.

For the third time today, he was going up to Mount Wilson, where he'd already spent the weekend installing new equipment with Albert. His home away from home. He needed to see it. What was left of it?

Mike sat in the front seat of Forrester's SUV while Roy and Dominguez climbed in the back. He didn't want to talk. He needed to process his suspicious thoughts. "What do you think?" he asked Forrester.

"About what we'll find at Mount Wilson?" Forrester looked at Mike out of the corner of his eye, staying focused on driving. "I don't know. I've never been up there. You tell me."

"That's not what I mean." Mike realized his thoughts were racing faster than his words allowed. "Do you think we'll find their bodies up there?"

"I'd rather catch them alive. But anything's possible. This whole thing's been bizarre."

Mike pushed the button to roll down the window and rested his elbow on the car door. The cool air on his face felt refreshing, and he took a deep breath. The streets of Burbank were quiet for 1:00 AM, more so than usual. Everything was closed, even the twenty-four-hour stores and restaurants. The curfew and lockdown had yet to be lifted, streetlights were still flashing red, and police and emergency vehicles were still blocking off side streets.

"Wow. Strange not to see any cars on the street," Roy said from the back seat. "Turn on the radio, I want to hear what we're doing."

Mike flipped on the radio, switching the band to AM and finding the 790 frequency. Jackie was talking to a listener about what had happened, giving her personal perspective on the loss of their FM stations.

They rode in silence for a few minutes, listening to Jackie play back call after call and answer listeners' concerns about what they would find when the sun came up.

Mike turned around to address Roy. "What will *we* do when the sun comes up?"

"We'll cover this in the news cycle. Our AMs will return to regular programming. Sorry to say, but we lost a lot of money and assets today. I want to pick up the pieces of what's left and start to rebuild. Don't you?"

Mike wasn't happy with that answer. He wanted the sun to bring a new day as if this one had never happened at all.

"Our investigation will continue," Forrester said.

"Will your investigation find out their motive and how they acquired these devices?" Mike had never considered himself a sleuth or amateur detective. Heck, until today, he hadn't been a conspiracy theorist either. But his mind had changed, and now, nothing could surprise him.

"We'll look into everything, I assure you." Said Forrester.

The drive on the freeway was a breeze, with not a car in sight. They followed Angeles Crest Highway and turned into the lot at Red Box ranger station. The lights from the emergency vehicles, fire trucks, and police and military vehicles were a sharp contrast in the dead of night.

The dismantled truck that blocked the path to the mountain this morning sat dejectedly on a flatbed tow truck. Mike imagined the tremendous challenge presented by the narrow road and daunting switchbacks. They would have had to back the flatbed all the way up the road in order to load the broken-down truck and remove it from the scene.

The staging area was bustling with activity, but no vehicles had been up to survey the target area yet. They were still clearing the debris from the road, as the vibration from the attack had loosened rocks on the side of the mountain, which were now obstructing the road further up.

The SUV weaved its way through the sea of vehicles and people. Forrester flashed his FBI badge at the security checkpoint, giving them access to drive up to the entrance of the mountain. The narrow road was still dark, and Mike held his head out the window, looking up at the remaining towers. They were barely visible but he could blindly describe them anyway.

His heart rate increased with every turn as they followed the lead vehicle, clearing the debris. It was a slow process, as they had to stop periodically to get out and move boulders that had fallen from the side of the mountain. They couldn't see the road well, even with their high beams on. Forrester wasn't familiar with the road like Mike was. He knew they had little more to go after the fourth sharp turn.

The snail's pace drove Mike's anxious thoughts. He wanted to get out of the car and run up the mountain. It would have been faster. He knew it wasn't a wise choice but his body didn't care. The scene resembled a moment straight out of a horror movie, and he couldn't help but feel a burning desire to rush towards the danger, ready to witness the impending destruction.

The lead vehicle came to a stop when they reached the open gate to Radio Road at the entrance to the city of buildings and towers. Forrester was still pulling up next to the first vehicle as Mike pulled the door handle and stepped out. He could have made his way through the dark, but he didn't need to. Just a few yards beyond the gate, it looked like a war zone, still smoldering with the glow of being attacked.

******

Roy stepped out of the back seat of the SUV and over to where Mike stood by the security gate to the restricted area, already surveying the carnage. Neither of them had ever seen anything like it.

"We have to wait until the FEMA crew gets up here before they'll let you walk in," Forrester informed Mike. "A team will sweep the area for the suspects and check for safety."

Mike struggled to hear what he was being told. The voices were muffled under the pumping blood mixed with adrenaline pulsing through his entire body. Even his toes tingled. He felt like his heart was going to explode.

He didn't know if he was angrier that all his work for the past thirty years had been blown to smithereens or that Albert, his protégé, was the mastermind behind it all. Mike wasn't a fan of the corporate world of radio and had no feelings for the company. Losing the radio stations wasn't Mike's concern. He had no stake in them except his retirement fund and some shares of stock he'd been offered as part of his compensation package. But the transmitters, the buildings, the history up here on Mount Wilson were his body of work in an industry he loved.

And it was all gone.

Destroyed.

The trucks carrying FEMA crews were right behind them, and soon, the top of the mountain was buzzing with activity. Mike and Roy were instructed to stay out of the way until they could determine it was safe. Mike imagined they looked like refugees from a hurricane waiting to be let back from where they'd fled so they could see their homes, with their bodies as close to the caution tape as possible without breaking the seal.

The SWAT team was right behind them and immediately began searching the area for Albert and the pirates. Mike desperately wanted to see Albert hauled away in handcuffs, even anticipating what he would say when the kid was paraded by him.

After thirty minutes of waiting, he was getting restless. An official-looking man approached them wearing a FEMA jacket and a hard hat with a headlight shining in their faces, blinding them to what was behind him, and Special Agent Martin Donaldson from Homeland Security appeared right beside him.

"We've conducted a preliminary safety inspection of the area," the FEMA official said. "There's visible damage to the concrete structures, cracks, and spalling. Some buildings have portions that have collapsed because of minor explosions and fires in the equipment. The structural stability of the towers is extremely weak, and they show signs of melting and vaporization, causing them to fall over partially."

The light was still blasting in their faces, emphasizing their expressions and wide-open mouths. Stunned by the reality of the damage from the intense heat, Roy had expected only the electronics to be destroyed and the power to be out. He hadn't expected to hear this. None of them had anticipated the damage the drones would inflict. But Mike knew. He'd done his research.

"A few of these towers will need to come down, and some of the buildings condemned." The FEMA official removed his hard hat and tucked it under his arm, so the light was now shining away from them. They'd been setting up portable lighting, and a tent was now standing at the entrance. "You can go in, but you can't stay long."

"What about the pirates?" Roy asked. "Did you find them?"

"If they're still up here, they're hiding," Donaldson said. "They may have gone down the mountain on foot once their transmission was killed."

Mike batted the caution tape to the ground and stepped over it like a runner at the finish line. He'd been waiting long enough. He needed to see it all for himself. He put the hard hat on that he'd been handed, pulled his phone off the clip on his belt, and turned on the flashlight as he walked down the road toward the buildings ahead.

Roy stepped back, deciding to wait by the car. He didn't need to survey the damage. He'd just be in the way with no idea what to look for and would just ask stupid or irrelevant questions. He had no business riding along on this journey, not at this level.

It was as if Mike was there all by himself. Forty radio and television transmitter buildings made up this little community hidden at the top of the mountain. Construction began in the late 1940s after World War II when television in Los Angeles sought a better signal. As the mountain attracted more television and later FM radio stations, the buildings housed them with a resident area complete with a small apartment for engineers who had to stay up there. There was even a small post office from way back when.

Mike approached the building that housed the transmitters for High Point Media's transmitters. It was a large concrete and steel structure with multiple transmitters inside it, all positioned in chain-link cages with locks on the doors to prevent competitors from touching their equipment.

But the door to the building was wide open. Was it open because of law enforcement or because Albert and his crew had left it open?

He stepped over some debris and tried flicking on the light switch, an automatic response to walking into the transmitter room. His four transmitters' gates were no longer padlocked. The smell of burned-out electronics stung his nostrils. It was dark, and his phone flashlight wasn't going to provide enough light to survey the damage the way he'd prefer to. However, simply by smelling the room, he knew there was nothing to salvage. He stepped out of the building and looked to his left.

A half dozen fire trucks and emergency vehicles now lined the streets. Crews began hosing the smoldering towers with water and fire retardant. Mount Wilson was always bustling with construction, but the noise the emergency crews made haunted him. He stood in silence, looked beyond the building, and saw the bumper of Albert's car parked on the other side.

He walked toward the car, inspecting it. He at least knew not to touch it, as the cops would want to inspect it for prints and such. At least, that was what he assumed. He walked around to the front of the car and scanned the ground surrounding it.

"There you are!" he said, spotting his drone, lying close to the building without a scratch on it.

He picked it up and examined it, happy to salvage something today.

The adrenaline was subsiding, and Mike shivered. The early-spring air remained chilly on the mountain, and he had neglected to bring a jacket. There wasn't anything else to see. There wasn't any equipment he could salvage, and he was just in the investigation's way. Would they catch Albert and his buddies? It's too soon to tell.

It was time to go. He was cold, sad, angry, and grieving the destruction of his life's work. He looked back once more at the building that housed his four transmitters.

"Talk about going out with a bang," he said to nobody.

******

In silence, Mike made his way down the dark road to where the SUV was parked, oblivious to the noise around him. Men were yelling at one another, assessing the damages, but he was lost in his own thoughts about what it would take to build four FM radio stations. He wasn't sure he had it in him.

He opened the door to climb into the back seat, shut the door, and let out a sigh.

"It's freezing out there," Roy said, blowing his warm breath into his cupped hands. He was already sitting in the front seat, with the engine running and the heat on.

"Yeah. I'm glad to get out of here," Mike said, thankful the heat had warmed up the car. "I found my drone though. Where's Forrester?"

"Probably still talking to the other FBI and FEMA guys." Roy pointed in the direction from which Mike had just come. "I heard them discussing the investigation. What they'd be searching for, procedures. It was interesting, but it got too cold, and I came in here. Thank God the keys were still in the ignition."

Mike looked out the front windshield and saw the group of FBI agents talking amongst themselves. He must've walked right by them and hadn't even noticed them. They stood in the headlight beams from all the vehicles parked nearby, visibly shivering with the cold.

As if Forrester sensed Mike's plea from the darkened car, he and Dominguez broke away from the group and dashed towards the SUV to get out of the cold. The doors opened, the chilled air and the heat clashing in the few seconds before they slammed the doors shut. They looked at Mike but said nothing.

He shivered, rubbed his arms, and said nothing in return.

"Let's get out of here and get you guys back to the radio station," Forrester said, putting the car in gear. "We can talk along the way. What do you think, and what do you want to know?"

Roy turned around and looked at Mike. "What did you see?"

Mike didn't want to talk much. He was still calculating the damage and what it was going to take to rebuild everything they'd lost. He was still cold and just wanted to warm up, but the conversation was unavoidable. "Everything's gone, Roy. There's nothing to salvage. It's going to take years and millions of dollars to get these stations back on the air."

Despite not feeling like talking, he was surprised at how easily his words spilled out. Roy didn't even look shocked. In fact, Mike thought he looked remarkably calm. The loss to High Point Media was catastrophic, not to mention the other groups of stations. Recovery was going to be costly and take a lot of time. Why was Roy so calm about it?

"I guess it's too early to have discovered the devices the pirates used to orchestrate this hijacking?" Mike asked Dominguez, sitting right next to him.

"The sun will be up in a few hours; then, we'll be able to expand our investigation. Hard to know this early on."

"I would have expected them to mount the remote gun turret lower down the road, not up here." Mike was thawing out, and so were his words. "It would've been further up the road than the truck barricade, but lower than the security gate. The camera would have detected our arrival, sending an alarm to the operator. Whether or not they were on the mountain, the gun would fire with a remote control. You won't find it higher up."

He was on a roll now. "The smoke bombs, cameras, and explosive devices could have been placed anywhere along the perimeter."

A light bulb went off in his head, and he immediately recognized Albert's genius. It had taken meticulous planning and execution to pull off this hijacking at five vastly different transmitter sites.

"Do you think they got away?" Roy asked.

Mike turned his head to look out the window. Why? That was the question that had been haunting him all day. The how of the pirates' operation was simple for Mike to reverse engineer, but the reason behind their actions was something he just couldn't figure out.

"What if it was just a game for them?" Forrester said. "Psychopaths don't always need a big motivation to do something criminal. Maybe what they were saying on the air was actually true. You can't believe what you're told, and it was all just a game."

"That's really sinister," Roy said. "The damage it caused for a game?"

They'd gotten to the freeway as the city was beginning to wake up. It was 3:30 in the morning, and a few all-night coffee shops and gas stations were lit up along the main streets, showing they were open for business. The emergency vehicles and police barricades had been removed from most of the side streets, and the stoplights were no longer flashing red.

"What's on the air?" Roy asked, taking it upon himself to turn the radio on to AM 790 to listen to Jackie.

"While the city recovers, they have lifted the curfew and the shelter-in-place orders," her sultry voice said from the speakers. "Stores, coffee shops, and gas stations are reopening, and we'll be back to business as usual soon."

The lockdown was over. They pulled off the freeway and stopped at a red light. One car crossed the intersection, and another was waiting at the opposing light. Mike welcomed the signs of life. Soon, the city would be bustling again as if this had never happened. The radio audience would talk about the hijacking, and personalities would use it to promote the power of radio.

As they approached the office building, Mike looked up at the huge signage with the company name on the south top corner. They'd only been in this location for a few years, and he'd been so proud of their engineering accomplishments. He had designed and built master control rooms and main studios multiple times throughout his career. He'd always embraced these multimillion-dollar challenges. Now, staring at the sign bearing the company name, he wasn't sure he had the strength to endure them once more.

They drove into the parking garage, and the static in the radio signal cut off Jackie's voice. Roy turned the radio off as they drove to the third level. The cavernous cement enclosure had few other vehicles, but the station vehicles were parked in their assigned spots. Mike opened his door and stepped out. He reached into the back seat to collect his drone, then slammed his door shut, the echo bouncing from one wall of the parking garage to the other.

Roy and the FBI agents stepped out of the car, too.

"We've got a lot of groundwork to do now. We'll be in touch." Forrester shook Roy's hand, then Mike's.

"It's time for us to start chasing leads and hunting down Albert and the pirates when the sun comes up," Dominguez said.

Mike's head was spinning again. He barely heard what they were saying. He wanted to ask them more questions, but he knew they didn't have the answers yet either. He just couldn't figure out why Albert did this. Was it really all just a game?

They said their goodbyes and went their separate ways. As Mike and Roy reached the elevator to the radio station, Mike dropped his drone into the trash can. He had no intention of flying it ever again.

******

"This is Jackie Shure. I am sure to be with you during this transition back to a somewhat normal life, with the curfew lifted and businesses opening up for early risers." She gave her listeners an update on traffic conditions, which remained light, but the freeways and streets were now open without restrictions. Schools would be in session, and businesses would be able to reopen.

"It's a relief to give you some good news in the aftermath of a traumatic day. We lost some great radio stations today, and speaking for myself, and I believe a lot of my colleagues, it's a very sad day. But we're working to get back to our normal programming soon, and I thank you for staying with me." She then played back a public service announcement listing the restaurants, gas stations, convenience stores, and urgent care centers that had reopened in the surrounding communities.

The simulcast with the emergency alert system had already ended, and most stations had separated their programming. High Point Media's four AMs were still airing the same program as they waited for their on-air staff and producers to

185

relieve Jackie and her producers. Gunner was back to business, relieving the producers and programmers who had stayed all night. He gave them the go-ahead to go home as fresh recruits were coming in.

"It's 3:45 in the morning, my friends. Who's still with me?" Jackie wasn't ready for it to be over. She'd found her sweet spot on the air. Now that the panic and chaos were over, she could relax and enjoy engaging with the audience that remained.

City officials had recorded statements once the notice of the curfew was lifted, but they had stopped making live calls. In fact, it was pretty quiet now, but Gunner knew it would heat up again when the next round of hosts got on the air. No matter the format, this was big news, so he knew they'd even have a spin on the hijacking, and how it all ended would be opined about on the sports station, the talk shows, and even the music stations.

"What about KSSP and my job?" Jackie asked. She had plenty of time away from the mic, taking full advantage of the recorded segments and calls from listeners expressing their relief and asking about the lost radio stations.

"We'll turn the internet streams back on and separate the AM programs at 6:00 when the jocks show up for their regular shows," Gunner said. He stood at the console with his tablet lying on the counter while he sent messages and texts, arranging the morning programs and giving them directions. "They can still be live and broadcast as usual. It'll just be internet radio for the time being."

"So, I'm not out of a job now?" Jackie was only half joking.

Gunner stopped what he was doing and looked at Jackie. He felt depleted and somber, a sharp contrast to how she was feeling. She'd powered through a marathon day of nonstop broadcasting, and even though she could benefit from a nap and some food, she was energized and ready for the next challenge.

"No, Jackie. I will not let you go to some other station in LA, so you'll be competing with me. I want something more for you, and I'm going to make sure it happens."

"Make sure it happens?" Jackie grinned, elongating the word sure. "I wonder how I can make that my new tagline? 'I'm Jackie Shure, making sure shit happens!'" She swished her head back and forth and side to side with a sassy smile and chuckled, and then her chuckling turned into giggling, and then her giggling turned into full-blown belly laughter.

It caught Gunner by surprise, and he laughed, too. "'Sure to make shit happen,' you mean."

Soon, they were laughing uncontrollably.

Out of breath, Jackie gained her composure, and Gunner got himself under control too, each of them bursting with a laugh as they tried to calm down. "We're punchy," she said, smiling at Gunner.

"It's been a long day. I needed that." Gunner smiled back. "Thank you."

"I sure aim to please," she said, and then they were back to the uncontrollable laughter.

The door opened, and Mike and Roy entered the studio, confused at seeing Gunner and Jackie so out of breath as they wiped tears from their eyes and tried to collect themselves.

"What's going on in here?" Roy asked, his gait transforming from that of a serious businessman to a graceful, almost dance-like stride. Mike had never seen this side of Roy, and from the look of it, neither had Jackie. But Gunner knew Roy had a fun side. He would cut loose often when they'd worked together in Sacramento. Los Angeles had made him too serious.

"Jackie is coming up with fresh taglines for her next big gig," Gunner snorted, holding back another outburst of laughter.

"I sure am!" Jackie said, holding up a hand as if to try to stop herself.

Mike looked confused. They'd just blown up their own radio stations; the perpetrators had gotten away. His life's work on Mount Wilson had been demolished. How could they be laughing at a time like this? He remained quiet, though. He felt like he hadn't laughed in a decade.

"Glad to see you back." Gunner looked over at Mike. "How does it look at Mount Wilson?" He'd never been there himself. That was Mike's domain. He didn't know what to expect.

"It looks like war." Mike stepped further into the room. "And we didn't find any bodies." He was obsessed with finding Albert. He desperately wanted to know why he did this. How long had he planned it, and where did he get the money for all the devices? During his research, he'd learned that the remote gun turret alone was almost two thousand dollars. "Those stations are going to be dead for a while, no doubt about that."

Roy attempted to lighten the tension Mike brought to the studio. "Everything is going to have to be rebuilt from the ground up. The buildings, the towers, and the components inside the buildings. It's going to cost a ton of money, but we have insurance."

"Insurance for this?" This was news to Mike. As his eyebrows furrowed, he shifted his weight and turned his feet towards Roy, adjusting his stance. "What do you mean we have insurance for this?"

"Let's meet in the conference room and talk about everything we know," Roy assured Mike, then focused his attention on Gunner and Jackie. "Whenever you can break free from the studio, I'd like to review the day and talk about what's next. There are a lot of moving parts and cleaning up we need to discuss. Tomorrow is another business day, and although it won't be business as usual, we'll need to hit the ground running."

Mike stifled the desire to roll his eyes at all the business jargon clichés that just came out of Roy's mouth. It must be conditioning, he thought. Never let a good crisis get in the way of making money.

He'd seen a different side of Roy today. He genuinely cared about his staff, the audience, the community, and even Mike himself.

But now Roy was all business again.

******

Once Mike and Roy left the studio, Gunner drew in a deep sigh of relief. He looked at his tablet and began typing a prompt for the AI.

"Let's get you a closing script so we can wrap this up," he said to Jackie.

"I don't want a script," she said, placing her headphones over her ears and nodding toward the door for Gunner to leave.

Taking a pause to consider it, he then nodded and smiled, confident that she had something profound to say to her audience. He may have coached her to be a great radio personality, but she'd elevated herself to a whole new level today. He was proud of her.

"I'll see you in the conference room," he said. "Don't take more than a few minutes, though. This is not the Jackie Shure hour. We still need to get back to reporting information. Keep it brief."

"Yes, boss." Jackie waved him off and flipped on her mic. There was no more quiver of nervousness in her voice. She knew exactly what she wanted to say.

"This is Jackie Shure, back on live for the last time..." She looked at the time on the wall in front of her. "... this morning, April second. It's nearly four AM, and I want to thank every one of you for being with us all day. And what a day it's been!"

There were no new developments. Her phones weren't lit up anymore. Social media posts had slowed down. Everything was quiet.

"We lost a lot of FM radio stations today, and maybe some people won't think that's a big deal. And maybe it's not. After all, there are thousands of radio stations. However, for those of us who work in the radio business, and especially those of us here at High Point Media, this was a day of profound change. I was a midday radio personality, a DJ if you will, just forty-eight hours ago, and honestly... I don't think I'll ever want to go back to that position again. Today, I had the honor of being a calming voice on the radio for millions of you. It was a wild ride, and I'm exhausted in every way imaginable, but as rough as it was, I'm thankful to have been here. I want to thank you for sticking with us, calling in, and sharing your stories and concerns. Your fears. We came together as a community and waged this war together. I don't know what the new day will bring, but it's time for me to sign off on AM 790 KLAR. I've been informed that the stations we lost will be rebuilt, but it'll take years to get them back on the air. Stay tuned as the rebuilding begins, and I make my moves. This is Jackie Shure, signing off, and sure to be with you again soon!"

Chapter Twenty-Four

The Fallout

4:00 AM

Mike took his seat at the table in the now-empty conference room. The FBI and lingering engineers and support staff had left, leaving a skeleton crew running the station. The wall of receivers had been turned off, creating an eerie silence. Mike sat with his eyes closed, appreciating the momentary calm. He needed to gather his thoughts now that Roy had asked him to share his eyewitness account of the carnage at Mount Wilson.

He took a few deep breaths, the air slowly going in and out.

Once he opened his eyes, he jotted down some notes on the legal pad in front of him, making a list of what would need to happen in order to start rebuilding the stations. He created a diagram, and estimated costs based on his knowledge of recent equipment purchases.

Mike didn't let Roy distract him from his project when the man sat down at the head of the table next to him. But the fresh coffee and a donut, now that distracted him. He hadn't thought about food most of the day, and his stomach growled at the smell of sweet maple frosting on a freshly baked donut and the bitter aroma of hot coffee.

"Where'd that come from?" Mike asked, eyeing the bounty in front of Roy.

"When the curfew was lifted, and coffee and donut shops opened," Gunner said, walking into the conference room, straight over to the refreshments on the counter. "I sent one of my team over to the one down the street to get some for us. I figured we'd all be hungry, but nobody was ready to leave yet until we sort stuff out."

Gunner's attention to detail always impressed Roy, even with something small like this. "Thank you, much appreciated. Get me the receipt, and I'll reimburse you for the expense."

"No need," Gunner smiled, pouring himself a mug of coffee and putting a donut on a napkin. "Jackie mentioned them on the air. No charge."

Roy smiled, too. "Even better."

Mike got up from his seat and went over to grab his favorite donut. Although he wasn't really a coffee drinker, he wasn't in the mood for a soda. He filled one of the station's promotional mugs and added a packet of hot chocolate to make it a mocha. Shelly had taught him that.

They sat at one end of the conference table, enjoying their warm beverages and donuts while making small talk about the Lakers, Clippers, Dodgers, and Angels. They soon found themselves discussing the weather as a way to fill the time until Jackie joined them.

Still glowing from the dopamine rush from her sign-off monologue with her audience, Jackie breezed into the conference room and headed straight for the coffee.

"Bless you, Gunner." She elected to skip the donut. She'd already consumed enough junk food today and wanted to cook herself a healthy meal when she got home. But she was in no hurry to leave. She wanted to hear about all that happened beyond the studio door this morning. She pulled the chair out from the table and sat down next to Gunner.

"Did I miss anything?" she asked.

"Just talking sports and weather," Roy said. Then he paused and studied each of them one by one. "You all went to battle for these stations today, and I for one could not be prouder of each of you than I am at this very moment. It was impossible to know exactly what we needed to do, and I want us now to be able to process the day while we decompress. I'm sorry everybody else is gone, but I don't blame them for going home. I am, however, happy that I have the three of you to sort this out with."

Jackie was the first to speak. "Can I be honest?"

"Consider us peers right now, and friends, nothing else," Roy said.

"I know this was a national emergency, causing fear and panic all over the country. I know we battled terrible threats and were under enormous pressure to kill the pirate broadcast. It was a lot of work, and I'm exhausted to the bone." Jackie paused, but then grinned. "But it was the best friggin' day in my whole radio career, and I thank you both, Gunner and Roy, for giving me the reins and the mic."

"It was the exact opposite for me," Mike said with a little huff. "This was by far the worst day of my radio career. All the work I've done was destroyed, and it'll take a miracle to rebuild it."

He shared with Gunner and Jackie what he'd seen at Mount Wilson.

"It was dark and cold and honestly looked like a scene from a disaster movie." Mike then explained the complicated and expensive process it would take to rebuild transmitters. "Assuming all goes perfectly, we'll be back on the air in a few years."

"If all goes perfectly," Roy reiterated.

"Yeah," Mike nodded. They both understood that they should expect whatever Mike estimated to double.

"What's going to happen with Albert and the other engineers who did this?" Gunner asked.

Roy filled them in on all he knew about Albert, the evidence found at his and the other alleged suspects' homes, and how the FBI would continue the investigation until they were found.

"So, you're convinced they got away?" Gunner asked.

Mike scoffed. "He's laughing all the way to the bank with his proof of conspiracies." Mike tried to contain his anger, but his exhaustion made it difficult for him to manage his emotions. He needed rest.

They discussed the stations on the air and what they thought should happen next. A hundred radio stations had been permanently taken off the air, affecting millions of listeners all over the country.

"The audience and the sponsors will find somewhere else to go," Roy said. "Trends will shift, and our success or failure to recover will depend on how we spin it. When we destroyed the transmission, it was game over for the pirates. They misjudged the power of radio."

"I agree," Gunner said. "Unraveling this mess will take some finesse and strategic pathways for better understanding. It's hard to know, so soon after an abrupt ending like this, how the sponsors or listeners will react."

"They're holding their breath, to be honest with you." Roy had kept in contact with major sponsors throughout the day with email updates and a few calls and texts.

"Will this have a negative impact on the radio industry as a whole?" Jackie asked.

"Depends on how we control our own narrative," Gunner said. "And I'll be working on that as soon as the sun comes up. Well, maybe after a good nap first." He grinned.

They all fell silent for a few minutes, lost in thought about the daunting task of rebuilding the stations after the hijacking. They all knew that life would never be the same for them. The past twenty-four hours had changed them all. Invigorating and exciting for Jackie and Gunner, terrifying and disastrous for Mike and Roy.

"We could continue to speculate until daylight, but we'd only be spinning our wheels," Roy said. The clock was nearing 5:00, and he couldn't stop thinking about heading home, getting some sleep, taking a shower, and then dealing with these pressing issues once again.

They discussed ending the simulcast at 6:00, giving the soon-to-be-arriving morning show teams time to prepare and get on the air. Commercials were already airing, and the internet streams for the FMs would start again simultaneously.

Roy explained that they'd already lost a lot of revenue that wouldn't be coming back. Layoffs were inevitable in multiple departments. "This is going to happen in all five markets, and there's no telling how we'll shuffle our best around so that we can keep them employed."

"This is going to happen quickly, isn't it?" Gunner was already contemplating how many of his team he would have to let go.

"Word from corporate is I'm going to have to make these cuts immediately, as in a few hours from now." It wasn't like Roy to be so candid, and he knew he was sharing information that the head office may not want him to reveal. But sometimes, remaining one of the people on the ground was more important, and he asked for their discretion.

"It's going to take someone with a vision to guide this ship beyond the piracy incident," Roy said, proud of his metaphor. "Gunner, how would you feel about being the captain?"

Gunner thought he was joking with the pirate ship and captain references. "The captain of what ship? Isn't that what I already do here with our programming?" The adrenaline that had kept him going all day had worn off, and his fatigue was making his brain feel foggy.

"Yes. You are the captain of this ship in LA, and you really came through for us today with your leadership, content production, and putting Jackie behind the mic." Roy gave Jackie a nod. "Great decision, by the way."

Jackie felt humbled. "Thank you."

"It was a juggling act inside a three-ring circus, and you kept every ball in the air."

"Okay, now I know you're losing your marbles," Gunner said. "What are you really trying to say, Roy?"

"We're in for a big change. We need solid leadership and a clear vision for the future. I think you're the guy for the job. I'm going to recommend you."

"Recommend me for what, exactly?" Gunner wasn't getting the message.

Roy smiled. "National program director for High Point Media."

******

Jackie's jaw dropped, and she squealed with excitement, moving her hips and dancing in her chair. Today, she'd turned into Gunner's biggest fan and was thrilled he was going to be rewarded for his talent and effort like this.

"Have the higher-ups already discussed this?" Gunner was stunned. A promotion was the furthest thing from his mind, and it hadn't been what he was vying for when this day got started.

"Are you kidding me?" Roy gave a little laugh. "We're still reeling from this catastrophe and how we're going to prevent the company from going under. Nobody is thinking about this."

"Then how can you offer me a job like this?" Gunner pushed his chair away from the table, picked up his mug, and walked over to pour himself another cup of coffee and grab another donut. He came back to the table and set them down.

Roy looked into his empty mug and circled the rim and handle with his finger, like he was reading tea leaves. "It just became clear to me that we're going to need someone passionate about radio, and with knowledge of a variety of formats.

Someone who can handle a crisis once in a while. It feels like a natural decision."

Gunner abandoned his snack on the table and paced past Roy, then spun on his heel. "You mean I'd be the head of all programming for all nine hundred High Point Media stations?"

"Well, less nineteen now," Roy said without turning around to look at Gunner behind him. "But yes, I would want to control all programming for all our stations."

Gunner said nothing as he digested Roy's response. He paced to the other side of the conference table and spun around again.

"What about Derrick McVay, the current national program director? You're just going to boot him out and replace him with me?"

"It's just an idea, Gunner, but one I wanted to know if you'd be interested in before I present it to corporate," Roy said. "And McVay has been hinting about retiring anyway, and with all of this, he might just look forward to making way for some young blood."

"Well, what kind of freedom would I have? Would corporate be breathing down my neck every day?"

"What would you want, Gunner?" Roy asked, amused by Gunner's pacing and heel turning. "You could choose where you want to live, what market you want to work out of…"

Gunner took a beat and thought for a minute, just looking at Roy, who was looking back at him. It was as if they were silently negotiating with one another. Gunner walked back over to his chair, sat down, and crossed his legs. He picked up his mug and took a sip.

"Obviously, it's not a done deal," Roy said, breaking the silence, "but you'd be the only candidate, and I'll petition the other market managers to agree." Roy's position in Los Angeles carried a lot of weight with the rest of the executive management team, and he was confident he could convince them to push this promotion through. He was determined to reward Gunner.

"Would I be able to make changes in underperforming markets?" Gunner already had some markets in mind. Program directors talked.

When Roy had brought him from Sacramento to be the director of programming for the eight-station cluster in Los Angeles, Gunner had thought that was the best he could ever hope for. He'd made it. But this... A national programming job was a bigger step up than he'd ever imagined he could reach.

"Slow down a bit," Roy said. "Let's get you into the position and see how it fits."

After Gunner had his first cup of coffee, his brain fog had completely disappeared. His eyes were looking at Roy, but his thoughts were elsewhere, playing out like a movie in his mind, programming a multitude of formats, working with countless personalities, and developing talent. It was a dream come true.

This debriefing had taken an exciting turn, and Jackie was ready for another cup of coffee herself. She wanted to celebrate for Gunner, who sat there in a daze, his face frozen in disbelief and fantastical strategizing. Breaking her junk-food ban, she indulged in a donut from the box before returning to the table, the soft pastry melting in her mouth.

"What are you thinking?" Roy asked Gunner.

"I'm not sure... This gig would be an incredible challenge. An incredible experience. But I'd really need to be in control and not a puppet." Gunner said, nodding his head. "But, if I did take the job, I'd stay right here in LA. My family is settled here, and I wouldn't want to make them move to New York or something. This is home."

Then he looked over at Mike and smiled. "Besides, I want to be here while we rebuild our FMs. I want to be around as it happens."

Mike pursed his lips and hid his expression by taking the last sip of his coffee. Gunner had no idea what he was in for. It would take months to clean up the transmitter sites and years to rebuild them.

"Excellent," Roy said, pounding the table with exuberance. "What's the first thing you think you'd do if you do accept?"

Gunner paused for a minute, then looked at Jackie. "I'd give Jackie a talk show of her own and syndicate it in all our markets."

******

Shocked by Gunner's answer, Jackie's eyes widened in surprise as she almost spit out her coffee.

"Wait, what?" She put her mug down and wiped her mouth with a napkin, checking her neck and blouse too, making sure she hadn't spilled all over herself.

"With KSSP off the air, I thought my job would be gone by tomorrow," she said. "Or, limited to streaming."

"That was never going to happen, not after your performance today." Gunner had already decided earlier that he would find a place for Jackie, regardless of whatever layoffs he was instructed to carry out. "And you know that."

"But a national talk show? Really?" This was exactly what Jackie had gotten into radio for. To host a radio show that mirrored her favorite host's impactful talk-show format. When she'd made it back to Los Angeles, she'd lost any and all hope of doing talk radio when she was given a show on a music station. From then on out, she wasn't unhappy. She loved being on the radio. But now, her dream was within her reach.

"Well, it's only going to happen if I actually get this programming job Roy is proposing," Gunner said. "But after today, I have all the confidence in the world that it'd be a ratings killer."

"Wow... I—I don't even know what to say right now..." she stammered while picking a nibble from her donut.

Roy and Gunner both chuckled at the idea of Jackie being speechless, while Mike sat quietly and weakly smiled, happy that something good could come out of all this.

"When do we start?" Jackie regained her composure and was ready to celebrate. "What's our next step?"

"Slow down, cowgirl," Gunner laughed. "We still have to make sure the national program director's job happens before you get your show. Roy was just asking me what I'd do first."

"Okaaaaaay..." Jackie said slowly. Her mind was already reviewing notes and ideas she'd been brainstorming. Today, those ideas flooded her like a tidal wave with each interview and shift in coverage of the pirate takeover.

She hadn't realized her attention to detail, interview skills, and ability to segue from one subject to another with ease was anything more than her doing the job that had been given her. It hadn't been an audition, but she'd recorded most of her live calls and interviews to critique them later with Gunner, as they always did when debriefing after a show.

She gathered her thoughts and forced her attention back to the room with the guys, smiling at Gunner and then at Roy. "When can we make this happen?"

******

"I don't know. I don't run the entire company," Roy said, leaning back in his chair and letting out a long sigh. It'd been almost twenty-four hours since the stations first went off the air. He was still trying to process the chaos and quick decisions, and grappled with the fact that he'd supported the plan to use the military to jam the signals, which had led to them destroying the company's transmitters. There would most definitely be countless meetings, memos, and all other forms of company bureaucracy to navigate over the coming days, weeks, and months.

Just the thought of it was daunting, and he wasn't sure he wanted to be in the thick of it. Although his role wouldn't be as involved as Mike's—rebuilding the engineering side of the radio stations—the business end of it all would rest solely on him in Los Angeles while he would also have to be responsive to corporate needs. They had five markets to rebuild, and that was going to require a lot of attention.

"I've been climbing the ladder of corporate success for twenty-five years," Roy said, "and when I made it to Los Angeles, I was appointed to manage a cluster of eight top-rated radio stations. I knew I'd exceeded my dreams and began setting even larger goals to achieve.

"The only other major market I'd want to tackle would be New York, and until today, I would have jumped at the chance." He looked at his friends. Really looked at them. "My kids are teenagers now, and I barely see them... I will not move farther away from my family. In fact, I told the CEO that I wanted to go back to Sacramento."

Nobody said a word or even blinked an eye.

Gunner was stunned. How could Roy offer him a big job if he was planning to leave LA?

Jackie saw her dream of a national talk show vaporize into thin air.

Mike wasn't surprised at all. He'd seen a different side of Roy today and felt like he'd known all along that something like this was going to happen.

Roy relaxed in his chair and looked at his empty mug, wondering if he should pour himself another cup. "I don't know. Maybe my ego loved the hustle, but today... today changed it all for me. Today wasn't about ratings, revenue, or contracts. We were doing real radio and worked as a team on an entirely different level. That's how I want the rest of my career to look."

"I understand wanting to be closer to your family," Gunner said. "But won't this be a step backward, to go from Los Angeles back to Sacramento? Wouldn't that be perceived as failure?"

Roy pushed his chair away from the table and took his mug to pour himself more coffee. He probably wouldn't go home to shower just yet. The business day would soon begin, and meetings to sort through the details of what the company was going to do would have already been announced. Then, he'd have to inform his own staff about decisions he needed to make. He had another busy day ahead of him, with no rest in sight. The best he could hope for was a nap on the couch in his office.

"I really don't care how it's perceived by anyone else. And I'm not done with radio, not in the least." Roy returned to his chair and sat down, mug in hand. He took a sip. "What I want is to find some stations in a small market to acquire and give them the old-fashioned way of doing business."

Still stunned by the news, the others sat silent and waited for Roy to give them a reason he would abandon them.

"The trip up to Mount Wilson did it for me," he said. "I couldn't shake it when we headed back down the mountain to return to the station. Mike is right; it looked like a war zone. But I couldn't stop thinking about my team and how we really came together. And it made me want to do something different."

"And that means owning your own stations?" Gunner was taken aback. Roy was a corporate man and a sales executive. He wasn't one to get his hands dirty in day-to-day operations.

"It's not going to happen immediately, but personnel changes are going to have to be made at High Point Media. There will be ripples in the organization. I'm going to take a proactive approach to owning my own company. I don't want to answer to a board of directors anymore, and a small market is the place to start."

"But you're abandoning us when we are about to embark on a huge undertaking," Gunner said. He couldn't mask his disappointment that Roy planned to leave LA. Who would take the helm, which would give him the leverage to run programming and promotions the same way Roy had?

"I'm sorry you feel that way, Gunner, but I'm not abandoning LA or the company. It'll likely take three to six months to make changes that'll transfer me, if they even approve it. There are a lot of things to consider, like where the manager of Sacramento would go. And the dust needs to settle here before that happens."

"Wow!" Jackie felt like she was being let in on a secret management meeting that she would never have been invited to before. "I think it's really exciting! The idea of buying your own stations to run. That would be something."

Roy thanked her for her enthusiastic support and reiterated that the plan would take years to put together, but in the meantime, he'd be near his kids and be able to have a family life again by going back to Sacramento.

"If they don't want to give me the transfer, I'll just go work for the competition," he shrugged, and they all laughed at the thought of threatening to go work for the competition. Roy felt confident the company would accommodate his request. He had a solid record of success with High Point Media, but he'd only shared with them his plans for the immediate future.

"I've been more honest with you guys than I should about what's happening at the corporate level. You three deserve to know what we're up against, but please don't feed the rumor mill that my long-term plans are to leave eventually. It's only conjecture at the moment." He gave them a wry smile, knowing he would eventually achieve his goal. He always did.

"What say you, Mike?" He looked over at Mike, who had sat quietly drinking his coffee, barely reacting to the news of promotions and management changes that had been announced. Roy hoped Mike had a strategy to get the reconstruction project underway and wanted to know his thoughts on how it should be tackled.

Mike put his coffee cup down and took a long breath. He wasn't taking what he was about to say lightly. He looked over, beyond Roy, at the array of receivers, powered off and silenced, and let out his breath with a sigh.

"I spent my life building these radio stations," he said. "And then it was because of me that they were destroyed. I... I don't think I have the... ability, or even the desire, to rebuild from the ground up."

✶✶✶✶✶✶

Roy and Gunner were jolted by Mike's announcement, but Jackie wasn't surprised in the slightest. As the chatter had gone around the table about all the career changes the other three had proclaimed and been awarded, Mike had stayed silent about his thoughts.

He formed his hand in the shape of a gun and winked while he pointed at the group. "Well, it's been great hearing how you youngsters' careers are going to skyrocket after this event. I'm happy you all had a career-altering experience."

He was being sincere but was afraid his words would come across as snarky. His energy had vaporized, and he was punchy now. He paused to change his tone. Seeing Gunner and Jackie rewarded for their on-air work today genuinely made him happy, and Roy's idea to return to Sacramento to be closer to his kids filled him with confidence that the man would support his decision, too.

"You guys are going to be great. I love this business too, but I have also had a career-, and I suppose, life-altering experience," Mike said. For the first time since his heart attack, he was finally prioritizing his own health and well-being. "My friend died today, and it could have been me. I don't know how I got lucky, and Tom didn't."

"I'm sorry," Roy said. He didn't want to lose his chief engineer. Mike Harris was one of the best. But Roy had a new problem he needed to address: if not Mike, then who would build these stations? "But I can't let you quit now when we need your expertise."

"Look, this is not a life-and-death industry, but today, it turned upside down, and my apprentice was responsible. I can't undo that. I can't fix it. I'm responsible. I know I am."

"Then wouldn't you want to rebuild it yourself?" Gunner asked. "Like a badass comeback?"

Laughter broke the seriousness of the mood.

"I don't need a comeback," Mike said. "The deconstructing and rebuilding of four... count 'em"—he held up his four fingers with his right hand—"four FM radio stations... that's going to take years to accomplish."

"Please, Mike, you can't stop now!" Gunner said

But Mike didn't want to go back to Mount Wilson. He didn't want to begin another engineering project that would take years to complete.

He shared that experience told him it would be a stressful project to undertake, and he didn't feel he'd be able to finish it without it taking a significant toll on his aging body. He finally wanted to honor his wife's request to retire and move to Hawaii, where he could simply tinker with electronics.

The others sat speechless. Once Mike mentioned his heart attack and his wife's pleading with him to retire, they could hardly argue with him.

"It's going to be a huge and complicated project to manage, and we have a very qualified team of engineers. Any one of them can lead it. In fact, they'll probably be chomping at the bit to get their hands on a construction project like this," Mike joked, bringing a bit of levity to the bomb he just dropped on them. He felt confident his engineering staff would relish the opportunity to build a radio station transmitter from the ground up, quite literally. He'd done it several times already and was comfortable letting it go.

"I'm sorry, I just can't believe this turn of events," Gunner said, not even trying to hide his disappointment. A radical shift was going to occur, and he worked so well with Mike that he'd been hoping he'd still be able to work with him. He'd counted on Mike to keep the studios functional and board operators well-trained on how to troubleshoot. Mike even accommodated Gunner with the simplest things, like installing digital clocks in the studio when the jocks struggled to read the analog ones.

"I've done enough. I turned my hobby into a long career, and I've loved every bit of it," Mike said, despite remembering several managers and ownership changes he wasn't very fond of. "Now I want to retire and enjoy my hobby while I still can. It's time for me to hang it up."

He knew that once he started an engineering project, it would be like a puzzle that he would have to see through to the very end, and he didn't want that for himself. Not again. Projects like these often took on a life of their own, and Mike had lost too many years keeping radio stations on the air. He envied Roy's idea of owning and operating his own station, but for now, he simply wanted to stop and put his feet in the sand, listening to the ocean instead of being on alert for dead air.

"I have just one important request to make."

"Anything, Mike," Roy said.

"Secure the transmitter sites. This day should sound an alarm in the broadcast industry. We don't want any other pirates to get the wise idea to attempt this again, and someone might, now that it's already happened."

"Most definitely. But I'm going to hold out hope that you'll decide to stay and take on this signature project anyway."

Mike looked at the time on his phone and shrugged.

"I'm going to go to Master Control and make the switch to separate programming on the AMs and activate the streams again for the FMs at 6:00," he said. The clock said it was 5:56. He only had a couple of minutes. "And that'll be it."

Mike stood from the table, and the rest followed suit. They'd said everything they needed to say and were feeling the weight of fatigue. Goodbyes, congratulations, hugs, and handshakes were slightly rushed as Mike had to get to Master Control to make the switch, and Gunner needed to coordinate with his morning-show teams before he went home to his family.

Mike left them and went back to the control room. He pulled his key ring off his belt and opened the door. This would be the last time he would enter this room. He took it all in, eyeballing each piece of equipment in the dozens of floor-to-ceiling racks that he'd ordered, purchased, and installed for the company. He turned the internet streaming back on and watched the monitor as it buffered.

Next, he discontinued the simulcast, which returned the AMs to their separate signals so they could return to their own programming on the dot at 6:00 AM. Precision was important, and Mike was a master of precision. The legal identification at the top of the hour played back on each station, and it was then that he knew his final task was done.

He looked around the room one last time, running his hand along the front of the components as if to say goodbye to a longtime friend. He stopped at the KSSP rack and peeled off the metal label with the call letters from the front panel. A keepsake.

Opening the door, he pushed the button on the knob to lock it and closed it behind him. Mike walked down the corridor and around the corner to his office. He didn't need to pack it. He had almost no personal belongings here. Just his bag of tools and testing equipment.

He picked up a box on the floor and emptied it of the spare parts and manuals he'd thrown in. Then he went through each drawer and shelf on his cabinet for any item that he wanted to take home. He wasn't about to leave anything behind.

He stood behind his desk and surveyed the small space. Having moved offices and built radio station facilities and studios countless times during his thirty years in Los Angeles, now he wasn't sure if he could bring himself to say goodbye. To leave. A tear welled up in the corner of his eye, and he swiped it away with his hand, placing his soiled shirt and coffee mug in the box with the other items and walking out of his office for the last time.

Chapter Twenty-Five

Off the Air

6:15 AM — April 2nd

Mike pulled out and away from the parking garage. The sun had risen over Burbank and the streets were already filled with cars of commuters heading to work or to school to drop off their children. The city looked as if nothing had happened. The signal lights were directing traffic, and the emergency vehicle barricades were gone. Stores and shops were open again, and city buses were picking up their fares at the bus stops.

A new day was beginning, and Mike hadn't been home since it started. Now, it appeared as if nothing had happened.

And yet, everything had changed.

He rolled down his window, feeling exhausted but free. It had been a long few days, and he felt as though he'd aged a decade.

He looked back at the building through his rearview mirror. High Point Media was prominently advertised at the top corner of the structure. Had he made the right decision? This would be a monumental project, and it would take forever, not to mention be extremely stressful. Shelly would kill him.

His thoughts raced. He second-guessed himself; something he rarely did when it came to radio. To drown out his thoughts, he turned the volume up on his favorite radio station, the oldies format. It was one of the few stations in LA whose transmitter wasn't on Mount Wilson, so they were still on the air.

First, it was the Doobie Brothers and then a song from the Rolling Stones. When "Help!" from the Beatles came on, he turned it off. He wasn't going there. He wasn't going back. But with the silence, his thoughts filled the empty space.

Mike ruminated on Roy's comment. *"We have insurance."* Mike knew what it was going to take to rebuild these stations. The industry disruption was likely going to require the government to investigate how broadcasters operated and had overlooked this level of security. It could delay the project for a lengthy time, and there was a possibility they'd never rebuild them and would just turn over the licenses.

But what about the debt? When Roy had mentioned insurance, Mike remembered one of Albert's many conspiracy theories about entities, whether corporations or governments, that would stage a crisis or attack in order to bury something else. "Like, how 9/11 was orchestrated by the CIA to get America into a war with Iraq, or how someone might set fire to their warehouse to collect insurance money to avoid bankruptcy," Albert had alluded during a late-night maintenance trip to the transmitter.

"Could High Point Media have orchestrated this takeover to collect the insurance and demolish the debt?" Mike said out loud, smacking his forehead with his right hand but keeping his left hand on the steering wheel. His mind began to swirl, and soon he felt dizzy, and felt the urge to pull over, but he shook it off. Thankfully, he had a red light to stop at. But he continued to theorize what might have been the motive. He couldn't help it. Mike was now a conspiracy theorist.

The questions appeared so rapidly he had difficulty separating them from one another. His heart raced, and his breathing became shallow. He had to remind himself to breathe. Mike knew he was having an anxiety attack and just wanted to get home.

He was headed in the opposite direction of morning traffic, so the traffic on the freeway was light. He was almost there, and then this nightmare would finally end. At least, that was what he tried to convince himself of.

But what if that was exactly what had happened? He couldn't help but wonder if the company was on the brink of bankruptcy and had a clause about a natural or man-made disaster.

Mike tried to shake the idea out of his head. It was too far-fetched. Who would do such a thing?

But the paranoia crept back up as he got off the freeway. Just a few blocks, and he'd be home. Back to bed. But would he be able to sleep? He was so tired his bones hurt. This drive home felt like the longest drive he'd ever taken. He wanted to put all this behind him, yet he knew that would never be possible.

His revelation that someone at the corporate level might plan such a criminal act was unbelievable, yet according to Albert, it was very possible in just about any industry or part of the world.

Even if it wasn't true, Albert had planted enough ideas in Mike that, although he was resistant and indignant about it before, he now couldn't help but think Albert had actually been trying to alert him, or fill him in, or perhaps even recruit him. He wondered how much the pirates had been paid to take over transmitter sites and broadcast their terrorist messages.

What else did they have planned? What was the "spectacular event" they'd threatened? *When we destroyed the transmitters, did we derail them, or were they expecting us to do it?* The evidence at Mount Wilson had all been destroyed when the site was blasted by the drones, and Mike would not be involved in the investigation.

He was reeling again.

Did Roy know?

Was he in on it?

He sure hadn't brought it up again, and Mike wasn't going to ask. He didn't want to believe that Roy was capable of anything nefarious like that.

But he would never have considered Albert for it either.

He turned down his street and pulled into his driveway. He turned off the ignition and sat in the quiet car for a few more minutes.

The job was done. It was over. He didn't know what else he could have done differently, except to have never trusted Albert in the first place with so much knowledge. But how was he supposed to know that Albert would turn out to be a pirate and steal his radio stations away from him?

He breathed in a sad sigh, sitting with the realization that the truth may never be fully known.

******

He couldn't get it out of his mind. Would the government have to pay to rebuild the radio stations because they'd ordered them to be destroyed? Would all of High Point Media's debt be erased as a result, or would they be given a grant to rebuild? What if it was actually just a huge public relations stunt for April Fools' Day that went horribly wrong?

He pulled down the visor and pressed the button to open the garage door. He looked beyond Shelly's car at his workbench against the far wall and the rack of monitors and equipment sitting next to it. He didn't even want to touch it. He'd never thought he would become a conspiracy theorist like Albert, but here he was in just twenty-four hours' time, his life and perspective turned upside down.

Mike felt a wave of regret wash over him. It was over, and aside from retiring and considering a move, he didn't know what he was going to do next. But it was time to go inside the house and see his wife. He hadn't communicated with her since before the destruction of the transmitters. He knew she would understand the significance of killing his babies, and he loved her for it.

Just as the thought crossed his mind, she opened the door that led into the house and peeked out at him, waving to him to come inside.

"I have breakfast waiting for you!" she hollered, making sure he could hear her.

Mike looked at her and smiled sweetly, appreciating her even more. He opened the door of the Explorer and stepped out. As he walked into the garage, he glanced over at his workbench. His monitoring equipment in the rack was still on. Without hesitation, he stepped closer and turned off the power. He was numb. He was free. No longer chained to the transmitters of eight radio stations.

But was he really ready to retire?

Shelly waited patiently at the door for him, the warm waft of breakfast filling the space. He walked over to her and greeted her with a bear hug. She was a breath of fresh air. He'd never been so glad to be home.

"What a day!" she said, and as if she could read his mind, she asked, "Are you okay?"

He smiled at his wife. "I am now."

"Why do you think Albert did this?"

His smile faltered, and for a moment, he looked away. "I doubt we'll never know."

The End

www.ingramcontent.com/pod-product-compliance
Lightning Source LLC
Chambersburg PA
CBHW071110100726
47908CB00008B/2327